What Amazon reviewers said about this book's prequel, *Truly Madly Obliquely*:

'Fast, witty and gripping ... what's not to like about this beautifully written book?'

'This is really funny, warm and captivating- a must read in these difficult times.'

'A genuine joy from start to finish. Laugh, cry and be very entertained.'

'The craziest, weirdest, funniest, spy spoof I've ever encountered.'

'Quirky, fun and a really entertaining read. A real page turner.'

Peterpink Publishing
Produced by Softwood Books, Suffolk, UK
Office 2, Wharfside House, Prentice Road, Suffolk, IP14 1RD

Text © Peter Spencer, 2024
Cover Artwork © Chloe-Mae Williamson
All rights reserved.
Without limiting the rights under copyright reserved above, no part of this publication may be reproduced, stored, or introduced into a retrieval system, or transmitted, in any form or by any means (electronic, mechanical, photocopying, recording or otherwise) without the prior written permission of both the copyright owners and the publisher of this book.
The story, all names, characters, and incidents portrayed in this production are fictitious. No identification with actual persons (living or deceased), places, buildings, and products is intended or should be inferred.

First Edition

Paperback ISBN: 978-1-0687068-0-6

www.softwoodbooks.com

For my granddaughters,
Binky, Pinky, Moo and Boo.

And Trudi Doppelgängerins Sophie and Hayley.

Also a cheeky grin at Freddie and his lovely family.

CHAPTER ONE
INCONVENIENT TRUTHS

It wasn't part of the plan. Never is. But we've all been there.

That flickering lightbulb moment when we discover that getting by in life will be trickier than we thought, because so many things we've always taken for granted suddenly seem to have gone out of their way to prove us wrong. Rule number one at such moments, if you happen to be feisty and female: never admit it.

Cue Trudi Penislow, aged twelve.

'Look, it's all right for you, Dad, you've had your time. It's my turn now, and it's not fair.'

Nor is it clear whether this mass of unknowns does actually end somewhere, or just splurges outwards, like when a huge rock gets dropped into a small pond.

It was a bad sign that Trudi didn't so much tap on Percy's office door as give it a good beating, as though it had behaved appallingly and thoroughly deserved it. Because she normally just wafted in, the poor chap could only wonder what the hell he'd done. Her way of dealing with things, and people, is generally pretty measured these days, because at heart she's a very nice person. But when she's on her high horse, getting trampled on is a clear and present danger, and it's as much as he can do to stay in his seat instead of diving for cover.

Trudi knows perfectly well that what's really got to her is anything but Dad's fault. And that telling a man who's only in his early sixties that he's over the hill is a bit spiteful. She already feels slightly ashamed of herself, but does feel better for getting it off her chest.

'OK, OK, Dad. I'm sorry.' She doesn't look it. In fact, when she's really, really cross her mouth puckers as well as her forehead, making her look like something between an anxious gnome and a shrivelled peach – which is actually quite funny, though Percy would never dare tell her, or even smile. Instead, he sits politely to attention, puts on his most concerned expression and waits.

'You do know what I mean, don't you?' The peach is looking more overripe than ever. 'About how I'm being totally shafted.'

'Yes, darling, of course I do, and I'm doing everything I possibly can to help.' Percy's sounding more sympathetic than he's feeling, though he's slightly mollified, and relieved that the storm might be starting to abate. Trudi's rage boiled over when she read on X that her range of options, both for overseas uni study, and her concert performances across Europe, if she decides to become a world-famous classical musician, took a hefty hit a few years ago. Not every young person has their adult education and subsequent glittering career prospects sussed before they've even reached their teens. Nor do they always take the implications of historic cultural and geopolitical decisions quite so personally. But Trudi is not every young person.

For a start, she's gone full circle in the look she goes for. After jumping through several fashion hoops, some of them pretty extreme, she's reverted to an obviously adult version of the Barbie look she went for as a little girl. This, equally obviously, is because pastel pinks laced with gold go best with her flowing blonde hair, brazenly blue eyes and all-year-round gently tanned complexion. A little part of her still hankers after the full-monty-tomboy lumpy boots and spiky hair phase that lasted a good three weeks. But, on the other hand, her loosely cut full-length dresses prove beyond any shadow of doubt that she's a fully-fledged grownup, who fully understands the ways of the world.

Bit of a maybe, that, as is the soft feminine mask. Behind it, like something between a naughty kitten and a hungry lion, lurks a steely and anything-but-demure determination to make things happen. She's inherited this, in different forms, from both her parents. And her oddly high, arched and puzzled-looking eyebrows leave no doubt that when she's on a mission to find something out, there's virtually no stopping her. Like when, at the age of six, she suddenly demanded to know exactly, not just vaguely, why Mummy and Daddy didn't really want her snuggling up all night between them. Their ducking-the-question suggestion that it was only because they quite liked snuggling up with one another got them nowhere, until they coupled it with the promise of an iPhone of her own at her next birthday. 'Cheap at twice the price if it gets the kid to bugger off and not spoil our fun', was Percy's take, though the words "mail" and "black" occurred to his wife. Then again, the fun Percy mentioned was a more fun thing to think about right now, faced with an angry twelve-year-old.

Meanwhile, Trudi's unlikely ally, Lady Casement, has learned the hard way how much sharper the wretched girl's become. The time when it was so easy to wind her up just by singing, or saying witty but annoying things, has definitely passed.

'All the world's a stage,' she had to admit to herself after a particularly snarly telling off, 'and the men and women, and parrots, merely players. Especially parrots.'

At that moment the relationship between rapidly maturing young woman and now older and wiser pet parrot was reset. Lady Casement will always be a haughty and often infuriating sulphur crested cockatoo, but she's got a whole lot better at buttoning her beak, when push comes to shove. Her strikingly white plumage, offset only with a dash of underwing and overhead yellow, looks as defiant as ever, but her unblinking stare is sometimes softened a bit round the edges. Trudi can see it, even if no one else can.

She can also see, though she'd rather she didn't, that Fangle's manners aren't going to improve anytime soon. The cat is affectionate enough, when he isn't on the lookout for kill thrills, but ridiculously energetic and really not fussed by the words "no" or "stop that" or even "I'm gonna fucking strangle you in a minute". These days Trudi does her best to avoid rude words, especially the f-word, but that b-word beast really can go too b— f—ing far.

Mum, known to adults as Viv, except when someone's made her

so cross that she becomes Vivienne, is pleased at Trudi's toning-down-the-language thing. She's also rather tickled by the way the girl casually flips between winding up and buttering up her poor, confused father. Odd that he puts up with it, really. Maybe it's because he's spotted that the uppity little madame takes in a fair bit more of the random stuff he comes out with than she ever lets on. But there's always the need for an anchor, a sensible grownup to make sure things don't get out of hand. Classic case in point: the build-up to Fangle's appearing on the scene.

After his predecessor, Fang, finally headed for the great cattery in the sky at the ripe old age of fourteen, Trudi's heartbreak wasn't going to be cured just by the mummy-fallback position of kissing it better. The girl made up her mind to follow in Queen Victoria's post-Prince-Albert dress code footsteps for the rest of her life, and Percy indulged her ridiculously, to the point of wearing an undertaker's hat, complete with a dark ribbon dangling from it, and an ebony armband. OK, that was rather sweet, if a little over the top, and Viv, too, certainly mourned moggie's passing. But the idea of buying her daughter a never-ending supply of black frocks, that she'd almost certainly suddenly decide looked awful, was beyond soppy.

'For heaven's sake, Mum. Fang really wouldn't want me looking such a fright all the time, would he? He'd want me to celebrate the life he had, not mope over the life he lost, wouldn't he?'

Convinced she could hear the girl saying this, probably just as she was opening yet another Amazon package stuffed full of yet more hideously expensive hideous dresses, Viv did the only sensible thing. A good Google search turned up a perfect Lilac Point Siamese kitten, and at least the five-hundred-quid cost would be a one-off.

'God, Mum, just how heartless do you think I am?' Trudi's fury, along with a fresh flood of tears, lasted as long as it took for her to fall in love with the pretty little bundle of two-tone fluff with the huge eyes. Just under two and a half minutes.

Of course, as the weeks passed and the creature found out how easy and what fun it was to rip things to bits, Trudi noticed reservations clawing their way into her unconditional love. And Lady Casement's suspicions hardened into certainties. Bad enough being verbally pounced on by a gobby human. Being actually pounced on by a crazy kitten really is too much. Nonetheless, the depleted trio did become an inseparable threesome once more.

'All for one, one for all?' Trudi spat through gritted teeth, as she watched Fangle scramble up one of her pretty William Morris patterned bedroom curtains, leaving a trail of nasty tears in his wake. As fragments of fabric floated downwards like little pink snowflakes, Lady Casement risked crooning *'oh for the wings, the wings of a dove'*, and the poor girl could only nod in agreement.

But today, as Trudi grips Fangle's deep-shaded front paws with one hand, to discourage scratching, and vehemently strokes his pale-shaded sharply arching back with the other, the parrot faces a moral dilemma. She really ought to warn Trudi not to take the cat's ferocious purring too literally, but the way his tail's wiggling so wildly is such fun to watch. He may be tightly wedged on the girl's lap now, but he could break free at any moment and scratch out any misunderstandings. Luckily, Trudi pops him on the floor just in time, as she's focused on getting a very clear message across to her father.

'Come on, Dad, you've got to do something. Or if you don't, I shall.' Torn between relief that the danger's gone away and disappointment that the show's over, Lady Casement settles for putting her head on one side and giving Trudi a knowing look. If there's a hint of a smirk in the bird's unblinking eye, she's doing her best not to let it show, but she has heard this sort of thing from Trudi before and seen how much hasn't come out of it. Percy, on the other hand, knows to take his daughter's tone seriously, and only wishes he knew how to help her.

'I know, darling, I know. But you see, the nation decided, for better or for worse, and no one really wants to go through the Brexit psychodrama all over again. Yes, I know all the opinion polls tell us the nation's changed its bloody mind, but the tosspot tendency among my old colleagues hasn't gone away. Even though they're now the government, with a healthy majority, they're still shilly-shallying round the subject.

'But I can't help but wonder whether your info might be slightly out of date.' Tentative, anxious not to provoke, he tidies folders and bits of paper on his desk. Playing for time as he hunts for just the right words.

'It's been a priority ever since we got in. Getting a better deal, chipping away at edges. Including ironing out complications for talented young people like you.' Hopefully that bit helped. 'But you have to accept that sorting the really big stuff will mean years of bartering. So it's got to be little by little. No way round it.' She's not going to like this. The bit-by-bit approach is one of her pet hates. Remember the day she decided her desk was much too small and babyish, and showed what she thought of the promise of maybe getting a bigger one when she was a little bit older by taking the bloody thing out into the garden and setting fire to it. Viv's face was a picture. Percy can laugh about it now, but at the time felt a bit hard done by at getting the blame for passing on such nutty genes.

He changes tack.

'Look, quite apart from promises my lot made in opposition not to do anything drastic, there's the small matter of ructions across the channel. And, however any of that pans out, they might not be terribly keen in Brussels to have us back anyway. At least not on our terms. Remember, we had the devil's own job to get in the first place.'

Trudi doesn't remember this, because she never knew it in the first place. Nor has she got anything much more than the vaguest concept of the polarising splits that led to our exit. Lady Casement is old enough to remember what it was like to be in Europe but not run by Europe, or at the heart of Europe, or the grumpy country on the fringe of Europe, but political developments have always rather passed her by. Like most parrots, she's fonder of the sound of her own voice than anyone else's.

To Fangle it's all virgin territory, the same as pretty much everything else in the world. All too much of it is to Trudi too, she's now realising. The problem of not knowing the answers to questions is made so much worse by not even knowing they existed in the first place. She's almost, but not quite, ready now to laugh at her earlier self and that phase in her life when she was convinced she could easily save the planet from global warming. All very well Feta Cheeseburg suggesting you're never too small to make a difference. OK, maybe nine is a bit young.

She can certainly manage a kindly smile at some of her other false dawns. Like her conviction, when nappies and the potty finally became a thing of the past, that she was sorted for life. While her memory of that turning point is a little hazy, on account of its being quite so many lifetimes ago, she'll never forget Day One at school. After waving goodbye to Mummy for what she knew would be ever such a long time, she turned boldly on her heels – it strikes her in retrospect – to go where angels fear to tread. The only real surprise was how silly and childish the other kids were. At that time, she still pronounced the word "arrogance" as "awwigunss", but did have an idea what it meant, and was very cross when Mummy suggested she might be guilty of it.

But of course, now that she's twelve, she's someone else again. And anyway, sorting her own future is less of a big deal than rescuing the whole world. Just a matter of being realistic, and channelling Mum's thought processes. But also latching on to Dad's more flamboyant, if not always more successful, way of looking at things, she mutters, 'We fail? But screw your courage to the sticking place and we'll not fail.'

Percy isn't meant to hear that, but he does. And can't help reminding the kid who came up with that line in the first place, and what it led to. 'Lady Macbeth isn't the perfect role model, darling,' he murmurs, gently. 'And her plan didn't exactly end well.'

'Hah!' Her snort means two things. One, though he may well have a point, that in no way excuses him for making it. And, two, that she's straight away off to the bedroom (that everyone has to understand is actually an office, that happens to have sleeping and clothing storage facilities thrown in). When she gets there, Percy knows, she'll knit her eyebrows so tightly that for once she won't look surprised. Until, on this occasion at least, she's opened her rose-gold Apple MacBook, googled furiously for a few minutes and got a lot of surprises. Quite big ones, actually. Not least, the near-certainty that he, as a life peer, former Prime Minister and active campaigner for better UK relations with the European Union, will pretty soon come up in her searches.

Percy's sensible enough, just about, to accept that any girl of Trudi's age is bound to believe her up-to-the-minute take on the world tips her father's straight into the bin. He's also respectful enough to admit that she's really good at working things out, but unwise enough to imagine she'll give credit where it's due. Flicking open his vintage silver cigarette case with the wonderfully inappropriate words 'to Brown Owl From 1st Newcastle Brownie Pack' engraved on the front, he pulls out an untipped Gauloise and selects his favourite Dunhill holder. Firing up one of his collection of pre-war lighters, in this case a silver S.T. Dupont, he smiles at something funny one of his Tory predecessors once said. After seeing off a particularly infuriating backbench rebellion aimed at thwarting efforts to keep Britain safely in Europe, John Major told a colleague a "full gloat" was merited.

Then again, the poor sod's efforts did end up going the same way as Lady Macbeth's. Percy's smile wilts.

CHAPTER TWO
SALT IN THE WOUND

'I've got a lot of respect for your way of doing things,'
Trudi announces as she almost goose-steps back into Dad's office. She's hardly aware of it, but the staccato bursts of words she's firing at him strongly suggest that his way of doing things does not deserve a lot of respect. At least not in the modern age. Sympathy, maybe, but that's about it.

Percy wanted to laugh at the girly Gilbert and Sullivan way his daughter was lifting her legs and swinging her arms like olden-days soldiers in red uniforms, but can't seem to rub out images of German troopers storming into Paris in 1940. The fact that the Allies did manage to drive them out again a few years later isn't much consolation right now. He wishes he were somewhere else – anywhere, really – provided she wasn't there too. Maybe his computer could double up as a shield, but it doesn't look as if it thinks that's part of its job description. Anyway, it's too late now, the bombs are already falling thick and fast.

'Thing is, you see, in your day writing stuff in the papers and magazines and things was the way to influence people. But these days no one really reads stuff in papers and magazines and things. And I know you make speeches in your olden-days place where the paintwork's trippy, the seats are red and everyone's about a hundred, but no one listens to what people say in parliament either.'

Percy adores his daughter, and, Viv's right, he is actually quite in her thrall. But he's only human. No surprise then that he can feel his hackles rising. The situation is not helped by Fangle choosing this moment to leap onto his desk, via his lap, in the process knocking his ciggie out of the holder and onto the carpet, causing one of those annoying little burns that'll be there for ever. The fact that only quite recently his dear lady wife threw out the tatty old mat and replaced it with something half decent makes it that much worse. Nonetheless, after he's given the damaged bit a good rub with the toe of his shoe, in a useless attempt to not let it show so much, he does try to keep his tone even.

'Sorry to learn that my life's work is utterly pointless, darling, but would you mind kindly explaining?' She's going to anyway, but with a bit of luck it'll be the sort of ill-informed infantile nonsense that can easily be chewed up and spat out. Fat chance.

'Well, you see, Dad, once upon a time people used to go to public meetings to hear politicians tell them what was going on. But we both know that was in the dark ages.' OK so far. 'Then came radio and telly, and people would sit down and pay attention to the news bulletins, and have their prejudices confirmed by what they read in their favourite silly newspapers.' Percy's still on the same page. But there's a big "but" coming.

'Fact is, no one can really be bothered with all that any more, or even the rolling news programmes, when they've got things like X or Meta or TikTok updating everything every minute of every day.' This is getting serious, but she might as well be hanged for a lioness as a kitten. 'We young people pass on all this intel straight away, on our own social media sites. And no one's going to tell us we're wrong, because we never are, because we are social, because the future belongs to us. And because we know best. Sorry, Dad, but that's just how it is these days.'

Sorry? Like hell. Glancing down at his immaculately manicured fingernails, Percy wishes they could help him out, but it's not really what they do. Instead he settles for lighting another fag, forgetting that the one he picked up from the floor is still smouldering away in the ashtray. He can count on one hand the number of times he's really lost his rag with his lovely and clever little girl. But what's getting to him isn't the bloody cheek of what she's saying, but the thought that she might have a point.

'Off you go now, dear.' He's doing his very best. Even the fingernails are trying to look calm. 'I'll think about what you've said and discuss it with your mother.'

Trudi takes one last look around the cluttered office with its battered period furniture, book-lined shelves and general air of huge but historic cleverness, briefly takes hold of his left hand, clocks why it's trembling, and gives it a gentle squeeze. OK, she might have gone a little far, but he needed to hear it anyway, because it was true. Well, most of it.

Percy stares blankly ahead, like a doddery old person who's totally lost the plot, and hates the fact that even the ciggie he's smoking, once so cool, is now so not cool. He stubs out the last remains and aims one last stamp at the burn mark on the carpet, which gets its own back by looking worse than ever. He actually gives it a V-sign as he snaps his computer shut and stomps out of the door.

Though Viv's only five years younger than he is, in some ways she hails from a different era. Yes, he's the clever one with the doctorate, the peerage and the proven track record of having actually made it to Number Ten. But his brilliance at dreaming up and selling strategies was all very well when he had tech-savvy teams of advisers, and the civil service, to actually make them happen. It's also throat-slittingly depressing, he has to admit in darker moments, that his journalism and speeches in the House of Lords aren't the platform he once enjoyed as Prime Minister. And now his own daughter's telling him he might just as well be planting daisies, or pushing them up. Shoulders back, head up, he cuts an imposing figure, that of a man at least ten years his own junior. But, as he gives his usual gentlemanly tap on her door and tries to stride in, his wife can't miss the hint of a stumble.

'Trouble at mill, dear?' The elocution lessons her snobby, aspiring middle class mum and dad put her through as a child have made her accent sound like it's just had a fresh coat of paint. But shocks can bring out the Lancashire lass in her. The smaller her husband's trying to make a problem look, generally, the bigger it is.

'My dear, do I look just the teeniest tad pre-Jurassic? Forgive me if I seem inquisitive.' Inquisitive? Percy's obviously beside himself. If he's got something on his mind that's easily sorted, like the settings have gone weird on his computer and he's buggered if he can figure out how to find anything, he always gets in a state, but this feels different. She hits him with a line he once used on Margaret Thatcher, in his much earlier life as a political journalist. 'Would you care to elaborate, Prime Minister?'

'Hell and damnation!' So much for his efforts at keeping up appearances. 'When I had the top job, I had people around me to paper over the cracks. I'd say do it and it was done. Now I've got to bloody do stuff myself I sometimes wonder where to start. John Prescott – remember him? He couldn't even work a keyboard, but didn't need to because he was Blair's deputy, which meant other people sorted the practicalities. Same as they did for me, back in the day.'

Probably because Viv's mind is racing like a puppy that's sniffing too many smells at once, she can't decide whether to tell him he's being a bit silly, which he probably is, or just plain stupid, which he generally isn't.

Certainly no need to suggest he grow a pair. He's as brilliantly kitted out in that department as he is up top. To this day she feels lucky to have landed such a cracking-looking guy, and in fact, if anything, he's grown into his own face. Those finely-chiselled features work as well for a man of his generation as his body's point-blank refusal to put on more than a few ounces of fat. Even the longish salt-and-pepper hair and rather dandified dress code do no more than add to his air of agelessness. But no man likes to think of himself as yesterday's man. And they're all a bit on the edge, she sighs, a male ego thing.

'I heard Trudi trotting along the passage earlier, darling.' The way her voice seems to tumble at least an octave as she names her daughter makes it sound like it was actually the Grim Reaper she'd heard trotting along the passage. Melodrama really isn't her thing, but his face is reading like the sort of novel that makes you want to top yourself. 'Has she, by any chance, said something to upset you? Maybe even to do with her being that little bit younger than us, and knowing that little bit more than us? Well, everything, actually. It's what kids do.'

Percy's relieved that he's never strayed like so many idiotic blokes do, given that his wife always seems to know exactly what's going on in his head before he's even got a clue. They've had their ups and downs of course during twenty years of marriage, wouldn't be human if they hadn't, but he's as sure as he ever was that when they got it together, he got lucky. At this moment the very sight of her clear dove-grey eyes has a calming effect on him. Different when's he's blotted his copybook one way or another and they go more gunmetal-grey. Fortunately, that's not all that often. He did wonder in the early days whether those slightly raised eyebrows that she passed on later to Trudi meant he was in a spot of bother, but he got the idea in the end. Meanwhile, he's always loved the slightly pointy chin that she's also been nice enough to share with her daughter.

She can afford to be generous, mind, as, besides the neutral accent, her parents handed her such brilliant genes that she could well pass as someone in her early forties instead of fifties. Wasn't that long ago that the guy serving in the offie asked for proof of her age, and got a bit flustered when Viv announced she didn't have anything to hand, but he could have a kiss instead. Percy doesn't do blokeish, but when he spots other men admiring her trim little figure, gracefully long neck and neatly bobbed hairstyle, none of which would look out of place on an art deco mannequin, he can't help feeling a bit smug. Illogically, improbably, it's happening again, which is pretty good considering that just minutes ago he was feeling like a swatted mosquito.

'The visible personification of absolute perfection,' he murmurs, apropos nothing in particular, from what Viv can make out. She has no problem with his habit of quoting Oscar Wilde at random moments, but couldn't help but laugh the day he did it once too often and Lady Casement fluttered onto his shoulder, peered into his face and said 'No one likes a smartarse.'

Right now, however, she's hoping her eyes are not flitting between shades, because, however oddly timed, her husband's words did sound like a compliment.

'Prescott may have been a bit of a prat.' Viv's tone is caressive. 'But that monster Thatcher managed to win three general elections without even knowing the price of a loaf of bread. So best not beat yourself up too hard. Besides, you've got pretty good at finding out how to do things for yourself now you haven't got a team of Sir Humphreys to wet-nurse you.'

As so often happens, the mummy-kiss-it-better thing works better on Percy than it would on Trudi, but Viv can see she's not there yet. What in God's name can the kid have said to him?

CHAPTER THREE
THE MOMENT OF TRUTH

Viv's office is pretty much the opposite of Percy's. While his is cluttered, contemplative and a bit curly round the edges, hers knows exactly what it's doing. Neat, efficient, elegant throughout, it looks as though it tidies itself up without even being asked. Her taste for William Morris wallpaper and fabrics is something she shares with Trudi, unlike the girl's pre-teen tendency to scatter clothes all over the place. This is to do with the obvious imperative of looking *just so* at all times – although, her mother's daughter, she does cram things back into drawers and wardrobes pretty quickly.

Unsurprisingly, the scrunched-up stuff tends to end up horribly creased, as well as taking up twice as much room as it needs, which confirms she's also her father's daughter.

The sense of unhurried but up-to-the-minute order in his wife's office generally helps loosen knots in Percy's brain. But today it accidentally yanks them tighter than ever. Ok, Viv's vision's not as wide as his, but she can at least see where she's going. And because she runs a successful polling company, which she built up from scratch all on her own, she gets how the tech works. He's always made a point of not grunting like old men do when they sit down, but, as he lowers himself slowly and sadly on to one of her dainty little two-tone green-velvet button-back art nouveau armchairs, Lady Casement's decision to perch on his head feels like a metaphor. And the bloody claws are digging into his scalp.

'Look, I do know loads about the potency but potential hazards of social media.' He's floundering, but those particularly raised eyebrows are demanding answers. 'God knows, I've written enough on the subject, but that's just the problem.' Viv folds her arms neatly across her lap, tilts her head in a question-marky sort of way, and waits.

'Fact is, writing about stuff is not the same as actually doing it. For God's sake, before getting into political journalism I did a couple of tours as a war correspondent. Remember?' She does.

'Do you seriously imagine that means I know one end of a machine gun from another?' She doesn't.

'I know what you're thinking. Jolly good thing too.' He manages the ghost of a smile, which dies in an instant as he reflects on Trudi's take on his efforts, and more or less his life's work. Certainly, everything he's been trying to do since he left Number Ten. 'It's not what the bloody girl said, it's the fact that she might be bloody right.' As he slumps despairingly forward, Lady Casement has the devil's own job to cling on. Though she's never thought about it much before, she's grateful for his full head of hair. Means she can use her beak to help her claws out.

By the time Percy's finished writing an article, it's always impeccably reasoned and perfectly easy to understand. Quite the opposite of when he's spilling out angst to his wife. At that point it's more like a kaleidoscope that can't stop spinning all by itself. Be tempting to put it on the ground and stamp on it, but that's hardly Viv's style.

'I suspect, dear heart, what you're telling me is that she knows how to really make use of social media, and you don't?' Percy nods glumly, then fires his final salvo.

'She also informs me that writing articles and making speeches in the Lords is a complete waste of time. Because no one takes any notice of that sort of thing these days. Yes, governments get things done, because they can, whether anyone's paying any attention or not. But no one else can make a blind bit of difference, at least not by the way I go about things. It's a bugger being nowhere, darling. A real bugger.' Lady Casement, who can never resist singing the right song at the wrong moment, wisely takes cover on one of the pretty little pale pink Tiffany shades close to the ceiling before fluffing up her wings and warbling an ancient Beatles song about being a nowhere man making nowhere plans for nobody.

Trudi steps back into the room just in time to witness Percy's reaction. Howling with rage, he lurches forward to the waste bin to grab whatever's in there to hurl it at the bloody bird. In the event, and no great surprise, the wodge of half screwed up A4 printer paper hardly makes the distance, let alone demolishes the target.

'Oh, come on, Dad, it's not as bad as all that.' It's obvious that it is, and all thanks to her. The sight of Fangle struggling to decide whether to chase his own tail or pounce on some imaginary prey sums up her own conflicted emotions, but in a fun rather than horrid way. She looks around helplessly and bites her lip, genuinely sorry for giving the poor man such grief. But at the same time she's seen enough older boys at school having idiotic teenage tantrums to make her wonder whether he's being a little bit silly. Mum's eyes tell her she's right, though she wishes for once she wasn't.

Viv allows herself a glimmer of an inward smirk at how alike father and daughter can be, but hopes it doesn't show. Diplomacy calls.

'I'm wondering if I've got this clear.' The perplexed look should help. 'Perhaps you've rather overstated your case, dear Trudi.' At this, dear Trudi looks affronted. 'And it's possible you've rather overreacted to what's been suggested, dear Percy.' His turn to look affronted. 'So between you, you've both rather shot your bolt.' The trick works perfectly. Now they're both against her.

'Oi, you're being jolly unfair.' Their voices are raised in unison.

'OK, we do hold different opinions,' Percy adds.

'But we can perfectly well agree to disagree,' Trudi points out.

Having wobbled their heads up and down like two nodding dogs on the back shelf of olden-days cars, they're both of them now glaring at Viv, who smiles back at them sweetly. Another line from Macbeth springs to Percy's mind, the one about daggers in men's smiles, but he keeps the thought to himself.

'There, what did I tell you?' Viv inquires, with all the mildness of a red-hot chainsaw slashing through a defenceless knob of butter. 'Now perhaps you'll tell me what's on your minds. Ladies first, Trudi.'

'Well, you see, Mum, I'd like to shore up Dad's brilliant and tireless efforts at softening the edges of Brexit with some social networking of my own.' Of course, she only half means the nice stuff about Dad, and after so many years spent in frontline politics, he can spot a forked tongue at a hundred paces. But he is a little bit appeased, and magnanimous in what isn't exactly victory, but can be seen as a points draw.

'Thank you, darling, I am humbled by your fulsome and generous praise for my limited efforts.' Well, she can take it or leave it. 'And I would be ever so pleased to learn what strategy you have in mind, er, going forward, if you'll pardon the cliché.' With the eyes of both her parents now firmly upon her and even Lady Casement giving her an unblinking, and what could almost be taken as a genuinely curious stare, Trudi clears her throat. Twice, but with more hesitation than threat.

'Some things are obvious.' The way she's shouting is meant to hide the fact that she hasn't thought out her plan in the absolutely minutest teeny-weeniest detail. 'It was stinky crinklies who voted us out of Europe, because they were stupid enough to think Britannia could rule the waves again, like in the dark ages.' So far, so uncontroversial, in her parents' eyes. 'But young people, people like me, have had to suffer because of their silliness. And, let's face it, tomorrow does belong to us, not to them. So it's up to us to make them see reason.' Still pretty much OK as far as Viv and Percy are concerned. In fact, they're both rather impressed at what a clear handle their daughter seems to have on the original hastily slung-together deal, after what they know is little more than a lightning look the available research material. But – and it's a big "but" – laying out the problem is not the same as solving it.

'Well, darling, what're you going to do about it?' Viv's tone is gentle, but deliberately not indulgent.

'Glad you asked that.' Trudi wishes she hadn't. 'I'm going to consult a range of experts and devise a strategy that'll really get people going. Quite possibly right back into Europe. You wait and see. I'll keep you informed on a need-to-know basis.'

This is all Viv and Percy need to know, for the minute. For all her brave words, the girl hasn't got a clue, and may never have. They vividly remember her effort of just a few years ago to put a stop to global warming, and how the little movies on the subject that she posted on TikTok somehow managed to enrage the Russians. In the event their counter offensive cancelled itself out when they started cancelling one another out, but it was enough to put the girl off dipping her toe into polluted ponds. With a bit of luck she won't be wanting to get downstream of anything too nasty again. At least, not until she's quite a lot older.

Sensing Mum and Dad's evident relief, Trudi tries ever so hard not to let her irritation show, as it would look like an admission of failure. So instead of telling them they're both thoroughly beastly she stares at nothing in particular and starts drumming her fingers in the manner of one considering options, action plans and certain victory. In the event, the hand she's doing this with was, until a few seconds ago, energetically stroking Fangle's head, which, as Lady Casement's noticed, he's not struck on. The way he finally wriggles free and savagely claws her suggests he's even less keen on tattoos being beaten into his brain.

Trudi's hurt, in both senses of the word. She's also hopping mad at the way Viv and Percy are smiling at her. A few weeks back, the word "schadenfreude" came up in a German lesson at school, and though she understood the concept at the time, only now does she feel what it's like to be on the wrong end of it. But the effect is to get her plotting more furiously than ever. She actually does have the germ of an idea, which she accepts may or may not work, but must be worth a go.

Ever since she was a little girl she's been having piano lessons with a rather remarkable woman called Miss Mism, who for years was nothing but a dopey old lady who happened to be a brilliant musician. But all that changed around the time Trudi launched her protect-the-planet mission. From being an inoffensive and generally incapable person, this teacher morphed, seemingly overnight, into a focused and formidable force twenty years her own junior and twenty times more deadly an enemy than anyone would wish to meet. Or, rather, not wish to meet, except on neutral ground and protected by at least a hundred heavily armed guards.

Well worth a punt then, Trudi decides, as she casts her mind over the woman's special skills, at the same time stuffing the wretched cat into the waste-paper basket. It's been looking for a purpose in life ever since Percy used what was in it to try and murder Lady Casement.

The more she thinks about it, the more convinced Trudi becomes that she's read her new ally's character correctly and got one vital thing right. Helping a twelve-year-old fight what could turn into a dangerous and dirty game would be out of the question for any normal, fully sane grownup. All systems go, then. Miss Mism is no more normal and fully sane than any reinstated counter-intelligence officer with a history of mental health issues.

CHAPTER FOUR
MISS MISM MISSTEP?

Miss Mism is a mystery, in many ways. For a start, even after having been taught piano by her ever since she was four, Trudi still doesn't know her Christian name. Assuming she's got one, that is. If cryptic crosswords are meant to be just about solvable by impossibly clever people, this woman seems to have been dreamed up by someone who's determined to prove everyone's really stupid.

Her quaint little thatched cottage is as good a place as any to start. Instead of the usual things inside the front door, like wellies, scarves, maybe a brolly or two, there's nothing to look at except an old, rather battered-looking but possibly extremely rare and valuable grand piano filling the entire living room. The only thing on the wall is an old, rather battered-looking but possibly extremely rare and valuable cuckoo clock, which she had modified years ago to play a piece of classical music. When she had it modified back it didn't seem much interested in what she had in mind, insisting instead on koo-koooing once in an hour, or thirty-eight times, or maybe not at all.

Next, there's the kitchen, where the nicest thing that can be said about anything is that it's functional. Not spangly new, not interestingly old, just as close to invisible as it's possible for anything you can see and touch to be. It all looks like it came from a second-hand furniture shop in the sort of town that no one would go to unless they'd got lost looking for somewhere else.

Then there's the upstairs. At the top of the narrow, creaky, pale-grey carpeted staircase, the pale-grey painted bathroom and bedroom are just as bad. The dangerously low ceilings are quite quaint in their way but still don't give much away beyond hinting that the place might be owned by an austere, maybe faintly eccentric, and probably oldish person. The collection of long, tight-fitting and faintly dramatic black dresses in the wardrobe strike rather an odd note, not least because they're all a size six, suggesting the wearer's as skinny as a rake, as well as unusually tall.

But there is one more smallish room on this floor, that's kept conspicuously off-limits by a Banham security lock. Anyone getting past that would be knocked out by the contrasting effect of what's in it, as well as how it looks. Laid out on and above the dazzlingly white desktop, which exactly matches the wall and ceiling paintwork, are no fewer than five computers, and a range of mysterious-looking high-tech gizmos and screens. No one would have a clue what any of it's for, unless they happened to be exceptionally well-qualified in modern espionage and dirty trick techniques. The final strikingly unexpected item is to be found in the rickety looking, but carefully padlocked outbuilding. In place of an old-fashioned sit-up-and-beg sort of bicycle with a basket attached to the handlebars, is a gleaming white brand-new Tesla sports car, said to be the fastest vehicle in the world.

Oh, and one other thing. Locked away in the boot is an AK-47, a stash of ammunition, and several grenades.

These days Trudi's generally pretty sure of herself as she picks her way along the hopelessly overgrown pathway leading to the front door, but this morning's different. She runs through in her mind quite how to broach the subject she's here to talk about, keeps coming up with a form of words, then getting in a muddle with them, then telling herself off for being so silly, then having to start all over again. Then, almost before she knows it, she's at the studded oak front door, tugging hesitantly on the rusty bell pull, crossing her fingers and giving them a quick kiss for luck. It's no comfort that being Miss Mism's only remaining piano pupil is an honour, now that the woman regularly swishes away, usually at the dead of night, in the direction of the MI6 headquarters by the river Thames, or Goonhilly, the unearthly and secretive communications centre on the far southernmost coast of Cornwall.

'Ah, you come most carefully upon your hour,' Miss Mism states abruptly, and steps aside to let her talented student pass. It was a while before the girl discovered, and that only thanks to lengthy consultations with Dad, that her teacher had a soft spot for Hamlet. Possibly, Trudi decided after a lot of thought, because she can be as bonkers as the Danish prince. As to the woman's frosty manner, she accepts that really is just her way. The fact that she's still lucky enough to get lessons at all strongly suggests that there's a soft spot for her too, lurking somewhere. She certainly hopes so, as, after battling though some of Mozart's trickiest passages and finally being told there are worse players on the planet, she sits on one of the hard kitchen chairs, accepts the offered mug of unexpectedly pleasant Lady Grey tea, and clears her throat. The girly harrumph is meant to sound clear and decisive, but is more like a confession that it's easier to have a tricky conversation with this woman when she's not in the room.

'Dear Miss Mism,' she's faltering already, like when she rang the bell only worse, 'you know lots of things that I can only guess at. Lots of things, actually, that Mum and Dad don't know either. So I'm wondering if you can possibly help with something that's terribly important to me.' All she gets for that is a pair of quite bushy eyebrows raised at a tilt so similar to her own that she half wonders if she's having the mickey taken out of her. On second thoughts, maybe it's the contrast between their intense blackness and the woman's ashen complexion and jagged forehead that makes her look like she's just seen a ghost. Same as Hamlet, come to think of it, on his bad days.

'Because you've always been such a brilliant teacher I've sometimes wondered if I might one day be able, just, to perform professionally.' Trudi's tone at this point is so sickly that Miss Mism's eyebrows are starting to look as if they're about to come unstuck, but it's too late to stop now. She gets a flashback to when, as a very little girl, she'd wanted a wee halfway through a meal in a restaurant. When Mummy suggested she hang on for a bit she leapt out of her seat and threatened to do it anyway. What worked then might work now. She presses gamely on.

'When Britain left Europe, life suddenly got ever so much harder for young people like me, and that really got me thinking. I know the government's doing its best for us, but the whole thing's silly. Apart from anything else, when it's nice and clear you can see France from Dover. It's no further away than St Ives is from Truro. Imagine chopping Cornwall in half! Wouldn't that make everybody cross? They'd think the world had gone mad, and they'd be right.

'So I'd be ever so grateful if you wouldn't mind awfully reversing Brexit for me.'

At this, Miss Mism noisily jerks her chair back over the ancient slate floor, pulls herself up to her full, imposing, height, and starts pacing round the room. Surprisingly gracefully for one who's almost certainly the wrong side of seventy, though her taut body and measured steps suggest she might have once studied ballet. Or, more likely in her case, some extreme form of martial art. What Trudi can't work out is why there's a hint of a smile wobbling round the edges of the woman's mouth, which normally looks so tightly clamped that nuclear isotopes couldn't get out.

It happens that, only the week before, Miss Mism had the Brexit barney with her section head at MI6. It only simmered down when she bet him ten grand that the UK would definitely rejoin the EU within five years.

'As if,' the man snorted, already mulling whether to put the money towards a new conservatory or splash out on a swanky cruise. He freely admitted that the Brexit legacy of extra bureaucracy and barriers to the Schengen Information System for intelligence sharing had made life harder for Britain's security services, and that sorting out the mess had been a Labour priority from the outset. But he'll always be a glass-half-empty kind of guy, while under it all Miss Mism's a glass-half-full kind of woman. Bursting his bubble will be more than a victory, she decides, giving her pupil a long, piercing – but, again, impossible-to-read – stare. It'll be a pleasure. Besides which, her suddenly puckered eyebrows clearly state, the bloke's a tosser and deserves to be proved wrong.

Sitting demurely, if rather stiffly, on the chair that's spitefully determined to give her a sore bottom, Trudi rubs her hands almost pleadingly up and down the kitchen table's rough wooden surface. She stops when she feels the irritating prick of a splinter in her left thumb, picks at it distractedly with her teeth and wonders if her inscrutable music teacher has any plans to tell her anything. Ever.

'We shall take arms against a sea of troubles,' Miss Mism smashes the silence without so much as a hint of Hamlet's do-we-don't-we dithering. 'And, by opposing, end them.'

'Oh, goodie, goodie!' Trudi claps her hands but immediately wishes she'd put it less childishly. 'Do we have a plan of action? How to, er, make the tide go out?' Sounds a bit better. Hopefully.

At this, Miss Mism sits down again, as abruptly as she got up, and glares fixedly at Trudi as though she were a whole classroom full of naughty children. 'Now gather and surmise,' she pronounces, as smugly as the boring old man in the same play. Switching now to another one of his speeches, she adds pointedly: 'By indirections we shall find directions out.' Trudi's pleased to hear this, she thinks, but wishes the woman would just get on with it.

As good luck would have it, newly invented words relating to the dark arts of the internet weren't around in Shakespeare's day, or if they could have been found they'd probably have meant something smutty. So Miss Mism has no choice but to switch to everyday English, which she generally does anyway after she's got the showing off bit out of her system.

'Well. My. Dear.' Her tone's more clipped than toenails could ever be, 'I. Have. Friends. Who make things happen. Who function in the shadows. On the fringe of legality. Not saying which side. But who don't do their work in Britain. Even though they might for once be serving Britain's interests.' At this she allows herself a ghost of a smile that's as wicked as it is worrying, before switching if off again and rapping out in her earlier staccato: 'What do you know. About bots? And trolls?'

Short though this speech is, it's long enough to get Trudi shifting more uncomfortably than ever in her annoyingly sit-up-and-beg seat. Though she's no less determined to do something about Brexit she's starting to wonder if Miss Mism was the wisest choice as co-conspirator. It's not the weird words that she's vaguely heard of, but more the glazed and crazed look in the woman's eyes. The poor girl suddenly feels tipped into the story one of the teachers told her in class about silly Pandora, and the box that should never have been opened. And the word troll brings back memories of innocent childhood days when Mummy used to read to her about billy-goats and the nasty monster under the bridge. The difference being that was just a story, and she was safe really in her nice pink bedroom with her pretty pink dollies and Mummy there to protect her.

Forcing herself to look calm, collected and altogether a woman of the world, Trudi hopes Miss Mism won't spot the funny face she has a horrible feeling she's making in her attempts to drive her eyebrows down to where they're supposed to be. If she did but know it, everything about her face is a giveaway, not that the ally she's wishing she hadn't chosen gives two hoots about that. When the woman sets her sights on something she's never let anything get in the way. Overwhelming odds? No chance of winning? No problem. It's where her glass-half-full thing can work against her. Indeed, it did just that at the point in her MI6 career when the only way out was out of her mind, and unplanned retreat into batty old-lady music-teaching weirdness. She only snapped out of it when the difficulty Trudi was facing in her climate change campaign gave her a chance to be a winner after all.

Her outwitting the Russians in that campaign got her fully rehabilitated, and her many successes since then have led to the closing of the file on her away-with-the-fairies phase all those years back. The shrinks trying to help her at the time decided it'd probably been triggered by some kind of trauma that she'd somehow managed to suppress, maybe for decades. What they didn't get to find out was just how peculiar she'd become after they'd given up on her. Recasting herself as a court musician from England's regency period and wearing dresses with fake bustles stitched in was only one part of the picture. She genuinely did need to be reminded, when Trudi showed up at her home each week, that she was there to learn to play the piano and not fix the plumbing. Also, she never seemed fully convinced that Lady Casement was actually a parrot and not a harpy eagle.

Trudi remembers, as a little girl, being so fascinated by Miss Mism's dress code that she asked Mummy why her teacher had such a big behind. She also remembers abandoning all hope of ever getting any sense out of the woman, on any subject other than classical music. Once a loony always a loony? She's kicking herself.

CHAPTER FIVE
PARTING THE WAYS

Miss Mism is kicking herself too.

Though she's outwardly as feminine as a zombie knife she's perfectly good at multiskilling. Meaning she can beat herself up inwardly, while at the same time staring fixedly at Trudi and busily channelling her spy's training in second-guessing and deception. Having spotted she's scared the girl by overplaying her hand, she's not going to break any more cover by backtracking too hard.

'Foolish creature. You didn't believe a word I said, did you? I grant my sense of humour is an acquired taste, but I'd have thought you were old enough by now to differentiate between fact and frivolity.' As much as anything else, the severity of her tone should be enough to trick Trudi into thinking she really was joking about the dark arts of social media manipulation.

'When you get home, start an X campaign. Full of reasonable arguments against Brexit. We've had enough chatter for one day. The rest is silence.' With this final flourish of Hamlet she pulls herself to her full height, clattering her seat back anything but silently. Trudi tries to be more ladylike, but spoils the effect by accidentally knocking her chair over and making a terrible noise.

On her short walk along the headlands back to Penislow Palace, she hopes the softly murmuring waves far below will help soothe her. They do their best to oblige, but are up against the wind, which goes out of its way to blow her hair all across her face. When one bit swishes her eye it starts watering, which is really annoying. She nonetheless does decide to set the anti-Brexit ball rolling with some nice, sensible tweets that are pointed but not inflammatory, and see how much of a following she can work up. No harm in that, surely? Certainly no dodgy dealings or illegal interference from shadowy forces operating from some other country. Reaching the house, still telling herself there's definitely no need to worry, she saunters up to the piano like a girl who hasn't got a care in the world. And plays Brahms' "Lullaby".

It would have worked better if Lady Casement hadn't fluttered down and messed up the music by treading on all the wrong keys. Shame also that Fangle joined in the fun by charging up and down the keyboard, clawing Trudi's hands out of the way. Disappointed that hurling the lid shut doesn't cut either of them in half, she settles for stamping up the stairs to work on her X campaign.

By this point Miss Mism has also headed upwards, fished out the Banham key she keeps clipped to one of her bra straps, fired up one of her computers and dashed off an email to her social media dirty tricks contact in the Philippines. She's proud, and MI6 was impressed, by the way she recruited him. After hours of trawling through an unusual dating website specially designed for ugly nurds, she decided on Doctor Strangelove. In his biog he explained that his nom de plume was sensibly chosen, as anyone who could fancy him really would have to be strange, even though he was probably the best techno genius in the market. His confession that his own idea of love had to be eclectic was easily explained by the photo on his page.

In response, she sent a fifty-year old picture of herself and claimed she never could keep her hands off seriously spotty men, especially if they're short, fat and knock-kneed, with a bald pate but hair sprouting right down their foreheads and out of their sticky-out ears. She only hoped, she added, thinking wistfully about how strikingly if oddly attractive she was back in the day, that he wouldn't find her too ugly. He didn't. And when, by way of virtual proposal, he promised he'd do anything to make her happy, she put him on the MI6 payroll. What she has in mind for him now is a seriously dodgy operation which will, in the end, delight almost everyone in the agency. The exception being her boss, who'll have lost his bet. Which serves him right.

'We're not up and running just yet, darling acne-ridden short-arse.' One of her coded sweet nothings that he seems to lap up. 'But it won't be long. And, when it is, I want you to be ready with a lovely army of bots to up the tempo, bit by bit. Then maybe a few tasty little trolls to give it some colour. Do you think you can do that for me, you luscious little sprouty-hairy weirdie?'

'Ooh, you are awful, but I like you.' Doctor Strangelove's extremely well-paid last lover was a severely autistic shackles-and-whip specialist with a soft spot for pigeons. No question, he's game for a laugh. Miss Mism knows, and she knows he knows she knows, that every message he gets from her gets him all sweaty and smelly, practically frothing at the mouth. She's proud of the way she grassed him up about the ever-so-rude thing he did that cost him his professorship at a Russell Group university. Though the badger that'd taken his fancy did manage to hang on to its virtue, it was really silly of him to film his attempt to take it away. Even more so to show her the footage. When she used AI to make it look like he'd got luckier than he did, and popped the doctored material onto the web as well as handing it over to the police, he fled the country. Which meant she'd got him just where she wanted, a nice long way away, panting and dribbling for her.

'Oh, and there's one other thing, you naughty knobbly-kneed knobber – just how I like 'em, by the way,' she writes saucily. 'Can you rustle up some nice, tame boffins, and maybe a half-brained hack or two, if that not too tautologous, to get us heaving and straining together to get Britain back into bed with Europe.'

'Rustle up?' He chortles, or pretends to. 'The Russell group's the place to start, then. Leave it with me. I'll leave no stone unturned, dear stony-hearted muse.' Such lightness of touch. Helps convince the lady he's a cool dude, not a greasy, frustrated, overgrown schoolboy.

That said, he knows exactly what Love-Of-His-Life has in mind. Or, rather, he thinks he does. Some random and unsuspecting person will set the ball rolling with a few tweets, and he'll set his fearsome army of bots on them. Within minutes there'll be thousands and thousands of likes and shares, all from bogus accounts, of course. But before too long real people will weigh into the debate, and, thanks to a certain amount of troll-generated traffic, they'll get more and more specific and bordering on plausible. Numbers will multiply still further and the whole thing will start to feel real.

The next step will be recruiting a couple of wannabe famous economists. PhD students will do nicely. They'll be fairly easily persuaded, by the dangled bait of worldwide academic recognition, to research the catastrophic impact staying out of Europe might have on the UK economy. Slow burn, barely perceptible in the short-to-medium term, but ultimately an existential threat to the British way of life. Given how terrifying their findings will be, and how they might shift the mindset of even the most fanatical of Brexiteers, there will be potential media interest. This will take skilful handling, probably entailing the offer of the material, on a strictly exclusive basis, to the political editors of at least three right-wing newspapers. The more they scoff at it, the more outlets of a different persuasion will take heed of and amplify the stakes involved.

'All total bullshit, darling heart.' Strangelove's still playing it ever so cool. 'But news is not what happens, but what gets reported.' More's the pity, he thinks, as he looks back on the splurge of publicity about the Old Bill's efforts to catch up with him not so long ago. "Hunt for the *unt!" was how the Daily Star splashed the story, with the strapline: "Clammy Cloister Monster? Clamp 'im In Irons." If he'd had any idea how much he'd been stitched up, and by whom, he'd have wanted to reduce the bitch-on-heat to a sizzled ember.

But he doesn't so he won't. And as Miss Mism shuts down the computer, with a grunt of satisfaction, Trudi opens hers, with a sigh of uncertainty. She scratches her head, quite hard, picks up her pink pocket mirror to check she doesn't look too much of a fright, then has a brilliant idea. It was the messy hair that did it. The image she got in her head was of a man with loads of messy hair, and when she remembered it wasn't Einstein, but the bust of a bloke Dad once took her to see in Highgate Cemetery, everything slotted into place. Or, rather, most of it. It took a moment or so more of intense concentration to get that he hadn't founded a rather expensive supermarket and clothing chain, and that he spelt his name wrong anyway. Then it came to her. Of course. Karl Marx. The point being, she's pretty sure there were words on his gravestone that would come in jolly handy. With a bit of help from her.

Percy's often in the past been left goggle-eyed at Trudi's googling skill. And he would have been now if he'd been there to see it in action. 'It's as though she's got at least a gram of cocaine up her nose,' he once complained to Viv, hastily adding that she'd better not have been at his little stash. But today she could have lifted the lot, judging by the lightning way her brain lands on its target, and her fingers fly. Even the keyboard seems impressed, given how long her expensive and sparkly fingernails are. Within nanoseconds she's there.

'Workers of all lands unite,' she reads aloud off the screen to Lady Casement. Not having ever been a member of the Communist Party of Great Britain, or Russia, or anywhere else, the bird just looks puzzled. Trudi presses on.

'Workers? Why shouldn't that be students? And I'm sure we can do better with the second line too. You have nothing to lose but your chains? Hey, let's make that ... brains. There, how's that for genius? Students of the world unite – you have nothing to lose but your brains! Snappy, huh?'

If Lady Casement's in awe of Trudi's brilliance she's got a funny way of showing it. After fluffing up her feathers and yawning loudly, she leaves a smeary response to the call of nature on the piano lid.

CHAPTER SIX
UNINTENDED CONSEQUENCES

Maybe to make up for her naughtiness, Lady Casement mentions, several times, that all property is theft.

Half a nanosecond's lightning googling is enough to confirm that the parrot slipped up there, as the line was not one of Karl's. But it sounds like it might have been. Probably worth putting in then, with a bit of clever updating.

'All Brexiters are bereft.' Because Trudi doesn't even look up, let alone give credit where it's nearly due, Lady Casement deliberately leaves another smelly little visiting card on the piano lid. But instead of apologising for her rudeness, the girl simply carries on scrolling through more stuff that the bloke did have to say for himself, and is chuffed to find that he did at least have a reasonable grasp of the obvious.

'According to this,' she announces, 'he could see, and I quote, that "social progress can be measured by the social position of the female sex." Well, well, well. If he really noticed that I can almost forgive him for his crime-against-fashion hairstyle.' Seconds later she's anything but forgiving when she stands up and spots Lady Casement's crimes against piano lids. Snatching up Fangle, she brandishes him at the stinky creature in the hope he'll do what cats are supposed to do to birds. It doesn't work.

Though this fails to end Trudi's crusade to reshape the destiny of the United Kingdom, Europe and the world, it does hold it up. Stomping off to the kitchen in search of cleaning materials, at the same time wishing there was a water butt in the garden to drown that vile bird in, she swears under her breath that the road to hell is paved with bad intentions. Particularly ones involving malicious damage to Bösendorfers.

'You all right, darling? You seem a little flustered.' Viv's attempt to get the mix just right for the casserole she was trying to quickly sling together before her next scheduled Zoom call is not helped by her daughter crashing around the place and tipping things out of cabinets and drawers. Everything in them is neatly placed. Or rather, was. Although most concessions to the twenty-first century in Penislow Palace are designed to be sympathetic to the building's Georgian architecture, the subtly pale green fixtures and fittings in this room are modern, stylish and, above all, orderly. Little wonder right now they're looking as furious as Trudi's feeling.

'That b-word bird's done her b-word business all over the piano,' she splutters, 'and I don't know where you've hidden the b-word cleaning stuff.'

'Dearest, I haven't hidden anything anywhere.' Viv's trying to sound calm, which isn't easy as the sudden commotion caused her to splatter drops of the wretched thick brown sauce God knows where. 'Perhaps you'd like to put everything back where you found it, and I'll clean up the mess.' At least the kid's tried. Just a shame she's as useless as her father at actually succeeding in this sort of thing. Two minutes later, having watched her mother deftly sorting out the piano, Trudi heads back to the kitchen and curses that she's given herself a much longer job sorting out the mess that she herself has created.

'Thanks,' she grunts, unwillingly, as Mum hurries out of the room, praying that the client hasn't given up on her and cancelled the conference.

'By the way, have you been out in the sun too much? You seem to have gone a bit blotchy.' It's not until the Zoom's well under way that Viv spots what the kid was on about. She toys with the idea of dying of embarrassment, but settles for switching off the computer camera just long enough to wipe her face.

Back now in her office (definitely not a bedroom, Trudi's had to remind everyone till she's blue in the face) she opens the computer, clicks on X and puts out her first power-to-anyone-who's-got-any-brains tweet. To the Marx and not-actually-Marx adaptations is added the simple slogan: "EU turn if you know what's good for you." Though being able to make out the words is hardly part of the cat or the parrot's job description, they both read the girl's body language accurately. Hard to tell if they're impressed, or alarmed, or just think she's being silly, but they are struck by the way she's pounding the keys as if she's using a rusty antique typewriter instead of the more user-friendly equivalent that you get these days.

A mile or so away, in her clinically white operations room, Miss Mism's also on the case. A little more calmly, admittedly, but the moment she spots the tweet, which Trudi's obligingly pinned to her X profile, she messages Doctor Strangelove.

She's grateful for his absolute refusal to do Facetime or Zoom with her, ever, presumably on the grounds that he's even uglier than the images of himself that he first sent her. Fortunately, this cuts both ways, as the man's pathetic vanity saves her the trouble of trying to explain any slight alteration in her own appearance over the last fifty years, but the downside is that she can't check out how he's looking. More's the pity right now because, given the time difference between Britain and the Philippines, at his end it's mid evening. Putting him midway through his fourth bottle of Merlot, leading to a certain clouding of judgement – both in his cyber warfare techniques, and in the sweet not-exactly-sweet nothings he chooses to send to Love-Of-His-Life.

'Shall I compare thee to a summer's day,' he oozes, 'I hope and I pray that you are not gay.' Like just about every wino who's ever spoken in the moonlit warmth of their cups and wished they hadn't in the icy chill of the morning, he thinks this'll really get her going. And the way the second line scans and rhymes so well with the first is bound to get her in the sack. Even his knobbly knees are twitching with excitement. But they go rigid when he reads her answer: 'Just shut it, you grubby, spotty, scrofulous little oik, and do as you're told.'

Funny how the drunken mind works. If you've just wrapped the car round a tree, probably best trot off home and it'll be good as new in the morning. But Doctor Strangelove does one better. After a quick fumble around on another computer, he stumbles on the programme lined up in readiness for Miss Mism's order and hits the "go" button. In the event, he presses the wrong one and crashes the entire system. Bit sobering, that, but at least the first machine still works. Better play for time then.

'Only joking, sweet Helen, darling of the Hellenes.' He's writing slowly and ever so carefully, with his tongue wedged between his teeth. 'Pretty soon you'll be able to check out your protégé's feed, and rejoice that yours is the face that launched a thousand bots. Or, as cockney news vendors used to shout, X-tra. X-tra.' Though Miss Mism has to admit to herself that what she's just read really is quite clever, she suddenly has the sickening sense that the bloody idiot might have, figuratively speaking, ejaculated prematurely. Probably does anyway, in the literal sense, not that that'll ever be any concern of hers. What does matter is the possibility that he's already launched the cyber campaign.

She calculates that the girl's cautious initial tweet, that went no further than suggesting now could be the time for young people to look to their own interests and get a bit serious about rejoining the European Union, will get responses. First off just telling her she's on the right track, or maybe just as politely telling her she isn't, but only getting shouty a fair bit down the line. On no account, until she's given Strangelove the definite go-ahead, are there meant to be any posts along the lines that anyone who still thinks leaving was a good idea needs a brain implant/should hang their head in shame/must be wiped off the face of the earth/be eaten by a swarm of locusts/be boiled alive in a vat of oil.

When Miss Mism rejoined MI6 after recovering from her nervous breakdown, that seemed terminal at the time, she got back her sang-beyond-froid that's been safely sealed in permafrost ever since. It's as though any possibility of uncertainty has been surgically removed from her DNA, along with mild anxiety, serious concern, or downright panic. But right now, they've been shoved back in, inflamed to the point of bursting every blood vessel in her body.

Though she's always treated her pupil as though she didn't give a monkey's about her, the opposite is true. Any notion of having children of her own was pretty much rubbed out the day she signed up to the secret service, as surely as if she'd married it on a promise to be faithful for ever and ever. But that doesn't stop her wishing she'd had just one little lapse along the way, and that Trudi had been the product. Or, more likely, given the time factors involved, the product's product. She's read enough to know that people are capable of loving their grandkids almost as much as the fruit of their own loins. And she accepts that her bond with this girl, no less real for being unstated, gets as close as is possible to plugging that gap in her life.

No wonder, then, that she took it to heart when Trudi looked frightened at the mention of bots and trolls during their chat about reversing Brexit. Of course the kid trades as a toughie, but she's anything but really. And the thought of seriously upsetting her makes Miss Mism's frozen-lake exterior melt, overheat and vaporise. Or at very least start smouldering. So the campaign's tempo must be upped on a strictly bit-by-bit basis, leaving the girl with a sense of being in control of it. At the idea of Strangelove screeching from standing start to max revs, her instinctive reaction's to get MI6 to fly her direct to the Philippines in a supersonic jet, parachute down to the loathsome creep's hovel and rip his head off.

However, the icily calculating spy kicks in just in time to get her channelling those protective instincts into precautionary measures mode. Gritting her teeth so hard that she worries she might end up at the dentists, she issues the clearest possible instructions to the man she pretends has won her heart but could so easily break it.

'Right, my knobble-kneed knight in shining armour, when you do get round to activating the artillery we'll hold our fire until it's be time to call in the cavalry. Just do my bidding, and dream of the rewards. Don't waste time squeezing those luscious little spots of yours, your squeeze will do it for you.'

Drunk though she strongly suspects the nincompoop is, Miss Mism knows he knows exactly what she means. For "artillery" read "bots", intended to wreak random havoc in the enemy lines, while the cavalry's the detachment of trolls, tasked with singling out specific targets. Their function will be to take issue with some of the more extreme anti-Brexit generalities now out there, and turn the tirade into something closer to a reasoned set of arguments. Though it'll take a little longer, it will be worth waiting for.

'But just remember this.' Miss Mism flicks the setting to bold. **'Do nothing until I give the order, and when I do it's to be a strictly one-step-at-a-time operation. We're doing it by degrees.'** That can't possibly be misunderstood by anyone in their right mind. Problem being that the booze, sploshing around with the ganja he smoked earlier, and the ecstasy tab he took at the same time, has got him tripping. If he doesn't lie down, he'll crash down, and probably crack his skull.

'Leave it to me, luscious lover,' he somehow manages to write back. 'Degrees, you say? Got plenty of those. Ha ha. Ha ha ha. Pippety pip.'

Miss Mism doesn't do God. But as that's obviously it for today she can but pray that if the bloody fool does scare the pants off Trudi by going too far too fast with the bots, the mitigating effect of the trolls might calm her down, if only a little bit.

She's not to know he won't be going anywhere before he wakes up tomorrow evening. And it'll be twenty-four hours after that before he manages to reactivate the cyber campaign that he's trashed.

If he could read Miss Mism's mind, which he obviously can't, he'd have agreed she's on to something. He really is a bloody fool.

CHAPTER SEVEN
ABOUT A BOY

For the next couple of days then, Trudi's take-back-control-back-again campaign is quite well behaved, perhaps a bit too much so. It feels odd, being disappointed and relieved at the same time, like wearing a pretty pink dress but horribly clashing shoes.

But it's still a scary time. And to stop herself from fretting too much, she's doing her best to enjoy one of her guilty pleasures, which she should be ashamed of but isn't.

Her dear little fluffy pussy is fond of his dear little fluffy mouse. Or, rather, fond of fighting it to the death and always winning. The battle always goes the same way. He taps it with one paw then pounces on it as though it were trying to get away, then rolls himself into a ball and savagely claws the life out of it. Which is stupidly easy as it's only a toy.

But what Trudi does to make it harder is rub the thing all over with catnip and then pop the end of its long, stretchy tail in Lady Casement's beak. Obligingly, the bird flutters above the kitten and dangles the prey just out of reach. At this point Fangle turns into a ravening lion desperate to capture a fleeing woolly mammoth and tear it to pieces. In short, he goes totally bonkers.

Trudi claps her hands and giggles like a naughty kid, forgetting that's exactly what she is at this moment. But she's also a battle-hardened geopolitical campaigner, alert to any funny business on the computer screen she's got open on her grownup and businesslike desk. Some might say, as it's pastel pink and decorated with pretty little swirly birdie images, that it's a bit girly. But they'd be wrong, obvs.

The little trick she's playing on Fangle does help keep her calm. But it stops working when killer kitten gives up on death and destruction, yawns and falls asleep, leaving Trudi with nothing better to do than give her full attention to the computer. She stares at it in horror, as, all of a sudden and all too clearly, something awful is starting to happen. Forget Fangle's silly game, this takes woolly mammoth moments to a whole other level. Only it's not one starving lion on her case, but a whole b-word pride of them.

Trudi looks around the room wildly, then paces round it rather more cautiously, as there's a lot of blingy clothing all over the floor and she doesn't want to prick her bare feet on any of the pins holding brooches in place. As she picks her way back to her thoroughly grownup and businesslike executive swivel chair, which just happens to be quite dainty and the same shade of pastel pink as her desk, she closes her eyes and clamps her hands over them.

Next, she cautiously parts two fingers in front of her left eye and gingerly opens it. Just a teeny bit, but wide enough to confirm that she really is seeing what she really wishes she wasn't. So much for Miss Mism making out she was only joking about her ghastly plot. As the scary tweets swamp the screen like autumn leaves in a hurricane, the poor kid flips from woolly mammoth to ostrich mode. Snapping shut both her eye and the computer, she fumbles for her comfortingly comfy pink crocs with the not-the-slightest-bit-childish Barbie logo on them, gets to her feet, and stumbles out.

After she's closed the heavy oak front door of Penislow Palace softly behind her, and wondered for the millionth time how Mum could possibly imagine a kumquat plant could grow in the porchway, she heads for her happy place. At least that's what the grassy headland a few hundred yards away normally is. Ignoring the fact that Fangle's still ever so cross with her and horribly prickly, she's scooped him up in her arms, knowing she can rely on Lady Casement to flutter along with them in the hope, doubtless, of more cat-baiting fun.

Sitting now in her favourite neat little dip in the ground that gives a panoramic view across the murmuring Atlantic rollers, she picks a few daisies and starts making them into a chain. Yet another deliberate ploy to head off panic by reminding her of the nice, safe, childhood which at the moment feels like she never even had.

Once again she's thwarted, as Fangle's decided daisies might not have as much play potential as pretend mice, but are better than nothing. Ignoring the fact that hissing is normally a cat thing, Trudi manages a human equivalent, as well as a number of those rude words that she usually avoids, especially in company. Seriously embarrassing then, when a slightly shrill but definitely manly drawl interrupts her flow.

'Hullo, are you all right? You sound a bit troubled by something.' Trudi looks up, as flustered as she is irritated.

'Oh, it's you, Tristan. Didn't hear you creeping up on me.' This is ungracious, but she's so out of sorts that the best defence has to be attack. Especially as he must have heard most, if not all, of the unbecoming b-words and f-words that were supposed to be for the smelly cat's ears only.

The two young people know one another, by sight at least, because they're both at Wadebridge secondary school. Trudi's a bit shy of him because he's so obviously posh, as well as older. For some mysterious reason, the way his longish hair curls over his forehead has a certain limited charm. And he's tall, and slender, and doesn't shout like the other boys. But he is still only a boy, even if he does seem to have quite good manners. For a boy.

'What're you doing here anyway?' Trudi's not sounding quite so grumpy.

'Well, you know, they let me off the leash now and then,' he answers, self-effacingly. 'Need to find my way around a bit, now that I've turned sixteen. Off to sixth-form college next term. Looking forward to it, actually, as they don't treat you like kids there.'

'Don't treat you like kids? But you're a sixteen-year-old boy! That makes you, in girl years, about eight ...' Though Trudi doesn't say this she certainly thinks it. Up to a point, at least. And she won't see so much of him, in future? Not that she cares two hoots, as he is only a boy. So what that he does look a little bit like one or two of those pinups she's got in her office-not-bedroom? What does that matter? He is, after all, only a boy. Quite polite though, for a boy. Not that that prevents him from interrupting her careful analysis of the situation.

'I say, hope you don't mind my asking, but you really do seem a bit ... how can I put this? Well, not quite tickety-boo? Anything I can do to help?' Just like a boy, Trudi thinks, barging in on my thoughts like that. But she has to admit to herself he's not really to know what a muddle she's in. And he did ask the question in a kindly and concerned way.

Lady Casement chooses this moment to swoop down from the gorse bush where she's been precariously perching, snatch the half-finished daisy chain from Fangle, swoop up again in a wide-ish semi-circle and drop it on the back of Tristan's head. Hard to tell whether this sort of thing is just any old parrot's idea of a bit of fun, or this particular parrot's way of defending her mistress from unwanted male attention. Either way, it lands so softly that he hardly notices. But Trudi does, and bursts out laughing.

When Tristan follows the direction of her eyes, he disentangles the offending missile from his thick and really rather graceful hair, and shares the joke, giggling in a thoroughly disarming way. What the hell? He's not so bad then. Besides, explaining her difficulty might help clear it up in her own head. After all, the boy's a virtual stranger and, thinking about it, she's hardly likely to see him ever again, as by the time she gets to sixth-form college, he'll be at uni. Or working the tills at Tesco for all she knows. So the sheer anonymity of the situation makes it like a priest's confessional. No harm can possibly come of it, then, even though as a sixteen-year-old boy (that's to say eight-year-old girl equivalent), he probably won't understand a word she's saying.

'Well, you see, it's like this.' She's faltering, which makes her cross with herself. 'I'm trying to get Brexit reversed. But I'm sure you can't have any idea why.'

'I jolly well can!' Suddenly, he's sounding cross too. 'D'you think I don't want one day to do whatever I choose in Europe? D'you think I don't know our lot got shafted by the old people who voted us out? Bloody silly buggers, the lot of them.'

The colour's rising in his cheeks, first in his anger then his embarrassment. 'But I do beg your pardon, Madame, such ungentlemanly language. Mea culpa. Unforgiveable of me.' At this, Trudi can't help but smile, both at him and to herself. If this is his way of pretending he didn't hear all those naughty words she hissed at Fangle, it's very nice of him.

What the hell? She is in need of a friend right now. Miss Mism doesn't feel at all trustworthy any more, and Viv and Percy will probably tell her off for not tipping them off about what she was planning in the first place. Anyway, there's an awful lot she needs to get off her chest, and there's not much point in taking someone into her confidence and then never seeing them again.

'Look, I only live a few hundred yards away.' Her tone is strangely strangulated. 'My mum always has a good supply of biscuits. Chocolate ones, incidentally. Would you care to join me in a little light refreshment?'

Tristan is sharp enough to spot that Trudi's casual manner and weird period movie performance is a way of covering a bout of shyness. Also, he's pretty sure that what she pretended was a question is a command, really. On top of that he's rather impressed, that someone he took as just one of the kiddywinks at school is actually a pretty savvy girl, with her ducks very much in a row. But, for the minute, he'll play the same game as her.

'Righto. Chop, chop, my dear.'

As she gets to her feet, clasping Fangle to her chest as though she were a medieval knight and the cat were her shield, Trudi accepts that what seems to be happening is exactly not what she had in mind with her original priest plan.

Against that, it is, always was, and always will be, a woman's privilege to change her mind.

CHAPTER EIGHT
THE KINDNESS OF STRANGERS

As the two young people, plus fluttering parrot and squirming cat, approach the front door of Penislow Palace, Tristan suddenly has a fit of nerves.

'I say, Trudes, old thing,' he wonders, in a failed attempt to sound a million degrees cooler than he's feeling, 'your parents have never met me. And everyone knows your dad's a bit of a swell. You don't suppose, do you, it might seem a bit funny you showing up like this with some random chap in tow?'

Trudi is not at all sure about being "Trudes". Or old. Or thing, for that matter. But it's well known in the school that Tristan comes from a super-posh family, so she's prepared to cut him a bit of slack. Especially as he is only a boy, albeit rather a nice one. More troubling is exactly what Dad will make of him. Thanks to services rendered to the nation as Prime Minister, and more particularly a service he once rendered to one of his successors, Percy does have a seat in the House of Lords. But being a life peer doesn't have the same ring about it as membership of the stately-homes-of-England brigade, and there's a slight chance that he might, if he clocks his young visitor's background, come over all man-of-the-people on him. Depends what mood he's in, of course. Alternatively, there's a danger that he might come over all happy-go-lucky chappie and offer him a drop of brandy. Or, more embarrassing still, some of that expensive white powder that he's still rather fond of, even though he's supposed to be a mature and law-abiding citizen.

Different thing with Mum. She'll be sensible and civil – a woman thing. But also protective of her innocent little daughter

– a mother thing. Trudi knows perfectly well Tristan is harmless, on account of his kindly eyes and his being only eight in girl years. But grownups, even quite clever ones, can be pretty silly. Best tailor the facts then, to the needs of the moment. Add a few stitches, and maybe take a few away.

'Oh, you'll be fine, Tristie baby,' she says airily, but with a bit of a tit-for-tat edge to her voice. 'Without actually telling any fibs, we might just give the impression we've known one another a teeny bit longer than we actually have.'

'Aha, twenty minutes not quite the ticket, eh? Point taken, old girl.' Old girl? Maybe later she'll point out that the twenty-first century has been up and running for a while now, and people do tend to live in it these days. But first there are the introductions to get through. Straight away, it turns out, as Mum's just appeared at the top of the wide curving staircase that leads down to the oak-panelled and slate-floored hexagonal mini atrium that forms the entrance area to the house. Though Viv's looking her usual elegant self, her hair impeccably bobbed as always, she slips her glasses off the second she spots the tall and rather good-looking young male visitor. Trudi notices this, and is slightly puzzled, but doesn't say anything. At least, not about that.

'Hi Mum, this is my friend Tristan. From school. Bumped into him by chance on the cliffs. He's going to help me with my, er, project. Isn't that nice of him?' She's trying not to gush, but isn't at all sure she's succeeding.

'So pleased to meet you at last, Lady Penislow. Such a pleasure. I've heard so much about you.' As she gets to the bottom of the stairs Tristan holds out his right hand and fixes her with his most endearing and charming smile. She shoots him a sceptical glance.

Suddenly the look on Trudi's face reminds Viv of the day she caught her red-handed tipping an entire bottle of Christian Dior perfume over her Barbie dolls to make them smell nice. She can't think what's the matter with the kid.

'Right, Mum, I'm going to make him a nice cup of tea and give him some of your lovely choccie biccies, if that's OK, then we'll get to work in my ... office.' Actually, she's left the room in such a mess that it almost looks like a young girl's bedroom.

'Just going to put the kettle on now, Tristan. Will you keep an eye on it for a mo while I pop up and powder my nose? Won't be a sec.' Trudi's already darting up the stairs.

'I'll show you where everything is. In fact, I fancy a cuppa myself.' Viv strides purposefully across the atrium, wondering what happened to that promise to put the kettle on, then sniggers to herself when she guesses what the problem was.

Trudi swiftly shuts herself away behind a pine-panelled door that has, in its time, had no fewer than four carefully printed-out embossed signs taped to it. The first, that had been there for years, simply said: "Trudi's Bedroom." The next, which sported a much fluffier design round the edges, read: "Trudi's Boudoir." Then came a plainer one that stated rather ambiguously: "Trudi's Room." That was finally torn down a few weeks ago, and replaced with the stark and definitely no-messing-around message, in bold type, incidentally: "**Trudi's Office**."

As she's obviously going to be gone for ages, Viv can take her time thoroughly checking out this complete stranger. Though he feels like a prisoner of war being cross-examined by an experienced interrogator, who has the power of life or death over him, he does his best to keep up the charm offensive, saying ever such polite things about how elegant yet practical the kitchen is. So much more so than at his little hidey-hole. Nice to hear of course, but Viv is keen to get down to brass tacks.

'So you and Trudi know one another from school, do you? Which year are you in?' If this thinly disguised and very specific way of demanding to know his age troubles Tristan, he doesn't let it show.

'Oh, I'm off to sixth-form college next term. Planning to get top grades so I can land a place in a half-decent uni, where I'll be studying techno wizardry stuff. Determined to be earning more than mater and pater by the time I'm thirty,' he announces airily. Arrogantly? The jury's still out.

'Oh, I see,' she stalls, not seeing, obviously. 'And what badly paid work do they do, dare I ask?'

'They just show people round our house, don't y'know? Parts of it are about the same age as your lovely place but it's a bit bigger. Well, far too big, actually. And impossible to keep nice and warm, like I bet this is in winter.' The mists in Viv's mind are gradually clearing. Ever since she was a far-from privileged little girl, and every bit as keen as this lad clearly is to do better in life than her parents, she's been quick on the uptake. So he's landed gentry, then, as well as four years older than Trudi. No surprise that she's suspicious. Good manners can double up as a mask for all manner of unmannerly motives. But, as she can't exactly ask him outright if he's a cad, she tries another tack.

'Techno wizardry, eh? What's that when it's at home?'

'Well, you know. I'm a bit of a geek, really,' he says, lowering his eyes in a particularly self-effacing way. Viv notices how long his lashes are, and thinks what effect they must have on the girls. On the potential cad spectrum, he goes up a couple of notches. Then down again, maybe, as he shares what's obviously a genuine passion for computer science and artificial intelligence. Also their potential to benefit humanity in general and him in particular, given the well-paid career paths they open for chaps with the right sort of top-notch degrees, doctorates and what-not.

This conversation goes on long enough for Trudi to snatch up the clothing scattered all over her room, scrunch it up into a delicate-looking but already overcrowded wardrobe, jam the doors closed without breaking them, hurry back down the stairs and start eavesdropping outside the kitchen. Fangle's settled for a bit of kip, for once, on her bed, but Lady Casement's fluttered after her and looks on the point of telling her off, probably loudly, for listening in at keyholes. Just in time, Trudi clamps her thumb and forefinger over the bird's beak, and her eyes open wider and wider as it dawns on her just how helpful Tristan could be. It was nice of him to pay attention to her problems with Miss Mism. Be even better if he could fix them.

She retraces her steps ever so softly across the atrium to the bottom of the stairs, then clomps back ever so noisily across the time-worn slates and into the kitchen. 'All better now,' she breezes.

'And what have you two been chattering about while I've been gone?'

Before either has a chance to answer, there's a weird and troubling noise coming through the pastel-painted French doors that are open to let in the soft summer breeze. Tristan anxiously cocks his head to one side for a moment, launches himself out into the garden and rushes towards where the high-pitched and clearly distressed-sounding squeal is coming from. Leaning breathlessly across the loosely looped wire stapled to a series of posts to protect the chicken run from foxes, he gently untangles a baby squirrel that's clearly fallen from the tree above and got well and truly stuck.

'There, no harm done,' he says, after he's reached up and carefully placed the little animal on an overhanging branch, watched it scurry safely away, and flicked back his long, slightly wavy and often unruly fringe. 'Same sort of thing happens to the wildlife in our gardens too. Can't stand to see defenceless little creatures suffer. Nature can be so jolly beastly cruel at times, but I always do what I can to help.'

He's certainly done all he needs to help his own cause. The jury's returned its verdict. He is not a cad. Viv's heart is won. Trudi's very taken with what she's just witnessed, too, though she worries slightly that he might be just a bit too kind. Sorting Miss Mism out may take a streak of ruthlessness. Meantime, both mother and daughter registered the way the noble saviour gentleman described the space outside his home. Ordinary folk have, at best, a garden. Whether it's back or front, or even all the way round, it's still just a garden. Singular. Any self-respecting aristo, by contrast, has *gardens*.

But before anything can be said about this or anything else, Percy strides into the kitchen and demands to know what the hell that strange sound was. Though it's two floors up, his office is directly above where they're all standing, so he, too, couldn't fail to hear the commotion through his open sash window. It was enough to make him completely lose his train of thought about the newspaper article he was writing, coincidentally, about how obvious it must be to anyone with a microgram of intelligence, why we must rejoin the EU immediately.

'A dear little baby squirrel got into difficulty. But, crisis over, thanks to our young friend here.' Viv's beaming at Tristan as though he's been a bestie since forever, and no other explanation for his being there can possibly be needed.

'Right. Good. Excellent.' Percy's tone is puzzled, and a tad suspicious. 'And our knight in shining armour is ...? Forgive me, I don't think we've had the pleasure.' He turns to Tristan.

'Ah, Lord Penislow, delighted to make your acquaintance at last. I've heard so much about you,' Tristan lies, charmingly. Trudi hopes he won't overegg it. Dad can be tricksy at times, though it is rather sweet of him to be as protective of her as Mum.

'This is Tristan,' Viv murmurs, in her most reassuring tone, 'he's a long-standing friend of Trudi's. From school.'

'I see.' Percy does not see. It's written all over his face.

'Now, how about we all have a nice cup of tea in the garden?' Viv replies briskly. 'And a biscuit?' We'd all like that, wouldn't we?'

Actually, as her husband makes plain by reaching for his silver cigarette case and holder, he'd sooner have a fag. Tristan watches him carefully, his face showing admiration, which turns into delight as Percy fishes out his lighter.

'Oh, I say, is that an S.T. Dupont? Vintage, isn't it? Would you mind awfully?' He lifts his arm in Percy's direction. 'May I?'

Percy obliges, and Tristan turns it over, almost caresses it, in his hand. He doesn't realise that doing this has the effect of extending, in Percy's direction, the hand of friendship.

CHAPTER NINE
THE LADY VANISHES

As the two young people disappear up the stairs, both adults agree Trudi seems quite good at choosing the right sort of friends. Percy's even prepared to forgive the young man not accepting a ciggie when he so obviously fancied one, though it's questionable whether Viv will forgive her husband for offering it in the first place.

'You did well, saying no to Dad,' Trudi murmurs as she turns the brass handle and opens the door to her – for heaven's sake let's get this right – workplace. 'Mum would not have been impressed if you'd accepted one of his precious, smelly cancer sticks.'

'Thought as much,' Tristan replies smoothly, making a mental note not to admit, at least not for the time being, that he's as fond of the fags as she seems to be of making daisy chains. 'But oh, I say, what a delightful be— er, office, you have here.' Looking around the room he can see she's gone to a lot of trouble to prove it's what it says on the door, but can't help but notice that she does actually kip down there. Given what a stickler his mother is for propriety, plus his own shyness, not to mention worries about what Viv and Percy might think, he's glad that she's left the door open.

But she nearly dies when she spots a frilly mauve skirt that somehow hid itself in plain sight during her lightning tidying operation. Nudging it as subtly as she can with her left foot under her gracefully pink-draped, if a little girly, four-poster, she hopes this won't have drawn attention to the wretched thing. It was only last week that she dragged the bed into the corner of the room, so she could shift her work station to the newly emptied centrally positioned podium. The bed looked thoroughly miffed at being pushed off its perch like that, but the desk was rather smug.

Trudi flips open the computer with as much flourish of a member of the royal family launching a ship. But she feels like a downtrodden commoner when she clicks on her X feed and clocks the look on Tristan's face.

'You do realise, don't you, old thing, that most of these masses of replies are from bogus accounts? Bots, we call them. I can see that you were trying to get people thinking, but all you've really done is get machines whirring. And not in a good way.'

'I know. I b-word know.' Trudi bites her lip and fiddles with the folds of her dress. 'Or rather, I didn't know, but had a horrible feeling.' Tristan wishes he hadn't been so blunt, and almost risks putting a comforting arm round her.

He doesn't, though he can't decide if that's because she might think he's being forward, or whether he's simply too shy. He carries on scrolling down the never-ending list of responses, while at the same time mentally scrolling through the list of etiquette tips Mummy's been giving him lately about how to treat damsels in distress. Happily, a couple of minutes later, his do-nothing-rash holding pattern gives him the thumbs up, as he's noticing stuff that might be genuine.

'I say old thing, looks like all's not lost.' He's relieved almost as much on his own behalf as Trudi's. 'You seem to have got real people talking about what you want them to talk about.'

'You mean I might be on the right track after all?' Though she grasps at this crumb of comfort, she's getting a bit tired of talking to the back of his head, and wonders if at any point it might turn into a face instead. It doesn't, because right now he's too busy facing facts. The good news of a moment ago is giving way to bad as the artificially generated nastiness is lowering the tone. Claims that all fucking Brexiteers need their fucking lobotomies reversed aren't exactly guaranteed to win hearts and minds.

'Ah. How can I put this?' It's Tristan's turn to start attacking bits of clothing, leaving his poor cuffs wondering what the hell they've done. 'I know you wanted to get a debate going, probably even a robust one. But, er ...'

'But not actually a b-word civil war?' Trudi cuts in. It's obviously impossible to actually crucify oneself, but she wouldn't mind trying.

'Once a nutter, always a nutter. I should've known better. You ask someone to help because you think they're your friend, then find out they really, really suck. Oh, sh-word, sh-word and sh-word, I've been so utterly b-word betrayed.' She's wailing like a witch watching her executioners light the bonfire.

'I say, steady on, old thing, only trying to help.' Tristan's pained protest wafts over his shoulder. 'I'm speaking more in sorrow than anger.' He's scared, and can but hope this bit of cleverness might calm the girl down a bit. It doesn't, as it's a line from Hamlet that Miss Mism's used on her more than once.

'That's one of hers too,' Trudi snaps. 'I wish I'd never met the b-word b.'

Tristan slowly swivels the chair to face Trudi, as he clocks that it's not him, after all, that's got her in such a bait. Good to know, as for a moment it had crossed his mind that she's been tricking the school all these years into thinking she's more or less normal, when she's actually stark-raving bonkers.

Flicking that naughty-but-nice fringe of his back into place is such a habit that he barely even notices he's doing it, though it does mean he can not only look in her direction, but actually see her. She stares back at him and reads the question, or, rather, loads of them, in his eyes.

'Not quite sure where to start.' Her dress really is feeling her pain now. 'Really not sure.'

'The beginning, old thing?' The helpless way her hands suddenly flop down and start hanging at her sides, and the little-girl-lost way her toes are pointing inwards, strongly suggest telling her it's time to buck up wouldn't play well. Might have been the first thought that crossed his mind, but could have been the last he ever shared with her.

Trudi wobbles, her head a maelstrom of fury fighting fear, then decides it's time to buck up.

She points him in the direction of the little pink faux-leather

Chesterfield sofa placed in the corner of the room nearest her desk and steps up onto the podium, feeling like that olden-days *Listen With Mother* lady who used to say: *'Are you're sitting comfortably? Then we'll begin.'* Not that Tristan will be comfortable for long.

Because he's now looking up at Trudi, he doesn't spot Fangle first stalking him, then taking aim at the laces of his swanky black, white and red trainers. But he does when the little monster moves in for the kill, curling into a ball and lashing out with all four sets of claws. His tight-fitting black jeans give some protection, but there's still a fair bit of collateral damage. To his flesh.

'Jesus fucking Christ!' Trudi looks at him, slightly shocked, while he looks at his left ankle, a lot more than slightly shocked.

'Oh, I say, old thing, ever so sorry about the, er, Anglo-Saxon thing.' Once again he doesn't want to blot his copybook with this nice young girl, and nor does he want to tarnish his reputation as an animal lover. But it did bloody hurt.

Trudi's so used to Dad's filthy language that she quickly forgives him. Also, she thinks what Fangle's just done was quite funny. Especially as it's someone else on the receiving end for once.

In his chivalrous way, Tristan's grateful that his suffering's helped to ease hers, though that doesn't help him warm to the beastly cat. Things improve a bit when Fangle decides enough is enough, springs onto his lap, snuggles up and starts purring. And when Lady Casement flies onto his head, leans across and shouts in his ear *'all's well that ends well'*, Trudi has a fit of the giggles.

The tension broken, at least for the time being, she snaps the computer lid down and tells her story. From the beginning. Tristan listens sympathetically, and as attentively as he can, though the little stabbings of pain he's still getting in his ankle are as distracting as someone with Tourette's syndrome shouting insults at him.

'The worst of it is,' Trudi grumbles, 'I haven't seen the b-word woman for days. She's just vanished. Off the face of the earth. I've been round to her house lots of times, but there's no one there. And there's no sign of her b-word car either. Expect she's gone off to start a b-word revolution somewhere, or something.'

Tristan bends down to pick up the cup of tea he'd placed on the floor, which Fangle miraculously managed to not knock over, toys with dunking his biscuit in it, decides it might be bad form, and asks what this Miss Mism lady actually does for a living. When Trudi tells him, the blue in his staring eyes contrasts so vividly with the whites that they look like bits of medieval Chinese pottery.

They'd probably have popped right out if Trudi had told him what mad MI6 agent Mism is actually up to at this minute. So it's for the best that she hasn't the foggiest.

As it is, she settles for distractedly dunking her choccie biccie in her tea. Tristan smiles and follows suit. They always taste better when they're nice and soggy.

CHAPTER TEN
THE ART OF THE FEMININE

Miss Mism is in the Philippines. And, in regard to anything happening back in Cornwall, in the dark.

From the moment Strangelove spouted that nonsense about his degrees and then fizzled out it was obvious. Trying to get him to help with Trudi's biff-Brexit campaign was about as foolproof as the Gunpowder Plot.

Sitting rigidly upright, she punished her ugly kitchen table by drumming her fingers on it for hours. A nod at Chinese water torture, as the buck had to stop somewhere.

While she'd never admit to anyone, least of all to Trudi, quite how much she cares for her, she got a knot in the pit of her stomach about how bad things could get. Should have steered well clear of the kid's idiotic fantasy. Shouldn't have allowed that stupid bet about rejoining the European Union to cloud her judgement. Also, totally unreasonably, she felt cross with the girl for asking her advice in the first place.

The finger drumming got more and more intense, as though it really was all the table's fault. Not that it seemed to notice, even when the hammering turned into a tattoo, beating out the bit everyone knows from Tchaikovsky's Nutcracker Suite. She even hissed out the melody, using a nasty one-word libretto. *Shit. Shit-shit-shit-shit. Shit-shit-shit-shit. Shit shit.*

But then, having done the woman thing of caring about a loved one's troubles, she switched to the man thing of trying to do something about them. Snatching up her latest model iPhone and tapping out the direct line to the bloke at MI6 that she took the bet with, she rasped out a request. Or rather, in that tone of voice, an order.

'Permission to go on overseas mission. Grant it. And grant it now. Someone's letting the side down. You're fucked if he's not fucked. Roger that?'

'Oh yes, my dear.' The man's drawl is suave, silky and double-edged. 'If it's rogering you're after we have just the travelling companion for you. Kindly get your ladylike posterior to SIS HQ ASAP.'

Miss Mism's assignments can be anything from teasing out secrets to carrying out assassinations, and, somewhere in the middle, training newbies. Teaching them all sorts of horrid things. Including, very specifically in this case, how to lay honeytraps.

Doctor Strangelove would be putty in her hands. Or, rather, in the hands of this new pupil of hers, who'd stared hard at her with a strange hint of recognition in her eyes before announcing her name was Davinia. 'Davinia Divine, some say.' The way she purred, lit a Sobranie Black Russian cigarette and blew several smoke rings at her was disturbing enough, but there was more to it than that.

Staring just as hard back, Miss Mism got another knot in her stomach, only this one came undone and started whirling around like a Catherine wheel. Because the lovely young lady was tall and lissom, with a flowing black mane, super-pale complexion and thick, quite high arched eyebrows, she looked oddly like herself in her younger years. Almost like she could be her own daughter, an impossibility as the nearest she'd ever got to having any fun was courtesy of Ann Summers. Not that that protected her from those infuriatingly distracting feelings she'd already had about Trudi.

Then her male side kicked back in, quite hard, and right in the midriff. Davinia was going to have to pretend to be her and get down to it with the target. A nice bit of footage would clinch it. What the men back at base would never know, as the sound would have been accidentally-on-purpose muted, was what Davinia said to this creature who made Munch's *The Scream* look pretty. She'd be getting him to pull himself together, pull out the stops on Trudi's behalf, and do so strictly by degrees. The right sort this time.

In the event, best-laid plans and all that, Doctor Strangelove does not get laid.

Davinia's life, so far, has gone in about as straight a line as the M25. Her dad, an overbearing, old, Old-Testament-minded country vicar, more into punishing people than loving them, grimly insisted on her leading a drearily fun-free life. Throughout her childhood and adolescence she read a lot, dreamed a lot, had a prim little bun and outlook to match, and wore glasses even though she didn't need to. But then came uni, where the scales fell from her eyes, and the specs.

She let her hair down in every sense, swopped Charles Dickens and Jane Austen for Ian Fleming and John le Carré, and decided that safe was definitely boring.

Nonetheless, she dutifully graduated in English Literature before giving the old man two fingers by jetting off to New York for a two-year Master's course. In Fashion. Pretty soon, everyone was telling her to stop wasting her time learning about the latest look, and start showing it off instead. On the catwalks. On camera. Guys were dribbling over her like bees round a juicily blossoming flower, which was fun for a while, as she'd been Miss Nobody at school. But what really thrilled her was the thought of her father's rage at the sight of her in magazines, or, better still, on huge, impossible-to-miss billboards.

But as her Big Three-Oh loomed she got bored, and something a trusted gay friend said to her really hit home.

'It's only the superficial qualities that endure, darling heart. Man's deeper nature is soon found out.' They both smiled, but in his jokey way he was reminding her that she did actually have a deeper nature. And it might have a bit more to it than just being the lust-after girl of every smelly bloke's dreams.

Back to London then, where she toyed for a while with starting a Satanic cult, to make the old bastard really choke in his dog collar. But after a while she decided that, as long as she was still fighting the man, she was still in a way tied to him. Clean break then. She went back to the stuff that helped untangle her in the first place, and – eureka! Spooks ahoy!

Of course she was a hit with the dirty rotten scoundrels who interviewed her. Sexy? Sultry? Savvy? Honeytrap hotel here we come! After the initial training, in code-cracking, pursuit avoidance and unarmed combat, her section head told her she was going to be sent abroad on her first mission, under the watchful eye of one of the toughest and most seasoned operators in the service. Such a thrill! She was more or less ready to die, if needs be, for king and country.

On the long flight over, she learned that it wouldn't come to that. In fact all she'd have to do was shag some sense into a colleague who hadn't done as much for king and country as he was supposed to, but may be on the point of doing too much.

But what Miss Mism didn't know was how events had moved on during the seventeen-hour flight from terminal three at Heathrow to the international airport at Manila. There was a problem with the in-flight wi-fi which, infuriatingly, didn't get sorted. And, thanks to an unexpected delay in the journey's first leg, there wasn't time during the stop-off in Doha to check Trudi's X feed. As a result, after the final touch-down, their leap into a taxi is also a leap in the dark.

Though it's no distance from Manila's glossy airport to Strangelove's grubby hovel, the two are worlds apart. In a matter of minutes, the shiny security of the terminal gives way to down-at-heel squalor, with vacant but dangerous-looking young men hanging around. The mature woman's relatively safe even though the light's fading, but divine Davinia is anything but.

Several of these dodgy blokes start closing in, only to find out the hard way how thorough Davinia's training was. Spotting their reflection in Miss Mism's eyes, she flips one of her stiletto-heeled shoes upwards, catches it in her right hand, swivels round and slashes a great gouge across the nearest bloke's forehead. Then she leaps in the air and floors two more with sideways kicks to their temples. As the rest of them run for their lives, she turns back to face her mentor as though nothing has happened, and casually asks her to carry on with what she was saying.

Because connectivity was still crap during the taxi ride, Miss Mism still has no idea what Strangelove has been up to. Not that this will be any concern of Davinia's for any longer than it takes her to boldly go down some dilapidated wooden steps, knock on a dilapidated wooden door, take one look at the dilapidated ugly man who opens it and boldly go back up again.

The million mental pictures she had of the guy she was about to seduce ranged from great hairy monster with, maybe, wooden leg, eyepatch and oozing scar on one cheek, to a heavily made-up little nancy with puffy cheeks and evil smile, perhaps venomously caressing an extra-fluffy cat. None of them, certainly, a girl's idea of the perfect partner for life, or even a bit of fun on a naughty night out. But this narrow escape brought back her father's off-putting words about what was in store for girls who did it with their boyfriends before they were married. A fate, he'd utter with a tragic shake of the head, worse than death.

And what could be worse than worse than death? Doing it with a man who's spotty, short, fat, knock-kneed and balding, with hair sprouting right down his forehead and out of his sticky-out ears.

'Ah, dear Miss Mism,' she breathes at the sharply raised eyebrows, 'espionage isn't for me after all.'

'And what, pray, is your chosen path, you batshit crazy, bull-headed, brainless little bimbo?' A smokescreen, designed to cover her real feelings about the girl, and what she'd been on the point of putting her through. Making her shag this monster suddenly feels like dunking a new-born baby in a barrel of untreated sewage. Not that Davinia even notices, judging by the way she lights another Black Russian and calmly blows a few more smoke rings before replying.

'Oh, that's simple enough.' Her exquisite lips curve beguilingly. 'I'm going to be a librarian.'

CHAPTER ELEVEN
WHO CARES WINS

Miss Mism's mind goes into overdrive. After a near-lifetime's experience in espionage, thinking quickly is second nature. In fact, several lightning judgements in the past have saved that lifetime from coming to a speedy and nasty end.

She focuses on her hopelessly conflicted feelings about Davinia being rescued from a fate worse than worse than death for approximately half a nanosecond, then jams them into the not-right-now file and concentrates on Plan B. If Doctor S can't be seduced into behaving himself, he'll have to be bludgeoned into it. Literally, if needs be.

'Right,' she rat-a-tats, 'if the angel fears to tread, the devil will do it for her. Stick around, kid, and watch me.' Davinia is intrigued. Now that her virtue is guaranteed a safe passage, at least until her next not-necessarily-tempting temptation, she genuinely would like to see what happens next.

'Lay on, Macduff,' she murmurs sweetly, taking one more deep and thoroughly satisfying drag on her ciggie. 'And damn'd be him that first cries, "hold, enough!"'

'That's my girl,' Miss Mism mutters as she marches towards the rough-timbered building and raps so hard on the door that bits of it splinter off and the corrugated tin roof rattles. There's a long pause, followed eventually by a shuffling sound from within. Hard to tell, when it does eventually creak open, what's hitting Strangelove hardest. Mortification? Mystification? Revelation, probably. But very much the wrong sort, now that Love-Of-His-Life has morphed into who she'll one day become, when time has done its worst. Sweet-Young-Thing is there again too, but ghostly presence behind ghastly destiny. After that first all-too-fleeting vision, he'd staggered back to his battered metal living room table, picked up a half empty bottle of cheap cooking sherry and glugged down the rest of it. Now he just stares at his visitors as though they were little green men who'd just stepped out of a spaceship.

'All women become like their mothers,' he finally manages to stammer out. 'That's their tragedy.'

'And no man does,' Miss Mism snaps back. 'That's his.' But Strangelove's words did disturb her. Something from long ago, maybe? But it's so faint that the "don't know" file is the only place for it.

As she steps into this glorified shack that could be any age except even vaguely new, Davinia smiles to herself at this elegant bit of Oscar Wilde chit-chat. But has no problem, in the circumstances, with stubbing out her fag on the inelegantly filthy wooden floor. Nor is she minded to go anywhere near any of the filthy wooden chairs. A pity, as she'd have loved to have sat back to enjoy the show, even though curtain up's a nasty thought, as in this place they're all as ragged, cheap and filthy as everything else.

'Right, Aguecheek,' Miss Mism snarls, 'get this into your unsightly, misshapen head. It's not just men who bullshit their way through dating sites, as you see. I am your phantom lover, turned nemesis if you don't obey my instructions, to the letter.'

Davinia lights another Black Russian and smiles to herself again. The Andrew Aguecheek character was one of her all-time faves, and she particularly loved how Richard E. Grant played him in a movie version of Twelfth Night. Of course, unlike Doctor Strangelove, he didn't look like every girl's nightmare. In fact, she's always rather fancied him.

'I told you to help my little friend in Cornwall.' Miss Mism's leaning forward so hard that her eyebrows are brushing his face. She so reminds him of the devil that he claps his ugly little hands together and prays for a long spoon.

'So what exactly have you done about it? And do you have any idea what happens to nasty knobble-kneed gnomes who dare defy me?' She ratchets up the fear factor by slipping out from a barely visible fold in her particularly severely cut black dress a particularly severely spiked knuckleduster. As she slips it every bit as severely onto her already half-clenched fist, he looks at the tatty little plastic crucifix that's hanging lopsidedly on one wall and gets where the tormented Christ nailed to it is coming from. Then his glance slithers over to a poor-quality, discoloured print of the Madonna on another wall, and he gets a kind of fellow feeling with her too, because she looks disappointed. But at last, he finds his voice. Quavering, but still a voice.

'Madame, I have done your bidding. How can you not know this? Yes, there was a delay, thanks to a technical, and ... er, bodily malfunction. But normal service was restored ... let me see now ... a good fifteen hours ago. Follow me to my operations room, please, I beg you, and see for yourself.'

Pulling aside an especially dirty drape pinned unevenly over a narrow and slightly wonky doorway, he leads the way into another, even nastier, room. Because there are no windows, it's revoltingly hot and there are horrible little insects buzzing around everywhere. Davinia's always been most particular that only horses sweat, while men perspire and ladies merely glow. But hanging onto that is a strain right now, as no one could realistically accuse the Niagara Falls of merely glowing.

The only light comes from a single bare bulb that's as filthy as everything else. The wide, misshapen and slightly rusty metal table is grumpily bearing the weight of a pointed pile of odd-looking electronic gizmos enmeshed in a jungle of wires. At first glance they look like a weirdly decorated Christmas tree. But close by is an instantly recognisable and relatively clean Apple Mac computer. There's also a shabbily framed photo of Strangelove in his professor's get-up at some bygone university do. Needless to say it's hanging, on the grubby but somehow colourless wall, at a tilt.

'There, what did I tell you?' Maybe feeling slightly empowered by the sight of his once-respected self in mortar board and gown, he manages a glimmer of emphasis as he opens Trudi's X account.

The facts speak for themselves, and the sound that comes out of Miss Mism's mouth is midway between a grunt and a growl. Like an XL bully bitch unwillingly suckling the runt of her litter.

'Yes, you have got your ugly arse into gear. But what about doing it by degrees? What happened to that then?'

'Degrees? Degrees? I've got so many letters after my name you can't fit them all into one line,' he mutters, with a sidelong glance at his image in his plumage. He tries to pull himself to his full height, but that doesn't take him very far upwards.

'And exactly how far up the spectrum are you, you brain-dead, broken brainbox? Last time I looked, the expression "by degrees" was defined as "in stages, little by little". A gently rising tide, not a fucking tsunami.' Strangelove's bewildered for a moment, then, as the mists clear, he's really hurt. His autism gave him severe problems in the noisy school setting, but the university environment was less challenging, and he'd finally convinced himself that no one would know about the endless fizzing and popping in his head.

'Ah, ah, yes, yes of course I might have misunderstood you, er, slightly.' More to the point, it's only now that she's reminded him that he has any memory at all of how that last exchange of messages finally petered out.

'Well, get this into your deranged brain now, you half-arsed half-loon, it's time to level out the floodwaters a bit with well-chosen trolls. With luck they can bring some sanity into this dialogue of the demented. We can't get the boffins or the scribblers in on the action until they've got something coherent to get their teeth into. Understood?'

It is. But it's also the last straw.

'Hence, horrible hag,' he screams out, 'you're not the person you said you were. I don't like who you are. In fact, I hate you. So there. So I'm not going to do what you say for one minute longer. So linger at your peril, you horrid, nasty, smelly poo-poo person.' Knobbly though his knees are, he does manage to stamp his foot, though it's about as effective as pointing a peashooter at a battleship.

'Very well, my friend, if it's war you want, then war you will get,'

Miss Mism's tone's explosive enough to sink an entire fleet. 'You wonder why your silly prank with your trousers round your ankles landed you where you are now, in this God-forsaken hovel? It was my doing. I have the Commissioner of the Metropolitan Police eating out of my hand, thanks to one or two little stains on his otherwise unblemished record, to which I alone am privy.'

'Talking of privies, we could always up the ante, could we not? After all, why stop at badgers? How about you had it off with a duck-billed platypus? Or a buffalo? Maybe even a pod of whales? Interpol would lap it up, and pursue you to the ends of the earth, if only out of curiosity. Something to look forward to, eh?'

Doctor Strangelove slumps onto a chair which is so dirty that it matches his mind. Then, holding his head in his hands, he starts to cry. And Davinia, who, let's remember, has a lot more front than experience in the ruthless world of espionage, starts to feel sorry for him. She even offers him a ciggie, in the mistaken hope that it might help. All her kindness does is make him cry all the harder. But it also makes Miss Mism love her all the more, so much so that she feels the need to hide it, by being more beastly than ever.

'Get to your feet, you acned acolyte of acrimony, and get to work. If I don't see results in a week you'll see the inside of the slammer in minutes, and won't see daylight again. Ever. Got that?'

He meekly lowers his head so far down that it looks ready to fall off, and holds out his hands like the naughty boy he knows he's been. At that, the women climb the steps back into the street and several young men run for their lives. One of them, in a desperate act of self-preservation, hurls himself into the path of a passing pedicab and offers the driver his wife, daughters and goats if he'll only spirit away these fiends.

Neither woman says much during the journey, largely because they're too busy hanging on for dear life as the creaking pile of twisted metal defies all the laws of physics by actually moving. But eventually they leave behind the scarily bendy, potholed streets and get to the nice bit of Manila, where they leap out and hail a proper cab that takes them the rest of the way in relative safety. Finally, as the car pulls up at the airport they make a dash for the departure area to catch the last plane out. The guy at the desk is on the point of telling them they're too late, but changes his mind when he spots a fat wad of cash in one of Miss Mism's hands and the trusty knuckleduster in the other.

Only when they're safely seated in the aircraft, which takes off barely two minutes later, do they begin to compare notes. It's agreed the Strangelove mission is done and dusted, which brings them on to Item Two on the agenda. Davinia's future. Accustomed as she is to the spy's life, always a double life, it ought to be second nature for Miss Mism to keep to herself her feelings towards the beautiful butterfly who's now in her care. But everyone makes mistakes.

'Friends like this, grapple them to thy soul with hoops of steel.' The words have slipped out of her mouth before she's had time to jam them back in.

'Ah, Hamlet.' Davinia smiles yet again. 'I do so love my books, so much more than I thought. But pray tell, who were you talking about?'

There'll be time later to beat herself up, for now Miss Mism's in damage-limitation hyperdrive. She plays for time by smoothing out her eyebrows, which are still slightly out of shape after their close encounter with Strangelove, then clears her throat noisily and slowly. It's like the warm-up act before the star performers hit the stage.

'My dear, I fear we in the service might have rather thrown you in at the deep end with what we were planning to put you through, but there's still a way you can be useful without sullying your purity. Books, you say? Well, rather a lot of ours need rather a lot of tidying up. We've got in a bit of a muddle about what we've been paying our agents, and whether we've got value for money. If you feel like sorting us out, we'll certainly pay you the proper amount.'

As Davinia's been feeling rather at a loose end since she handed in her notice at MI6 at least an hour ago now, and has yet to receive any job offers from the British Library or some equivalent, this does strike her as a maybe way forward. Hence the spark of interest in her eyes, which gives Miss Mism the slam-dunk opening she was hoping for.

'Of course you'd be able to do the work from home.' She's sounding so casual she could be talking about the price of lentils at Lidl's. 'Which means you could settle wherever you fancied. In Cornwall even, if you want a room with a view. It is quite pretty there, and I expect I could help fix you up with somewhere. Just a thought. Up to you of course.'

'Dear Mr Forster,' Davinia sighs. '*A Room With A View*. Sounds amusing. Diverting. Very well then, the rolling breakers beckon.'

Miss Mism isn't going to slip up again. Which is why she just nods, as absolutely matter-of-factly as she's absolutely not feeling.

CHAPTER TWELVE
WHATEVER NEXT?

The moment they get back to Cornwall, Miss Mism's on the blower to Trudi. She's as calm as you like, certainly a lot more so than Davinia, who's not used to hurtling down motorways at speeds of up to a hundred and sixty miles an hour.

'Now, young lady,' she raps out with her usual pretend indifference, 'come round to me. Instantly. Time for an update on your project. Which, I am prepared to concede, did not start exactly when or how I had in mind.'

Trudi is intrigued. The woman's tone may not have changed, but her tune has. Grudging though the admission was, it's the nearest thing she's ever come to an apology. For anything. Glancing at Tristan, who's dropped round for his own update, she promises to be there in a jiff.

'Oh, and by the way,' she adds, 'I hope it's OK if I bring a family friend. He is in the loop.' Tristan smiles at hearing his status spelled out so clearly. He certainly cemented relations with Percy, who opened the door to him on his arrival and offered him another ciggie. His whispered response, that he'd really love one but Trudi would kill him, had the man grinning all over his face. The little bunch of flowers he'd picked for Viv on the way made her like him that little bit more too. Luckily, she didn't catch the secret he'd just shared with her husband.

'Very well,' Miss Mism raps back. 'I have a colleague from the service here too, who's also up to speed on operations.' During the short walk up and down the grassy hills and knolls, speckled with pretty pink thrift flowers along the cliff top, Trudi more than once reminds Tristan not to turn left, as he'd fall into the sea. At the same time she's trying to picture this accomplice Miss Mism now seems to have in tow. Another scary person, she guesses, possibly a Sean Connery lookalike brandishing a Beretta, or some short-but-deadly bloke who uses his boomerang-style hat as a lethal weapon. In short, anything but a glamorous-looking young woman who looks straight out of Vogue magazine, circa 1924. Unsurprisingly then, when she lets them in, Trudi's intrigued, and Tristan is in love. Or thinks he is. A boy thing.

He can't stop staring at Davinia's intense blue/black eyes, which contrast exquisitely with her pale and perfect complexion. The strong, clear features of her face are rounded off, or, rather, squared off, with her no-nonsense, slightly angular jawline. And as she sweeps her lustrous ebony mane back it shows off the graceful nape of her neck to advantage. Also, she's tall and slender, same as him. To cap it all, she's effortlessly blowing rings within rings from the Black Russian that she's smoking today, through a mid-length cigarette holder that exactly matches her hair.

In the young man's eyes, that's beyond swoon-worthily, get-on-your-knees-and-propose-marriage-worthily, cool. She reads all this in his doe-eyes and smiles at him in a kindly, perhaps slightly condescending, way. Of course she's used to this sort of attention from young men, but not usually ones who must be a good ten years younger than she is. Yes, he is pretty, but for God's sake let's get real here.

Trudi looks from one to the other and is slightly put out. She doesn't exactly get the upspoken messages flitting between them, but does feel like stating plainly: 'He's my bestie, not yours.' But then she's distracted, as her glance hovers between Davinia and Miss Mism, by an odd quirk in the way they both look. They seem to share a subtle but distinctive kink in their left earlobe, which she'd barely even registered in all the years she's known her music teacher, but which now strikes her as, well, the sort of thing that runs in families. Of course it's just a coincidence, as she's already been told the relationship between the two of them is purely professional. Anyway, she's got other things to think about right now.

Davinia, meanwhile, is much more interested in Trudi than she is in Tristan. And, for different reasons, the hint of jealousy on the girl's part cuts both ways.

'My dear,' Davinia drawls disingenuously, 'dare I ask what is your age?' She's guessed at least fifteen.

'Twelve. And quite a bit.' All things are relative. Trudi's birthday was a good month ago.

'May Jesus rot in Hell.' Davinia's blasphemy is quite deliberate. She's thinking, hard and hatefully, about her puritanically domineering father, and the emotional straitjacket that he had her strapped into until she escaped to uni.

Yes, he did encourage her to read and, yes, books will be her passion as long as she lives. But throughout her school-age years she was little more than a shadow of her mother. Any ability to think for herself, still less to talk about anything, was bolted down in some kind of subconscious silo. Though this kid hasn't even reached her teens, poor Davinia suddenly feels like an untidy-looking cygnet gazing at a fully-fledged swan.

'Tell me about your father.' She's like a shipwrecked sailor grasping at anything floating. 'Does he try to, er, influence you in any way?'

'What? Dad? No. He's just a bumbling old ex-Prime Minister who totters along in his nutty sort of way, and leaves me to get on with it. Think he's a bit scared of me.' Even her eyebrows are grinning cheekily.

'But he does try to help when I ask him things.' Slightly more thoughtful now. 'Not that he always gets the answers right. Pity really. He does know loads of stuff, but he's a bit too clever for his own good, as well as a bit mad. Oh, and he smokes too much. With a ciggie holder, by the way, same as you.'

'And your mother?' Davinia's almost given up hope.

'Oh, she's much more sensible than Dad. For a grown-up, she's really quite, well, grown up, if you see what I mean. When I ask her things she quite often gets the answers right. Which can be quite helpful sometimes.'

'But she doesn't boss you around, just tell you father knows best, dear?' Though this is supposed to be a question, it feels more like a suicide note.

'Boss me around? Not really her style. She did once chase me round the house with a lethal weapon in her hand, but that was partly my fault I suppose. Mums do tend to be a bit funny about little children eating every single one of the jam tarts they've made for all the kids who're arriving any second for a birthday party.' Trudi smiles at the memory. 'I locked myself in the loo till she'd calmed down and started brushing her hair with the weapon instead of threatening me with it.'

Davinia's feelings are as mixed as a giraffe crossed with a jellyfish. She hates Percy and Viv for being just the sort of parents she so wishes she'd had, but can't wait to meet them. These days there's a comradeship between smokers. Especially ones who use holders. There's a good chance she'll hit it off with the mother too, so long as she remembers not to barge in and eat everything in sight.

Her thoughts are interrupted by Miss Mism exploding into the room like a whole shopful of lethal hairbrushes and giving Tristan a swipe on the bottom sort of look. 'Who, or what, are you?'

The young man has by now pulled himself together and more or less accepted that his love affair with Davinia probably won't take off just yet. So he's also able to pull himself to his full height, which is pretty much on a par with Miss Mism's. Holding out his right hand, he gives the usual can't-possibly-fail guff about being delighted to meet whoever it is at last, after hearing so much about them. Hoping, maybe even praying, that what he's heard isn't all bad, Miss Mism softens somewhat. The handshake she returns does feel like a clawing vulture, but she has noticed his nice eyelashes.

'Well, I'm told you're up to speed on our little venture. So you'd better come with the rest of us, to take stock of the situation.' As he steps into her gleaming white operations room with all its up-to-the-minute electronic gadgetry, and the row of clocks on the wall giving the time in different parts of the world, Tristan's knocked out by how different it is from with the rest of the cottage.

Trudi just gawps, as she's never been in there either.

Miss Mism presses a couple of keys on one of the computers, and a switch built into the pure white desk, and swivels round. So does everyone else as a panel on the opposite wall slides silently to one side, revealing a huge screen with Trudi's X feed on it. All the time there are new entries and responses, which now run into the hundreds of thousands, and which are looking very different from how they did only yesterday.

'Gather and surmise.' Her tone's very different from when she last said that to Trudi. This time she's looking like Monty must have done after the battle of El Alamein. Putting the frighteners on Strangelove really has worked, as the trolls he's brought have done their stuff. It's a win-win-win, beyond her wildest dreams. And the thought of her bet-loser of a section head having to stump up beats all the jam tarts any mother ever made for anyone.

Davinia can't believe how easily Miss Mism made this happen, without even having to have it off with the ugliest man in the world. She finds herself wishing she'd had a mum like her to show her the ropes instead of the woman she was saddled with. Looking back on it, the poor love was so under the thumb that she might just as well not have bothered to exist at all.

Of course you can't change history, but even just an older relative would have been a help. Someone she could have turned to ... Davinia heaves a bottomless pit of a sigh and stares forlornly at the big screen.

In place of all that shouty nonsense there's now a proper debate going on. People with letters after their names that look genuine are making informed and sometimes fascinatingly novel points, breathing fresh life into what had been a sterile and boring dialogue of the deaf. Not just in this thread, incidentally, but across the nation at large. Each of these thoughtfully sensible contributions is drawing more and more people in. At this rate it looks like the tens of thousands could multiply into millions, as though a dribbly little stream's suddenly turned into an ocean.

Trudi stares and stares at what started as, looking back on it, her rather silly idea of imagining everyone in the whole country might take notice of something she had to say – and finding, as if by magic, it's all coming true. She and Tristan raise their arms and slap their palms. Forget high-five, this is a five million.

CHAPTER THIRTEEN
THE PACE QUICKENS

As the days pass and the numbers joining in on her X thread continue to grow and grow, including more and more people Trudi thinks she might have heard of, it's starting to look like she really has cracked the code. And, sitting brightly to attention over the worn, knotty but lovely old stripped pine breakfast table, she shoots a pretend casual glance in her mother's direction.

'Mum, you do polling stuff. You noticing anything happening Brexitwise? Just wondering.'

Having been on intimate terms with her daughter for a good twelve-and-a-half years, Viv spots the edge in the question immediately. Even when Trudi was no more than a bulge in mummy's tummy she was a wilful little creature. Percy used to prod the sticky out bit sometimes, and they'd both smile at the way the barely formed infant kicked back.

'Why do you ask, darling? I'm just wondering too.' The difference being, in Viv's case, that she really is wondering whether her hunch is right, and that there's something Trudi might care to share with her. 'Well, since you ask, we got the results back from a survey last night that showed significantly more buyers' remorse than anything we've seen since the referendum all those years ago.

'This seems to be on the back of a fair bit of media interest in the subject, and a number of surprisingly thoughtful opinion pieces written by journalists whose minds had been closed for years. And a fair sprinkling of academics adding their two penn'orth. Of course there've been plenty of headbangers on the other side of the argument churning out the usual old rubbish too.

'Still, it's interesting. Almost as though some outside source has given the commentariat a good nudge and set the ball rolling. As to who or what might be behind it all, your guess is as good as mine. Or maybe, just maybe, yours is just a little bit better? Talk to me, Trudi, you have your mother's ear.'

'Er, well, Mum,' ever so clever though she's been, Trudi's still a bit nervous. 'Yes, my guess might be a little better than yours. You remember how cross I was a little while ago about Brexit? And how I was going to, er, fix it? Thing is, I have given it a go, on X. And, erm, I got Miss Mism to lend a hand.'

Viv splutters, gets a coughing fit and spills coffee all over the white blouse she's wishing she hadn't chosen for the Zoom call she's got booked in twenty minutes.

'Miss. Bloody. Mism?' she finally manages to snarl. 'Loose cannon? That woman's a rogue thermonuclear bloody device. Just off to put this bloody thing into soak, and change. Then perhaps you'll bloody tell me everything.'

As her mother marches out of the room, hastily unbuttoning her blouse as she goes, it occurs to Trudi she should have broken the news rather more gently. Four bloodies, practically back-to-back? And this from someone who hardly ever swears. Not such a surprise though, thinking about it. After all, Miss Mism has rather rung the changes over the years. First, the brilliant but barmy music teacher. Then, as if by magic, the lethally effective one-woman defence force. Useful, but unsettling. And finally, the rehabilitated and deadly counterespionage expert, trusted by MI6, feared by enemy intelligence agencies across the globe. The perfect person to have on side, then? Except that the common thread through the woman's phases is that she's not one to do things by halves. Oscar Wilde's line "nothing succeeds like excess" could have been written for her. She simply doesn't have a "steady as she goes" setting.

'Yes, Mum, I can see what you're getting at,' Trudi falters, as Viv sweeps back into the kitchen. 'Must admit she scared the frilly knickers off me when I first asked her to help. Still, all's well that ends well?' This last bit is directed at Percy, who's just ambled in with a hungry air and a fag on the go. She feels the need to get him on side, and Shakespeare references usually help.

'Battle's lost and won, then, eh?' He always enjoys getting in on the act, and is pretty sure his daughter will pick up on that line from Macbeth. But he also picks up on the tension in the air, and could have sworn Viv was wearing something different not half an hour ago. He shoots slightly anxious questioning glances at the two of them as he pours himself a cup of coffee, which is his idea of breakfast. Trudi glances back, also slightly anxiously, and produces the iPad that all this time she'd sneakily had on her lap. When she opens her X feed it's Percy's turn to cough, splutter and spill his drink all over the place. Doesn't matter quite so much in his case though, as he's wearing a black shirt.

'Fucking hell, Trudi,' he finally manages to gasp out, not noticing his ciggie's dropped out of the holder and lighting another one. 'How the hell have you managed that?'

'With a little too much help from Miss Mism,' Viv cuts in sharply.

'God. Not Miss fucking Mism. Tout se fucking explique. The woman's a genius, but also a fucking nutter.'

'She seems to have got results though,' Viv has to admit. 'Just look at this latest poll. Shows the nation's mood is shifting. Surprisingly quickly. Or perhaps not so surprisingly.'

As Percy peers over his wife's shoulder at the page she's just opened on her iPad, he feels like the earth really is flat, and he's just fallen off the edge of it. That conversation he had with Trudi last month. The one about how his way of going about things might just as well go back into the ark where it belongs. Speeches? Articles? Pah! Social media is the way forward. It's a consolation, but not much of one, that if things really are spiralling out of control, he at least might be able to help.

'Well, there's no point in crying over spilt milk,' he admits, then half changes his mind when he notices his shirt's all sticky. After hurrying up the stairs and into his and Viv's gloriously huge bedroom with its soft pastel-shaded walls and original paintings of beautiful sunsets and crashing waves, all done by local artists, he heads into the en suite bathroom. He doesn't risk putting his shirt in to soak in the sink as there's already a white blouse in there. Instead, he dumps it in the conveniently large wicker laundry basket, puts on another one – pale blue with pink flecks this time – checks how over the bloody hill he looks in the full-length mirror, half hates the magnificent sea views that are just as lovely as they would have been thousands of years ago, and does his best to stride back down again. If he's going to be a phoney at least he's going to be a genuine one.

'London. Now.' A bit of his old self is kicking in. 'Time we paid a visit to my old mucker Percival. Handy that he's managed to make it to Number Ten.'

She's surprised. Even a little bit impressed. Normally Dad's just … well, Dad. Writing stuffy stuff on his boring old computer, and regularly burning holes in the rugs in his office with fags that he's dropped. Easy to forget then that he was once Prime Minister, and to this day has mates in the highest of high places. At this moment Lady Casement flutters in, perches on her shoulder, peers at Percy and somehow manages to look a little bit impressed as well. Though it could just be because she thinks his shirt's rather cool.

'Not sure if he ought to respond by shifting government policy in tune with shifting public opinion, or to arrange a security detail to protect you from headbanging Brexit bulldogs who might get on your case. Maybe both. That's if he can manage either.' Percy tails off.

'Thing is, he's a dozy old fart. Only got the party leadership because everyone else was so crap, and Labour only got in because the Conservatives collectively took leave of their senses.

'How could they possibly think the punters wouldn't notice that abolishing income tax would mean the NHS would have to be dismantled? And wouldn't mind about free education being replaced by student grants for everyone over the age of four? Even their whacko wheeze of transporting all asylum seekers to slave camps in North Korea didn't strike everyone as desirable. Or even feasible, come to think of it.

'Turnout at the election was at an all-time low, by miles,' Percy adds, thoughtfully. 'Apart from their crap policies, they'd got through twelve Prime Ministers in two years. None of them chosen by the voters, obviously. And each one dottier than the last.'

'But your, er, old mucker Percival actually is the Prime Minister?' Trudi's eyebrows flicker. 'And he is supposed to be able to, well, you know, do things?'

'In theory, yes.' Percy's pause screams in practice, no. 'You did once meet the man, when he was Foreign Secretary. Don't you remember?'

'Him!' Trudi shouts. 'The bloke with a nose like Pinocchio when he's on a fib-fest? See what you mean, Dad.' Her voice is softer now, but nearly as pessimistic as her father's. 'He's about as much use as Ken in a crisis.' Viv manages a nervous smile in spite of herself as she spots the reference to the Barbie movie. It takes Percy a little longer, but that's partly because he's working on an idea.

'He did buck his ideas up a bit when I got him back on the ciggies, but I'm told he's off them again. Maybe I can entice him out to the Rose Garden and switch his brain back on. It's his bloody dominatrix of a wife buggering him up. Makes Bloody Mary look like Mother bloody Teresa.'

Trudi's mind wanders for a second back to the days when she had a pretty little swear box, always at the ready to cash in on Percy's indiscretions. What with what he's just said, not to mention Mum's straying from the straight and narrow a few moments back, she'd have been well on the way to getting those sparkly pink trainers she's been after for weeks.

'When we going then, Dad?' The way she raps out the question is a way of proving, to herself at least, that she's in charge. Annoyingly, the way Lady Casement clambers onto her shoulder and peers sideways into her face implies that she can dream on.

'The sooner the better,' Percy announces. 'Tomorrow, I think. The only question is whether we question Miss bloody busybody Mism before we go.

That question answers itself, as the sound of the Westminster chimes booms round the house. Viv glances up at the discreet little screen linked to the CCTV camera at the front door. Percy grumbled when she first insisted on having it installed, calling her a para-nurd nurd. But later he realised how useful it was when he wanted to pretend to be out when really boring people turned up, like the vicar.

'Talk of the bloody devil,' he gasps, 'here she bloody is. And who the hell's the belle she's got with her?'

'Oh, her,' Trudi smiles. 'That's Davinia. She's divine.'

CHAPTER FOURTEEN
LESSONS LEARNED

Viv eyes Davinia cautiously. She reminds her of someone. Someone from another life, maybe? She can't place her. But she can see that the cigarette holder the young woman's so casually dangling between her fingers is strikingly like Percy's. Also, she can't miss the fragrance – to put it politely – of the Black Russian sticking out of the end. Even more stinky than her husband's Gauloises. He'd better not copy her.

Percy isn't tempted, though he does wish he was that good at blowing smoke rings.

As a well-mannered, if at times slightly dotty gentleman, he makes a point of not seeming too interested in Davinia's remarkable good looks and excessively figure-flattering ankle-length midnight-blue dress. Or of the matching wide-brimmed hat that she's wearing at an angle that subtly shrouds one eye and half her face. But there is something else about her that gets him thinking. Something that also reminds him of someone. Like with Viv, someone from a past life. Except that, unlike Viv, that someone he has in mind – it's a couple of seconds before the penny drops – is himself.

It's to do with upbringing, he decides after a couple more seconds. His own was slightly confusing as it wasn't until he found out, as an adult, that he'd been adopted. Which was why he'd spent his entire childhood feeling like he'd misread his own birth certificate and turned up at the wrong house when he left the maternity ward. And it wasn't until he discovered his real heritage that he decided he wasn't a phoney after all. Likewise, with this woman, all that front feels more like a stage set than anything more solid. Curious. In fact, curiouser and curiouser. But that'll have to wait, as he's got more pressing priorities on his mind, like keeping Trudi alive.

'Well, woman,' he barks at Miss Mism, 'you've certainly put my daughter in the firing line this time.'

'And I've got her what she wanted,' she replies, just as haughtily, and looking him straight in the eye. This doesn't give her a crick in the neck, as she's pretty nearly as tall as he is.

'But at what cost?' Percy's sounding slightly less sure of himself.

'You can't make an omelette without breaking eggs.' Miss Mism's sounding slightly more sure of herself.

'It is a truth universally acknowledged that a young girl in possession of a good idea must be in want of an ally,' Davinia purrs sweetly. Recognising where that comes from, Trudi claps her hands and twinkles her eyes at her.

As it's the first time Percy and Viv have heard their glamorous visitor speak, they're both struck by her vowels that are so rounded that they come out of her mouth like tiny balloons. Percy in particular, as he was a broadcaster before entering politics. Viv, with her intuitively feminine ear, can't help noticing the faintly flirty-teasy undertone, though Percy wonders whether behind that there's also the tiniest hint of something else. Like, maybe, she's trying to make out she's someone, but secretly worrying that she might actually be someone else. Miss Mism simply laps it all up, but crams adoring glances at Davinia and Trudi right back up her optic nerves. Focus! Focus!

'Yes, well, Jane Austen is all very, er, well,' Viv snaps. 'But what we need to assess is whether it's a good idea to expose a twelve-year-old chi... er, girl, to a likely backlash from bigots who've set their ugly faces against what she's trying to achieve.'

'Interesting literary and historical fact,' Percy muses. 'Many people attribute the omelette and eggs line to Lenin or Stalin. But in fact it seems to come from Robert Louis Stevenson, just before the turn of the nineteenth century.'

'Shut. Up.' Viv's in full Vivienne mode.

Percy can see a white flag is called for, and is careful not to say anything about keeping red flags flying. Or anything else. Just for the moment it's not only Trudi's survival at stake.

'I do take your point, however,' Miss Mism says, mainly to Viv, 'and am wondering whether we should take the matter higher. A trip to Legoland perhaps?'

'Legoland?' Viv demands.

'You know – or rather, it would seem, don't remember – it's where my bosses hang out. That funny-looking place south of the river. Vauxhall Cross, otherwise known as the headquarters of Britain's Secret Intelligence Service.'

'Funny you should say that,' Percy's found his voice again. 'We were thinking of taking a trip to where I used to hang out. That funny-looking place north of the river. Ten Downing Street, otherwise known as the headquarters of Britain's Prime Minister.' His play-fighting with Miss Mism's gone on as long as they've known one another, though it isn't always particularly playful. Especially not now.

'Glad that's agreed then,' Trudi chirps. 'Can I ride in your super-duper motor, Miss Mism?' She's never been in it, but has heard it's quite fast.

'Sounds altogether charming,' Davinia drawls. 'I could go with you, delightful Percy and darling Viv, and get to know you both better.' She's yet to learn that she's letting herself in for two-hundred-and-fifty miles in one of the slowest, and oddest, cars on the road. But rather than repeat that hair-raising experience in the Tesla, she'd be happy to travel in a wheelbarrow. Not that there's all that much difference, she'll soon find out, between that and a beautifully restored and prettily painted but still sixty-year-old Citroen 2CV. Known to many, affectionately or otherwise, as the 'Tin Snail'.

She'll also find out, even sooner, that there's more to Fangle than a pretty and adorable little pussycat.

Judging by the way he's been stretched out and softly snuffling in the cosy little wicker basket that he arrived in, and is still just about big enough for him, he hasn't found the humans' conversation especially interesting. But then he opens one eye and spots how the art deco charms loosely attached to Davinia's silver bracelet glitter and sparkle as she gesticulates while talking. Beyond interesting, this is prey, to be captured and butchered, if not necessarily eaten.

Springing up from the mosaic-tiled floor to the subtly-toned pale green work surface, he tautens into the kill position. The terrible twitching, both in his clenched back legs and his tail, indicate that attack in imminent. Or, rather, would have done, if anyone had been watching. Because they aren't, the element of surprise is absolute. And, equally absolutely, Davinia's kitchen cred is crushed.

It's said that when England's King Edward II was murdered, in a particularly nasty way, his screams could be heard from outside the walls of his castle prison. Though just about every aspect of that story is now disputed, there's no getting round it. Davinia's squeal was piercingly, bloodcurdlingly, loud, much like the sound a baby might make if Dracula pounced into its pram.

Miss Mism nearly lets slip her true feelings as she leaps to her feet and whips out the knuckleduster, before hastily slipping it back into the folds of her dress and settling for shooing the cat away. Having seen it all before, many times, Percy and Viv simply snigger. But Trudi's reaction is more complicated, because she sees Davinia as, well, not old exactly, but certainly a grownup. Watching her adulty mask slipping like that tells her something she hadn't thought of. No matter how ancient a person might be, you can still find the kid inside if you scratch them hard enough. Or rather, as in this case, if your cat does.

Meanwhile, Percy picks up the fag, still amazingly in its holder, that shot halfway across the room when Davinia had her near-death experience. He has a sneaky puff before giving it back, and decides he was right earlier on. These black numbers really are gaspers. Even though the woman has just exposed her soft centre, and is finding it a struggle to rebuild her supercool image, she's also pretty hardcore.

'Well, that was amusing, was it not?' Davinia's drawl is more pronounced than ever, but the huge smoke rings she's blowing look like mushroom-cloud images from early atom bomb tests.

'The rest is silence.' Miss Mism's casual-not-casual way of hiding behind Hamlet again gets Trudi thinking a little bit more. These two are supposed to be no more than colleagues, yet there's something almost protective in the way the older woman is trying to move so swiftly on. Fangle doesn't exactly help matters by keeping the show on the road for a bit longer. Reaching out for Davinia's wrist with one of his front paws, he gently pulls it towards him and starts licking the injuries he's just inflicted. A guilty conscience? Everyone thinks how sweet this is, except for Viv, who suspects the little monster just likes the taste of blood.

'Right, well, that's enough drama for one day,' she announces. 'Expect us at yours, Miss Mism, around ten in the morning. We'll take Davinia, and Trudi can show you where the place is.'

It's a double-fronted, four-bedroomed Georgian flat in the best bit of Camden Town, close to Primrose Hill, handily doubling up both as her London office and somewhere for everyone to stay when they're in town. And because Trudi has a seemingly supernatural ability to find her way around, ever so much better than either of her parents, or even Google Maps sometimes, it seems sensible to Viv to let her act as Miss Mism's guide. Had she any idea how fast the bloody woman drives she'd sooner the kid walked than got within a hundred miles of the Tesla. But that won't become clear until she finally makes to Camden, only to be told that they'd watched an entire movie and still had lots of time left over while they were waiting.

Though she's trying ever so hard to shake off both the terror she felt when Fangle got his claws into her, and her embarrassment at having shown herself up as such a wuss, Davinia's still wobbly. So it's a great relief when, far from hurtling up the drive, they stick to a gentle amble.

But there's method in the Mism madness, to do with the thought of having Trudi to herself for hours and hours, without the distraction of having to giving her a bloody piano lesson. Taking off in her usual way would have put the kibosh on that.

Everything changes as Penislow Palace disappears out of sight, and in seconds they're skidding round the bends at ninety. Davinia decides it'd be even worse to be crushed under a tractor than savaged by a kitten and does what she vowed at the age of eighteen never to do again. At least the woman picks up the words 'deliver us from evil' and eases back on the throttle.

Not that slowing down to eighty-five is exactly dawdling.

CHAPTER FIFTEEN
WHEELS WITHIN WHEELS

After a long night of dreaming about lions, tigers and carnivorous dinosaurs, Davinia wakes with a glorious thought in her head. She isn't facing a kamikaze car crash in the Tesla. This helps her to slip her mask of faintly amused indifference neatly back into place.

But it falls off again the minute the Penislow party belches and lurches up to Miss Mism's front door. She has such a fit of girly giggles that the Black Russian she's just lit falls out of the holder and, on its way down, burns a hole in her dress. Not that she'll notice it until she's halfway to London, many hours later.

When this happens, Viv will get a rush of schadenfreude, because, stepping out of her pride and joy, she immediately spots what the cheeky madame's finding so funny. Ok, it was out of character to buy a Citroen 2CV, more so still to replace it, when the thing eventually died, with an even older one. But that's not the point.

Percy had to admit, after the recon job, that the paintwork was rather fetching. Best not mention that getting a proper car would have been an even better idea, but there is something sweet about Viv's way of letting her hair down. Normally so sensible, efficient and practical, her little indulgence is colourful in every sense. Davinia picks up on that.

'But, darlings, what simply glorious little pink butterflies your, er, machine has all over it! And how delightfully they tone with its interestingly watercolour pale blue, er, bodywork.' The thought of spending God knows how many hours in this ghastly contraption has wiped the smile off her face. But at least the bloody cat won't be there too, as Percy's told her that the lovely lady-what-does obligingly doubles up as a pet-sitter. Clearly a masochist or a nutter.

The back of the car seems to shrink as she squeezes herself in. The only way to get even vaguely comfortable is to wedge up tightly on one side and half stretch out her legs across the weirdly elasticated seat. And there's something hateful in the way the vile machine responds to her body weight by tilting downwards, as though she's just put on about fifteen stone. She'll want to kill it when she adjusts the folds of her dress and spots the burn mark.

It'll be no consolation when Percy cheerily tells her the 2CV's designed to let a farmer drive easily and safely across a ploughed field with a top hat on his head and a bag of eggs on the passenger seat. Still, when he admits that Citroen stopped making them before she even turned two, she feels she's won the argument.

Miss Mism has taken the obvious precaution of setting off first, with her ever-so-excited passenger. Though Trudi's never been in this car before, she has a hunch it's faster than Mum's, on the grounds that it couldn't really be any slower, except while it's idling in neutral.

As she settles into the Tesla's neatly streamlined front passenger seat, Trudi lets her mind travel through time. Yes, it was naïve of her to think she could just reverse Brexit with a snap of her fingers. Which is why, to allow more time for the reforms she'll have brought about to fully bed down, she'll take a nice relaxing gap year before heading for uni. But looking back on things it strikes her that right from her make-believe world of dear little dollies to almost the present day, her whole life has been a glorified gap year.

Suddenly she's struck by another gap, in the bit of the car where knobs, switches and dials usually are. Apart from a computer screen there's just one half-hidden button that Miss Mism fiddles with before easing up the road. Once out of sight of the dear little 2CV, Trudi feels like she's in a beetle that's suddenly opened its lumpy back and switched to wing power.

The bit on the screen that gives the car's speed has obviously muddled miles per hour with kilometres, as they can't possibly be going that fast. Also, the telegraph poles on this stretch of road must be closer together than usual, given how they're whizzing by. Then, when they hit the dual carriageway out of Cornwall, she's intrigued by how slowly everyone else seems to be going.

Then, in about a quarter of the time it usually takes, they pass the speed camera not far short of Exeter. Trudi glances anxiously over her shoulder, but when it flashes at them twice, in what looks like a fit of extreme rage, Miss Mism only smiles at her. In a forlorn hope of distracting her into slowing down, just bit at least, she risks a question that's been much on her mind lately.

'I'm ever so grateful, er, I think, that you agreed to help with my Brexit campaign.' She's faltering already. 'But I didn't really expect you to go to quite so much trouble. Also, you disappeared completely for a while, and I can't help but wonder where you went, and why?'

Deftly undertaking a row of high-powered sports cars in the outside lane, then weaving between several road hogs in the middle bit, seemingly just for fun, Miss Mism thinks about how much she dares share with the girl. And how best to not let on about her silly granny fantasy.

'I have long thought Brexit was a damaging idea from the nation's point of view, not least because it inhibits our intelligence-gathering capacity. This has been a matter of serious debate between myself and one of my respected colleagues at MI6.' Respected? That tosser? But she's choosing her words carefully.

'Truth of the matter is,' the gruff tone's not really convincing, 'I have always been rather fond of you. Actually.

'And, yes, when I discovered my endeavours to advance your cause had gone slightly awry, I took Davinia to, er, the Philippines. To set matters straight.'

Trudi goes very quiet. She has sometimes wondered if Miss Mism likes her a teeny bit more than she's ever let on, perhaps even respects her, just a teeny bit. Could be why she came within a gnat's of actually saying sorry about messing up. But flying halfway round the world? Her voice, when she eventually finds it, is ever so tiny.

'Thank you. Thank you ever so, ever so much.'

Miss Mism's eyes flap wildly open, but her mouth stays firmly shut. And the time-lapse between either of them saying anything starts to feel as wide as a mountain range. Eventually, stumbling towards the foothills, Trudi changes the subject.

'Don't suppose you'd fancy, would you, driving just the teensiest bit less fast?'

'Tush.' Miss Mism is no more one for speed limits than she is for heartfelt sentiments. 'The law was ever more honoured in the breach than the observance.' There, good old Hamlet. Nice and safe. She smiles gleefully as another camera flashes at the Tesla.

This happens oftener and oftener as they hit London. And, by the time they finally pull up in the underground garage near the flat, where Viv rents spaces, Trudi's totted up at least two hundred points and a good lifetime's disqualification.

She clambers out of the car, astonished that she's still alive, only to be told to step round the vehicle and read what it says on the back. She wonders exactly how much you'd have to pay for a number plate that reads M16 OOZ.

'Wait and watch,' Miss Mism calls through the open window as she fiddles with the button she'd pressed before setting off. Trudi obeys, but can't think why until what she's looking at swivels on some kind of invisible axis.

In place of hideously expensive M16 OOZ, there now appears flagrantly illegal FUK U2.

CHAPTER SIXTEEN
WHO YOU KNOW

Trudi has a flashback to when Mummy, as she then was, took her for her first piano lesson.

At that time, all those years back, the pillows sewn into the inside of Miss Mism's dresses strongly suggested she was funny in the head. And now, whirling around in her crazy made-up world of spies and lies, nothing much seems to have changed.

On the other hand, the woman's reaction to Viv's fancy apartment and office space, in what is after all one of the swankiest bits of London, is oddly, well, normal. Given that her own home is a crime against good taste, about as cool as a T-shirt worn back to front with the label showing, Trudi's always assumed the woman had had a style by-pass at birth.

Then again, maybe she thinks the same about design and décor as she does about the law of the land. Fine for other people, just not for her.

As she steps through the front door, Miss Mism looks approvingly at the ornamented high ceilings and airy spaciousness of the pale-green decorated living rooms. She also takes a closer look at the contrasts created by the large gilt-framed prints of lush sunsets painted by JMW Turner, side-by-side with blown-up political cartoons spanning everything from the Victorian period to the present day. Next, she slips off her shoes and curls up her toes, to get a better feel of the deep-piled mid-green carpeting. Then, when Trudi swishes back a William Morris printed curtain to reveal a ninety-eight-inch television screen, she grins like a schoolgirl.

'Right, dear,' she announces as she lowers herself into the deep-green velvet sofa directly opposite, 'off you go and make us a cup of tea. Then we can watch a movie, er, or two, er, or three, while we're waiting for the others.' Busying herself in the state-of-the-art kitchen with its shiny bronze-effect up-to-the-minute appliances, Trudi decides that sitting still and watching other people instead of her risking their lives is a very nice idea. Pulling out from the classy Whirlpool fridge-freezer a couple of chocolate ice creams, she knows exactly what to plump for.

'We're going for *The World Is Not Enough*. You'll love it when the speedboat shoots out of the side of your office building into the Thames. You might even tell me which bits could be true and which are obviously made up.' Miss Mism allows herself another smile as she settles back into the sofa. She'd put her arm round Trudi if she dared, but just quietly sitting with the girl for a whole two-and-a-bit hours' worth of viewing feels like an entire warehouse full of ice creams.

When the movie's over, the two of them while away another contented hour or so as Trudi shows Miss Mism round the other rooms, then points out the versatility of the Yamaha Clavinova digital piano, whose relative littleness is the one admission that the flat really isn't as big as Penislow Palace. She's just getting to the end of her favourite bit of, appropriately, Schubert's *Unfinished Symphony*, when the key turns noisily in the front door.

Because she's not to know that these hours spent together have been some of the happiest Miss Mism remembers in her whole life, Trudi can't make out why she whips her shoes back on and tautens like a bowstring. A bit disappointing really, as they seem to have bonded as never before. But then she's distracted by what's left of Davinia stumbling in, followed by a hungry, but far more serene-looking, Percy and Viv.

'Hello, everyone, what took you so, er ...?' Trudi doesn't bother to finish the sentence. Five microwaved instant meals and not a lot of chatter later, everyone heads off to bed, and to an interesting variety of dreams. Tonight, Davinia's are full of hurricane-tossed seas and being lashed to the mainmast of a ship that stubbornly refuses to move at more than a millionth of a knot.

Next morning, bright and early (especially by Trudi's standards), they call an Uber to swing by Downing Street, then across Vauxhall Bridge to MI6. The decision to leave their own cars in the garage is something of a relief to Trudi. To Davinia, it's a gift from the God that she so flatly refuses to believe in.

As Percy's already arranged security clearance for his wife and daughter, getting to the front door of Number Ten is relatively easy. The gaggle of TV crews waiting for some boring foreign bloke or other barely spare them a glance, though, rather sweetly, the old guy who lets them in recognises the former Prime Minister from back in the day and gives him a typical ex-serviceman's salute. And a smile, which goes down well. He makes a quick call, then points towards the stairs and says respectfully: 'Up top. You know the way, sir.'

Once inside the prime ministerial flat, Percy looks round at the dullness of it all and is absolutely not surprised. Sir Percival Spectacle always was drearily suburban, and since his attractive but domineering wife made him give up the smokes, he's clearly lost half the will to live. Trudi looks at him in surprise. When she last saw him, she couldn't take her eyes off his remarkable nose, which she felt at that time made the Eiffel Tower look quite petite. What she can't get over now is that she still can't get over it.

'Ah, Sir Percival, delighted to see you again.' She's trying to behave. 'And, boy, have I got nose for you. Er ... news.' Oops, fallen at the first hurdle, but Dad comes to the rescue. Simply being back in his old watering hole has sharpened his wits wonderfully, and he covers his daughter's faux pas with a ridiculously loud coughing fit. Sir Percival looks suspiciously from one to the other and hopes he didn't hear what he suspects he just heard. With a forced kindly smile, he welcomes the girl.

'My, how you've grown.' Trudi does her best to return the smile, but can't help feeling disappointed that that's the best he can come up with. After all, he is supposed to be clever enough to run the country. Percy decides best move swiftly on.

'Well, me ole mucker, my daughter here seems to have got the anti-Brexit ball rolling nicely. The polls have been consistently showing for long enough that a clear majority of punters now wish we hadn't left. And, thanks to her efforts, we're definitely nudging up to a critical mass. So how about it? What say you grab the British bulldog by the horns and announce we're having a crack at getting back in?' Percy knows full well what a scaredy-cat Spectacle is, and always was, probably even when he was supposed to be a raunchy teenager. So he's not surprised to receive a limp-wristed, bordering on buggered-if-I-know, kind of response. But he does have an ace up his sleeve that's done the trick in the past.

'Of course, I quite understand you have to be cautious.' Spectacle spots the glint in Percy's eye and feels an even greater need to be cautious.

'But it is a lovely day. So how about we grab a bit of, nudge-nudge-nod-and-a-wink, fresh air in the rose garden? Maybe alight on some sort of solution? Not like we're at the fag-end of a parliament.' He doesn't quite tap the side of his nose with all these subtle-not-subtle hints, but Spectacle's resistance is already crumbling. The tiny, just-visible glow in his cheeks is like the first glimmers of seismic activity in the build-up to a volcanic eruption. Both Viv and Trudi know exactly what Percy's game is, and think he's completely shameless. Not that they mind, just this once.

Once they're all out in the soon-not-to-be fresh air, both men's eyes are on fire. Percy's well prepared, with, in addition to his fully-stocked cigarette case, three spare packs of Gauloises. The same wicked trick worked wonders when he used it to get the man to do as he was told three years ago, and he's pretty confident it will again. Spectacle knows he knows, and is literally gasping to be proved right. A faraway, dreamy look comes into his eyes as he watches the first fag being placed in the holder and used to light the second one. His hands tremble and very soon only the whites of his eyes can be seen as he inhales, and inhales again. And again. And again. This is putting his marriage on the line, as it did last time. Against that, he sighs contentedly, 'Who says a fag doesn't beat a shag? You bastard.

'Seems only yesterday,' his eyes look weirder than ever, 'our golden retriever jumped up to the kitchen table and nicked a sponge cake my mum had just baked. He wasn't stupid, knew there'd be hell to pay, but reckoned it was worth it. Couldn't believe it at the time. Can see where he was coming from now.' Though she's pleased that Percy's ploy is working, Viv can't believe how weak and stupid men are. But Trudi's prepared to cut the guy a bit of slack, on the grounds that having a nose like that must mean he's got an uncontrollably powerful sense of smell.

Whatever the reason, Spectacle seems to have morphed from inert chrysalis into fluttering butterfly. Divorce? Who cares? After pocketing the other packs of ciggies, he announces loudly, and in the earshot of a young intern who happens to be engaged to a top political journalist, that reversing Brexit is definitely a runner.

'Won't happen overnight, but we've been forging better links and lifting levels of cooperation ever since we got in, as you know. And thanks to your charming daughter and her magnificent social media campaign, now could be the moment for the decisive push.' Trudi claps her hands, as does the intern, who'd spotted her stuff on X, now puts two and two together and puts in a lightning call to his fiancée. She calls her junior colleague who's been kicking his heels out in the street for hours, and when, some thirty minutes later, the Penislow party steps out of the black door, one camera rolls. After the shouted question 'Oi, Trudi, you gonna get us back into Europe?' the other cameras fix on her. More than that, the bloke who got the ball rolling follows her up the street and begs her to come into the studio for a sit-down interview.

'It's only just up da road, luv.' He's breathless, but on it. 'In numbah fore Millbank. We'll put you on straight away. Great bein' a star, innit?' Percy looks at him slightly sadly. This junior producer, who looks scarcely out of his teens but is almost certainly a graduate, Cockney accent or no, doesn't even recognise him. This is bloody galling, but at the same time he's slightly ashamed of thinking about himself when his daughter should be his first concern. It certainly is Viv's.

'Which organisation do you represent, pray? And how can you possibly know what we've been talking about in Number Ten?' Though she's giving him a gunmetal glare the bloke is unfazed.

Cheekily he hits her back with 'In dis place da walls 'ave ears. Dat line's from 'amlet, by da way, but da bard weren't da first geezer to use it.' His way of pointing out that though he was born within the sound of Bow Bells, he did get a degree in English before the masters in media studies.

Percy's suddenly curious about this chap, in spite of everything, and so's Trudi. Viv just wants to throttle him.

CHAPTER SEVENTEEN
LOST AND WON

The Cockney intern survives the seven-minute walk from Downing Street to Number Four Millbank.

Not that he has an easy ride, as father and daughter take it in turns to fire questions at him. By the time they're dodging the cars and buses between Whitehall and Parliament Square, it's established that he works for the latest start-up TV outlet, called "Free Up Connected Knowledge News", and as they weave through the traffic again to get to Millbank, the Cockney lad smirks when Percy points out that the channel's long name can shorten to FUCK News.

'Yeah, I know dat, and so does da boss. But da fing is 'ee's like Puck in da dreem. Got a wicked sense of 'umour, right? You might 'ave 'erd ov 'im, 'is name's Jonny Breeze.' Percy starts.

'Heard of him? I worked with him for years before I went into politics. He's a good egg, in his off-the-wall way.' At this, the young producer looks at Percy long and hard and his face scrunches up. First with fevered concentration, then with embarrassment. But by the time they reach Abingdon Green he's figured out how to cover his tracks.

'Must admit, Lawd Penislow, arve orlways bin a great admirer of yours. Reel prividlidge to finally meet ya. An ov course yer'll get ta see yer ole mucker again in a minnit. 'Ee's frontin' da show dat starts in arf an 'aar. We can orl 'ave a nars cuppa in da rest-rong in da numbah fore basement before de interview.' He knows he's chancing his arm, but is pretty confident the gamble will pay off. The more so as the hurried text he bangs off to Jonny gets an immediate cheering emoji back.

Viv finally has to give up as the five of them settle in their armchairs in the timber-floored cosy bit of the restaurant, and Percy and Jonny start on a good old chinwag about the good old days. But they know this isn't exactly a social call, and in no time the conversation gets round to the interview with Trudi.

'Well, gal, you up for it then?' The abrupt question gets an abrupt response.

'Do bears do poo-poos in the woods? You think I've come all this way just for the fun of it?' Over his half-glasses, Jonny's grizzled and absurdly thick Denis Healey-style eyebrows rise in genuine surprise. And delight, as he can see he's got a bit of a scoop on his hands. He nonetheless shoots Percy a jowly but reassuring grin.

'Don't worry, me ole china, I'll take it gently,' he mutters. Viv gives him the full gunmetal. 'You bloody better, or you'll wish you'd never been born.'

It being the middle of the silly season, there's not much around. Which is why Jonny decides to lead off with the Trudi interview as soon as the boring old news segment, stuffed with the usual murders, motorway pile-ups and international disasters, is out of the way. It is at least long enough, just, for Percy to prep Trudi.

'Do not, repeat, *do not* on any account, give him the full low-down on what happened in Number Ten, darling. Just say we all had a nice chat and Speccie seemed reasonably receptive to your plea to up the tempo in tightening ties with Europe. Go any further than that and the press office will deny everything. Worse than that, the silly old sod will probably do as he's told and break his promises. Meaning we'll have achieved Sweet Fanny Adams. You follow me?' She nods, and, as the adverts roll, marches across to the guest seat in the on-air studio.

Jonny grins at the swinging arms and doesn't even need the autocue to tee her up as he's already eating out of her hand. So he should be, she thinks, grateful nonetheless for the make-up lady's last-minute touch-up job, but well satisfied that her long, pastel-pink dress offsets her blonde hair so nicely. She'd originally pinned on her little silver brooch with the EU emblem on it, but then took it off, as the colours really didn't go with anything else. Definitely a good move, under these unforgiving lights.

Sitting pertly to attention as Jonny does his introductory spiel, Trudi inwardly rehearses her lines. She's thoroughly grateful for all those starring roles in school plays, as they taught her how to get a script into her head and keep it there. And, sure enough, when he finally asks her how it went in Downing Street, she's word-perfect.

'Well, I must say,' she's using her best queen-of-the-fairies voice, 'we all had a nice chat, and old Speccie did seem reasonably receptive to my plea for closer ties with Europe.' Staring through the glass in the control room, Percy nods with satisfaction.

'I like to think a man as well-endowed as he is has a nose for wise advice.' She's getting impish. Staring even harder through the glass in the control room, Percy crosses his fingers. 'Of course he's bound to be cautious.' There's a devilish gleam in her eyes. 'But hopefully in the end we can smoke him out.' Percy doesn't know whether to laugh or cry, but settles for avoiding the gunmetals. He can almost hear them shouting 'I told you so!'

Trudi gets into her more sensible stride after that, patiently explaining how much more difficult the original Brexit deal made life for all soon-to-be undergraduates who had any thoughts of overseas study. Likewise, any professional musician wanting to perform outside our borders. Which did rather get her thinking about all sorts of drawbacks stemming from our pulling out. Before long, thanks to a combination of her high-octane tone, and the height of the stool she's sat on, Jonny more or less forgets he's talking to a twelve-year-old. And after what seems like only a few seconds, though it's actually a good ten minutes, he's thanking her sincerely for her time and bidding her farewell. As the adverts roll and she skips out of the studio, Percy gives her a huge high-five. Viv goes for the full Mummy hug.

'Not a foot wrong, darling, even though you were very naughty about the cigarettes.'

'And the nose.' She's having an eat-all-the-birthday-tarts flashback.

'But you're supposed to be nervous in your first TV appearance.'

Percy's more put out than he likes to let on. 'Me, I was wetting myself. Kept the footage for months, just to remind myself how crap I was.' Trudi's tactful enough not to go back over their earlier conversation about young people like her being so much more media-savvy than stone-age relics like him. Viv half reads her mind and decides to bustle them away before she does it anyway.

It gets a bit more complicated when they step out of the FUCK News studios only to be waylaid by several eager young reporters from rival channels. As the slow news day hasn't got any faster in the last half hour, they're all after a slice of Trudi action. But, though she's on a high now, Viv can see she'll swiftly be on the wane, and is strongly minded to tell them all to bugger off. In the end they compromise on a mini on-camera news conference, known in the trade as a huddle, here and now, in the corridor. Spotting an odd little pointy sculpture that'd turn his daughter into a unicorn if it looked like it was growing out of her head, Percy shuffles them along a bit. Then, barely ten minutes later, the whole thing's done and dusted and they're headed for the building's imposing front door.

Turns out the trial-by-telly was the nice bit. Because, when they step into the street, there's an unruly gaggle of all-too media-savvy right-wing oiks shouting rude things at them. They must have clocked the FUCK News interview, because they're certainly on a mission to tell this bloody bitch that she's a disgrace to Englishness and needs to shut her shitty gob. Viv's body language instantly becomes the human equivalent of Fangle's when he's moving in for the kill, but, as good luck would have it, a black cab's just pulling up and letting someone out. They're in it, in a flash, and gone.

But flash is the operative word, as a couple of snappers who happened to be nearby caught the horrified expression on Trudi's face before the cab door slammed behind her. Also, a quick-thinking Sky News cameraman shot the whole thing, including the yobbos' nasty shouts and horrid gestures.

'Bugger and buggeration. The shape of things to come?' Percy's way of breaking the silence says it all. So does Viv's tightly clenched mouth. Likewise the trembling in Trudi's lower lip. Mummy holds her tightly and Daddy looks like he's just swallowed a whole nest of wasps. Not a lot more is said in the mercifully quick journey back to what suddenly feels like an MI5 safe house. A relief to all that London traffic always thins out during the summer holidays.

Davinia opens the door and blows them a smoke ring. Her way of saying, presumably: 'I suppose not much happened when you met the Prime Minister with the intention of radically altering the course of British history?'

Percy, who'd been dying for a fag since before they even entered Number Four Millbank and is now puffing ferociously, blows several clouds' worth back at her. His way of saying: 'Whaddaya bloody mean nothing's bloody happened, when the bloody universe just imploded?'

Miss Mism, who's standing behind Davinia and staring anxiously at her phone, looks up sharply. Percy's face is a scary confirmation of a long text message that ends with the words, 'Swivel-eyes on the warpath. Closing in already. You know what to do.' To help calm her nerves she reaches in the folds of her dress for the trusty knuckleduster and clenches her fist round it. She also mentally wraps the forefinger of her other hand round the trigger of the AK-47 that's stored, as always, in the boot of the Tesla.

But this masculine rage is nothing to the woman's instinct to protect her young. It's as though Miss Mism has transformed into a swooping dragon with poison-tipped claws, flames gushing out of enormous jaws, and slitty eyes burning round the edges.

'The female of the species is more deadly than the male.' Her words, oozing out of her mouth like poisonous gas, don't have anything to do with anything, from what any of the others can work out. Percy's tempted to run his hand across her forehead to check she's not feverish, but has the feeling that she might bite. Or flick out a long, lizard-like tongue and actually eat him.

Eventually the battle of the sexes within her subsides, and the somewhere-in-the-middle bit wins out. After all, it's too late now to wish she hadn't egged the girl on. Besides which, it looks like the Downing Street visit actually is set to make a difference. For better and for worse, however.

Spectacle's spectacular pronouncement wasn't just overheard by the intern who tipped off his fiancée, but also by the Foreign Office's man in Number Ten. He could hardly wait to pass it on to his boss in King Charles Street, who terrified his secretary by dancing a jig round his office, uncorking a magnum of his best champagne, glugging half of it down straight from the bottle and whooping like a demented dervish. Given that getting back into Europe had been a key departmental objective ever since Britain pulled out, the bloke did rather gild the lily when he got on the blower to MI6. And they did the same when they shared the news every bit as quickly with opposite numbers in Brussels and beyond.

'The intelligence community is gratified by the latest developments. That's the good news,' Miss Mism announces, as they all sit down to a nice cup of tea. Or rather, in Trudi's case, a comforting choc-ice, and in Percy's a fat swig of brandy. To go with his third ciggie since getting out of the cab.

'And the bad?' Viv's steely tone matches her eyes.

'Ah, yes, well, you see …' For once Miss Mism isn't sounding like Good Queen Bess spurring on her chaps before the Spanish Armada. 'You see, er, my mob put in a precautionary call to the domestic lot across the river, and they put out a few feelers about certain political groupings. And, er …'

'You mean MI5 are on to something?' Percy cuts in. 'Like, neo-Nazi nasties on fucking manoeuvres? With Trudi in their fucking cross hairs?' The penny's just dropped. He couldn't figure out how come those yobbos were on their case so quickly after the TV gig. He can now.

CHAPTER EIGHTEEN
OPPOSITE EXTREMES

The tea, choc-ice, brandy and cigs all help. A bit. But not all that much, in spite of Miss Mism's efforts at calming everyone's nerves.

Davinia wins the prize for looking the most chilled of all, but this is largely because MI6 accepted that, due to primitive public transport arrangements west of the Tamar, she'd better be allocated a vehicle. Meaning she can Uber it down to Vauxhall to pick up the nice, sensible Mini that she'll be able to just jump into and drive back to Cornwall. In complete comfort. And safety.

'Well, what do we know about these neo-Nazi scumbags then?' Percy, having downed two more fat balloons' worth of brandy, and lit his sixth ciggie since getting out of the cab, is ready to hear the worst.

'Ah. As it happens, I do seem to have more intel,' Miss Mism tells him, scanning her phone and opening a briefing note from MI5 that her boss has just forwarded to her. 'Straight from the horse's mouth, so to speak.' She clears her throat.

'The new far-right group, that rejoices in the title Supremely Helpful Intelligent Testimony Party, has an interestingly eclectic set of policies, which can only be described as nationalistically incoherent.' She clears her throat again. Only this time it's more of a rasp.

'Their central complaint is that England isn't English at all any more, while Scotland and Wales are a clear and present danger.

'And their central demand is that all migrants, whether hitherto deemed legal or illegal, should be jetted off to the north pole and jettisoned without parachutes.

'This they judge to be proportionate, humane, and fair, as no one's suggesting anyone should be denied the right to register formal complaints, or relieve themselves, or both, during their descent.' The more Miss Mism reads, the more her ever-widening eyes seem to blot out the rest of her face.

'Now, to present a flavour of these people's thinking, here are verbatim extracts from their manifesto. *People of Cornish descent will be treated as a special case. In spite of the racial impurity stemming from their Celtic heritage, they will be granted the privilege of working an eighty-hour week, on an unpaid basis, of course, for owners of white vans who were born and raised in Essex.*

'But in the spirit of our party's common-sense, moderate approach to international affairs, we have no plans to declare war on the European Union. There is little question of special military operations, even against the French, regardless of our traditional enmity to the quisling surrender monkeys.

'That is not to say that we are prepared to neglect any aspect of our green and pleasant land's security. Defence spending must be immediately increased to eighty per cent of the nation's budget, to adequately protect our precious shores with modernised Martello towers at five-mile intervals. Also, submarines, meshed razor-wire and land mines on all beaches.

'In addition, we plan to upgrade Hadrian's wall, and all Norman fortresses protecting us from the Welsh, to twenty-first century standards.

'On domestic policy, we are calling for the immediate restoration of hanging, flogging, foxhunting and bear-baiting. And the introduction of national service for all boys over the age of eight. Girls will attend compulsory courses in knitting, needlework, and obedience to husbands.

'Finally, we are adamant that inferior foreign cocaine should no longer be imported from South America but manufactured to English standards. In England.'

Miss Mism curses herself for not having the trigger of the AK-47 at her fingertips, on the grounds that a gun in the hand is worth an arsenal in a boot, but says nothing. Percy might have been better off holding his tongue too, but doesn't.

'Supremely Helpful Intelligent Testimony Party? Well guess what? That contracts to the acronym SHIT Party? Supremely appropriate, I'd say.' There are times when Viv, too, could do with a machine gun, but she settles for ignoring him.

'Right, we've got a bunch of dangerous nutters on our case. Question is, how many of them are there? And how well organised are they? Perhaps most pertinent of all, how violent are they prepared to be?' As she speaks her arm snakes instinctively round Trudi, who suddenly has a longing for nappies, dummies and tuck-up time for tinies.

'Well, I'm coming to that,' Miss Mism replies, carefully, as she closes the note on her phone and spots that another one's just come in. 'Once more, you heard it here first.' She clears her throat yet again, even though it's crying out for mercy.

'These vile people are small in number, but dangerously well organised and alarmingly up to speed on technological developments. Our intelligence suggests they have, up until now, disregarded the social media campaign orchestrated by the former Prime Minister's daughter as beneath suspicion. Because no one cares about a silly little girl—'

She's interrupted by a howl from Trudi that she's not f-wording silly and not f-wording little. Anxious gnome and overripe peach aren't in it, her face has gone so dark and shiny it looks like a toffee apple.

'Of course not, dear,' Mum says, soothingly, 'but we'd better hear the rest. Forewarned is, after all, forearmed.' Trudi does the not silly not little girl's equivalent of a retired colonel's harrumph, furiously folds her arms and gives Miss Mism a "get on with it, then" glower.

'It seems they've had a speedy rethink on the grounds of the silly little girl suddenly turning into a media personality.' A million times more than that, to Miss Mism's mind, though she's careful to keep her tone even. 'Her raised profile stems not only from her television interviews, but also a range of feature pieces already appearing about her in the online editions of national newspapers.

'To make matters worse, although the, ahem, SHIT Party has scarcely more than a couple of dozen paid-up members, it does have links with other, demonstrably more numerous, organisations. And with a bit of help from X, Telegram, Meta and the rest, it can pull together protests and demonstrations anytime, anywhere. It is unclear at this stage where the money's coming from, but, unquestionably, the promise of vast quantities of beer and drugs unfailingly motivates the football-supporting fraternity.'

Closing the link on her phone, Miss Mism looks like a masked executioner with a great big axe and a longing to chop off lots of heads. But Viv calms her down.

'I set up my polling company, as little more than a kitchen table operation, before Percy and I were married. And it's still registered in my maiden name, meaning there's no way of connecting this place with any of us.'

'Likewise, my little house in Cornwall, and Davinia's, but the same does not apply to Penislow Palace.' Miss Mism's upping the bloodlust again. 'A lightning Google search and there it'll be, plain as daylight. My people can beef up security arrangements, which, let's face it, don't really exist at present, but we can't turn the place into an impregnable fortress.'

'I want to fucking murder the fucking lot of them.' Percy, who's been hissing and rumbling like a semi-dormant volcano, suddenly goes full Vesuvius. 'String 'em up by the fucking neck. Give the fuckers a taste of their own fucking medicine.'

'Yes dear, I'm sure we all feel much the same, but that's not really an option, is it?' Right now, Viv wishes it was, but she's feeling like a trodden-on worm. 'Passionate Remainer though I've always been, I really don't give two hoots right now whether we return to the European Union or float off to Mars.'

'Yes, that's the mother in you talking.' Percy's taking deep breaths, between deep drags. 'And of course you're right, keeping our little treasure safe is our number one – indeed our only – priority.' Looking from one parent to the other, Trudi runs the fingers of one hand down her nose and carefully eases the squidgy bit at the tip from side to side, as though she's checking that it is still there. It's something she's always done when she's really scared, ever since she was a baby. It feels like an essential precaution now, as it's perfectly obvious no one can possibly, actually, keep her safe. Unless, that is ... Unless? It's Miss Mism's talk of impregnable fortresses that's got her thinking.

'Just off to the loo.' She jumps up and scurries out of the door, rummaging for her phone in the discreet but deep pocket in her pink dress. Connectivity being as it is in Cornwall, she utters a heartfelt prayer to all the pagan gods she can think of as the beep-beeps go on and on and on. But at long last ... yessssss! A surprised but delighted voice drawls a cheery hello.

'Tristan, dear, dear, Tristan, lovely Trissie baby, I have the, er, mother of all favours to ask of you.' Trudi's words are sploshing out in bigger and bigger spurts. 'I know it's a total f-wording cheek but you see, we're in a spot of f-wording bother up here in London. And it'll be even worse when we get back to Cornwall. You don't s'pose, do you ...? I know your mum and dad don't know us, but I'm sure they're lovely people. And, even though it's a terrible imposition, I'm just wondering ...'

'Yes, of course Mummy and Daddy will be delighted to receive you, and there's oodles of room in the west wing.' Tristan's voice is like a lovely warm mug of cocoa. 'Bit of a bitch to heat in winter, but in summer it's just the ticket.' Trudi slurps up the words, so enthusiastically that she can almost feel them dribbling down her chin.

'Right now, it's all yours. Oh, and by the way, last time our humble abode was used as a film set the techies fixed the defence thingies in the entrances. Hadn't worked for centuries, but tickety-boo now. So we're as safe as houses. Quite big houses, actually. Well, sort of castles, really. So why not tootle on down and dream of Manderley. Or perhaps not, thinking about it. Be a shame to set fire to the place.'

The stupefied silence at Trudi's end goes on. And on. Tristan starts to wonder if the dashed signal's jolly well conked out. Won't be the first time. Or the last. Or has he said something out of turn? Has he sounded like a bounder or something?

'I say? Hello? Er, Trudi, dear, you still there? Haven't said something frightfully upsetting, have I? Frightfully sorry and all that. Didn't mean to presume. Just, we saw something on the goggle-box. You looked frightfully unhappy, and Mummy and

Daddy felt ever so sorry for you. Be delighted to help and all that. If it's not too frightfully forward of us. Wouldn't want impose, don't y'know?' Never mind spurts, Tristan's gushing like a waterfall, but he can't seem to stop himself, even though he has a feeling he's sounding sillier and sillier. Perhaps even a teeny bit snobby.

'You see, Mummy and Daddy are keen amateur anthropologists, and your lovely, er, Dad is a sort of lord. Well, the other sort, and so they're ever so frightfully curious to see what lords like him are, er, like. Er, if you see what I mean. Oh, for God's sake, if you are still there, please say something. Even if it's only jolly well push off.' At this, Trudi's thoughts do, finally, cascade into words.

'Tristan, you're a treasure! Thank you thank you thank you thank you! Mum and Dad will be so pleased to meet your, er, Mummy and Daddy.' She's remembered that royals and aristos always go for the kiddie way of talking to and about their parents, even when they're really quite old. Certainly old enough to know better. But she accepts the need to make allowances, especially given the unusual circumstances. Not that that stops her making a small, slightly defensive, point of her own.

'Actually, my dad is both sorts of lord. He'll explain when we get to yours. This should be in about three hours. Or ten,' she adds, thoughtfully. 'Depending which car we come in.'

CHAPTER NINETEEN
CULTURES CLASH

Lord Daddy and Lady Mummy are about to get a shock, as Trudi's well out on her timings.

By the time the Uber's arrived, Miss Mism's sorted everything. Stowing her phone back in a similar, but much more take-no-prisoners sort of pocket than the one Trudi has in her pink frock, she orders everyone else to hop in, and instructs the driver to carry on to Lombard Road, SW11 3BE, after dropping Davinia off at Vauxhall Cross.

'Yeah but, no but. Yeah but ...' Viv tails off, as she's got a horrible feeling she's sounding like the Vicky Pollard character in *Little Britain*.

'But me no buts, or even no-buts.' A hint of a smirk's playing round the edges of Miss Mism's mouth. 'That contraption of yours is, to put it at its kindliest, conspicuous. So it's staying out of sight for as long as is needed.' Though Viv can see the logic here, she's really quite upset.

But Davinia is ever so pleased as she gracefully eases herself out of the Uber outside the MI6 headquarters, and spots a shiny new Mini Cooper S with a contrastingly grey-looking balding bloke in a grey-looking overall standing next to it. He waves the keys at her and bows like an olden-days family retainer. 'Here you are. All yours, milady. The makers tell me it's "Enigmatic Black". Hope that's to your taste, ma'am.' As always, she's careful not to set fire to the wide brim of her slightly floppy hat while lighting the Black Russian that's already in its ebony holder. She looks at him briefly, and at the car for a good deal longer, before switching into Grand

Duchess mode.

'I think you'll find His Holiness the Pope is of the Catholic persuasion. And Her Enlightenedness Barbie is cleverer than Ken. Does that answer your question?' It doesn't, but long experience has taught the man that he can't go wrong with a polite and thoughtful nod.

Hiding inside the grande dame is a little girl, who so wants to burst into song and do several cartwheels. Davinia did manage at uni to scrape together enough money, just, to get herself a car. But it was a twenty-year-old rust-bucket, and no one was less surprised than her when it finally died, halfway through the last summer term.

After starting this little beauty's engine, she presses knobs randomly, and lights go on and off, the windscreen wipers flicker into life and the seat goes backwards and forwards, but finally her window does open. Meaning she can follow up her kindly farewell smile with a regal wave of her elegantly gloved right hand. Next, her elegantly shod right foot pumps hard and repeatedly on the accelerator, but she waits until the man's safely out of sight before ever so gingerly easing away from the kerb. Cautiously coasting across Vauxhall Bridge before turning left into Grosvenor Road, she dares herself to give her lovely new motor just a little bit of welly on the M4. Maybe even sneak up towards eighty, if she's feeling reckless enough – not that it's really her call.

'Well, Minerva Mini, what do you say to that?' Like most cars, Minerva Mini isn't big on words, though Davinia's convinced the soft purring sound from the engine is her way of saying "Yes, please, and thank you for naming me after the Roman goddess of wisdom". It also seems safe to assume that her new four-wheeled friend agrees that the Mism motoring method is best avoided.

Fifteen minutes later, Percy's feeling much the same about getting his head lopped off. Taking the opportunity of scratching it while he's still got it, he shows Viv a scary text that's just come through. 'Who the hell does this manic Mism woman think she is,' he mutters, 'the queen of bloody hearts?'

Trudi, who's sitting on the other side of him, peers down at the words "the chopper awaits", glances up at a very visible sign by the roadside, and claps her hands. 'Dad, silly, silly, silly Dad, what does that say?'

Before he has time to answer the driver mutters over his shoulder: 'This where you wanted dropping off, sir? Battersea Heliport?'

'Er, yes, of course.' Percy's doing his best to sound like he knew that all along. And isn't the slightest bit relieved that he's not on the point of dying a swift but gruesome death. Viv gives him a look that's something between despair and tenderness. She and Trudi lean forward slightly and mouth to one another, at the same time, the same word. 'Men!'

The rotor blades are already about to start turning as the three of them hurry into the cabin. And as the pilot does his final checks he cheerily calls out, 'Wind's just right, everyone, should be there in forty-five. Good to know there's somewhere in the grounds to touch down.'

Miss Mism really has done her homework. The aerial view of Tristan's not-remotely-humble abode indicates it's a mock-Georgian nod at the classic Norman Stone Keep castle design. The pretty much empty bailey area within the outer walls is big enough to land a good couple of dozen large military transport helicopters.

Peering down from one of the deep redbrick crenelated walls, Lady Mountie-Molehill says what even quite posh Americans sometimes say when they're surprised: 'Well, I'll be doggone.'

'Quite agree, egad. No sooner the word,' her thoroughly true-blue, my-people-came-over-with-the-Conqueror husband drawls.

'These crazy limeys sure as hell know how to hit the gas,' his wife replies, thoughtfully. The Mountie-Molehills are a handsome couple, easing into middle age but looking gloriously well on it. And they're a beautifully snug fit, first and foremost romantically, but, as good fortune would have it, financially too.

A drawback of coming from any of the nation's oldest families is that successive wars, income tax hikes, death duties, and a smattering of dumbo descendants have left nearly all of them strapped for cash. Meaning their homes, once very nice places to live in, have generally turned into millstones round their necks. Those that haven't already been passed on to the National Trust, or accidentally-on-purpose torched then turned into multi-storey car parks or supermarkets, are bordering on impossible to keep up. Little wonder that the once all-powerful and grandly titled De Montagne-Petitescollines had felt obliged to shrink their name along with their bank balance.

Against that, being a descendant of a family that made it big in the Texan oil boom of a more recent era has lots of pluses.

The Connaught ó Súilleabháins fled the Irish potato famine in the 1840s and scratched a living for half a century as two-bit farmers on a scrubby smallholding not far from Houston, grateful simply to not be dead. Then came the day when they were astonished, and ever so pleased, to discover they were sitting on a gusher that would keep on gushing. But their grievance lived on against Perfidious Albion for not coming to their country's rescue when the crops kept failing all those generations ago.

No surprise then that they cursed themselves when, against their better judgement, they'd allowed young Maeve to study at Oxford, only to discover she'd got it together with a filthy Brit with a fancy title. But that all changed when they found out he'd only got his stately home because King Charles the Second gave it back to his ancestor as a consolation prize for losing his right arm, left leg and both testicles in one-to-one combat with Oliver Cromwell.

Seeing as the wart-faced bastard's brutal massacres of Irish people have made him a hate figure for centuries, the now stinking rich ó Súilleabháins decided "my enemy's enemy is my friend". Rebuilding his rotting family home? In olden days style? What the hell? Why not?

So Lord and Lady Mountie-Molehill now live in their ridiculously huge historic-style home with all its wonderful modern conveniences, apart from central heating. They both thought leaving this bit out was jolly silly, but the American cousins were adamant that it just wouldn't be authentic. Seemed odd that they hadn't spotted that mock-Georgian architecture cladding a tumbledown real Georgian mansion, built round the original

Norman ruin wasn't quite the ticket either, but beggars can't be choosers.

In keeping with the times, Lord Jiminy Mountie-Molehill rather approves of his son mixing with the local populace, and was curious from the outset about him befriending this young Trudi girlie, especially as his father was apparently a sort of lord, but the wrong sort. He'd never met one of those before. Lady Maeve was more sceptical, out of long-standing family loyalty, but was won round when Tristan told her that this Lord Penislow chappie really did have Irish roots. So when he showed them on the Sky News website how the family had been shouted at by a bunch of yobbos who were extra-horribly English, the matter was decided. The fact that the place is big enough to house half a regiment without even noticing made the decision easier.

Thanks to the once again not-totally-authentic high-speed lift, whose entrances are cunningly disguised on all levels as bookcases, the couple is on the ground floor and heading out towards the helicopter in a matter of seconds. Tristan, who heard the racket even through the earphones he had plugged into his Fender amplifier so he could practice his Jimi Hendrix riffs on the Strat without driving everyone nuts, swiftly joins the welcoming party.

Anxious not to appear forward, he resists the temptation to give poor Trudi a great big hug, but does risk putting his hands on her shoulders and giving her a little peck on the cheek. He gets a cheeky grin back and is ever so grateful. His father, sticking by his idea of the spirit of the times, ducks the formality that'd usually go with greeting a person to whom one hasn't been introduced, but who happens to have just landed on one's property and stepped out of a flying machine.

'Good trip? What? Jolly good to meet you and all that. Untoward circumstances, don't y'know, but you're frightfully welcome. Ready for a snifter? Jolly old yard-arm time, what?' Spotting that Percy's struggling not to gawp, or giggle, or even just climb back into the helicopter and do a runner, Maeve tries a more casual approach.

'Why, howdy partner? You sure as hell got your sweet asses into gear this fine day. Whaddaya say, like, to a drop of hooch?' Percy stares from one to the other. But spotting that they're both trying to say the same thing, apparently by way of welcome, he gives the mid-Atlantic card a go.

'Charmed to meet you both. Of course The Pond is so wide, but we understand the special relationship with our colonial cousin buddy buddies. They say jump, we say how high, right?' Then, turning to Lord, as opposed to Lady, Thingamajig, he adds, 'Shame Good King George was off his rocker, otherwise history might have been turned out very differently. Very much for the better, many might say.' Unsurprisingly, this doesn't exactly do it for either of his hosts. And, as Trudi and Tristan have already sloped off for a good catch-up, it's down to Viv to sort things out.

'My dears, please don't mind my husband's manners. He has got an odd way with words, but is quite harmless, really. And we both truly are extremely grateful for your kind hospitality in what is, without question, our hour of need.' Percy, whose brains have at last kicked back into gear, has another go.

'As ever, my wife is absolutely right. And without doubt we humble Brits have always revered the magnificent American model encapsulated in the Gettysburg address. Just a shame our own noble traditions that go right back to the Magna Carta are now being traduced by anti-democratic elements.' Seeing that he is doing better this time, he delivers his punchline.

'So what I say is "God bless America", and "Rule Britannia". United we stand. Onward, arm-in-arm, to victory!'

Not for the first time, he's over-egging it. Though that's obvious to Viv, she can see that Jiminy and Maeve both seem to have swallowed it. A relief that Trudi's not in earshot, as she'd have spoilt everything by stamping her feet and telling Dad he's being ever so, ever so, *ever so* silly.

CHAPTER TWENTY
OVERWHELMING ODDS

It's not Trudi's style to admit it when she's feeling a bit out of her depth. It's not as if she was all that fazed by being in Number Ten Downing Street. Or talking on live telly, for that matter.

But, stepping through the magnificently wide half-glazed heavy oak doors of the *excuse me, humble abode? I don't think so* mansion, she feels like she's just stepped into a Tardis. The marble-floored entrance area's so huge, has so many heavily ornamented pillars, and has such a high ceiling that it looks like a cathedral, for God's sake. Big enough for several gods, actually. Tristan, who first-off struck her as a nice enough lad, then turned out to be a useful ally, now seems to have turned into an alien, who might at any moment pull off his human-like mask, and reveal a perfectly circular and scarily scaly head, with one great big staring eye and sticky up bits on each side of his forehead. Glancing round at the place he rather takes for granted, as he's been here all his life, he can sort of take her point, and does his best to put her at her ease.

'Oh yeah, we play footie in here sometimes. Really annoying when the ball gets stuck on the ledge by the skylights, but we usually manage to shoot it down with a crossbow. Eventually.' Trudi says that's good to hear, but wonders whether people living in a place like this might just as easily shoot down the occasional servant with a crossbow, just for fun. Tristan picks up the vibe, and has another go.

'Come up and see my axe. I'll even do something with it, if you don't mind awfully. You like to tinkle the ivories, don't you? Well, I have my moments too.' Trudi has a bit of a silly old dad moment, as she doesn't immediately get the connection between her playing the piano and Tristan chopping down trees. But, after what seems an interminably long walk through interminably long corridors, hung with an interminable succession of implausibly enormous paintings of definitely dead people, Tristan pushes open a door and the penny drops. Not only that, the red Fender Stratocaster guitar on its stand does look reassuringly tatty. It's for the best that she doesn't realise that it only looks battered because it's half a century old, and so stupendously collectable that it's worth an absolute fortune.

Trudi sits in one of the reassuringly normal-looking and slightly scruffy off-white wicker armchairs, and, after he's switched on the amp and done a lightning tune-up, she's impressed, but in a nice way, with what she's hearing. In keeping with the transatlantic flavour of the day, he plays *The Star-Spangled Banner*, which, because he does it really gently, is quite pretty. Next, he subtly fuses it with *God Save The King*, which, thanks to a hefty bit of boogie-woogie, is quite listenable-to. The twangly-wangly bits that he works in also sound pretty cool, thanks to his skilful use of the tremolo arm. When he rounds off the performance with a gloriously bouncy version of *Barbie Girl*, she moves her opened hands and outstretched arms about from side to side, in that really silly way kids used to when the hand-jive was all the rage. She's not even aware that she's doing it until Tristan glances up and gives her the smiley equivalent of a big hug.

Though she can't help blushing, she does feel strangely bonded to Tristan, in a sort of brother-and-sisterly way – which is absurd, given the social chasm dividing them. She really can't put her finger on it, but the fact that he doesn't do the bloke thing of playing on and on at her is a definite plus point. Putting the guitar back on its stand and switching off the amp, he spots that she's looking a bit more chilled, and comes out with something else that might strike a chord. Metaphorically speaking.

'I'm rather fond of reading as well. D'you fancy a gander at our library? It's a bit stupidly big, you won't be surprised to learn, but does have some jolly good stuff.' Though Trudi's always well up for any kind of room with books in it, she feels once again like one of Jane Austen's unmarried and strapped-for-cash young women when they finally get there. It's not as ridiculously huge as the entrance area, but the ceiling's still a good fifteen feet high. Which is why, after yet another route march past yet more dead-person portraits, her mouth actually drops open. Even more embarrassing than the sitting-down-dancing routine.

Spotting that once again his friend is a bit taken aback by the over-the-topness of his ... OK, not exactly the humblest of humble abodes, Tristan does another speedy damage-limitation job. The library is so big that it has not one, but four of those ladders on wheels, essential for finding anything much above head height, but he tells her this technology is in fact dual-use. Thanks to their extra-long glorified bicycle chains and rotatable handles, they can be moved about even from the very top, which, he explains, makes all the difference.

'Means we can stage medieval battle re-enactments in here, don't you know? Daddy and I pop mixing bowls on our heads, arm ourselves with plastic swords, and charge Mummy and the housekeeper. Dashed annoying really – they use broom handles as lances, and often beat us. But it's still jolly good fun. Go on, let's have a go!' Trudi assumes he's joking, until he opens a large mahogany chest decorated with images of knights in shining armour, and pulls out loads of silly boys' toys. Kitted out and raring to go, she leaps up the steps of her pretend mighty steed, charges him before he's really ready, and knocks him right off his perch.

'I say, old girl, that's a bit, well, you know, unsporting, what?' It's not surprising that he's not ever so pleased at losing quite so completely, and quite so quickly. Though the carpet's absurdly thick pile protects his body, his pride feels mortally wounded, as the library door's just opened to reveal Mummy and Daddy and Mum and Dad grinning like so many beastly hyenas.

'Female of the species? More deadly than the male?' Maeve doesn't recognise the line Viv's just quoted, but does get the idea. And agrees. In her own way.

'Yay, sister! *Annie Get Your Gun!*'

Though Percy accepts that the real-life Annie Oakley of the Buffalo Bill Wild West Show was a crack shot, he winces a bit too visibly at the racism and sexism built into the old movie about her. He squirms at the thought that he might have goofed again, but rather to his surprise, Jiminy gives his arm an understanding squeeze.

'Wouldn't remotely suggest Americans have smaller brains.' He's murmuring ever so softly. 'But you might have had a smidge of a point about Good King George, what? Not saying the memsahib isn't a jolly good egg, mind, because she jolly well is.' Nodding energetically, Percy does his best not to look as surprised as he is relieved. The more so, as the high-five that Viv and Maeve just gave one another suggests they are at least agreed that girl power is good power. He also has the impression that Tristan might be getting over his little snit about being bested by Trudi. The rueful smile in his face is a good sign.

Given there's no knowing how long this exile from Penislow Palace might go on for, this upgraded special relationship is especially welcome when Miss Mism arrives with the news that the situation is a good deal trickier than any of them had imagined. Not that she hasn't already confirmed that she's equal to pretty well everything that fate throws in her path.

Before heading for the M4, she swung by the MI5 headquarters just up the road from where Trudi made her TV debut, and casually left the Tesla on the double yellows right by the building. Having switched numberplates to the rude version, and left under the windscreen a sign clearly indicating that she had diplomatic immunity, she was not impressed with what she came back to, just over an hour later.

The towaway truck was bad enough, but nothing to the bloke crouched over one of the car's wheels, getting ready to strap it up with bits of metal. To make matters worse, he said in the monotone jobsworth voice that's enough to bring out the murderer in the most respectable of citizens, 'Just doing my job, Madam.'

'Oh really. Well, I'm just doing mine, and it's a lot more important than yours.' Miss Mism followed this up with an extremely hard kick in the back of the man's head, then, stepping over his crumpled form, she started the car and shot off in a deafening screech of tyre rubber. A woman and her little daughter passing by both put their hands over their ears in horror, but her teenage son yelled applause. And vowed to do the same, and even better, in a couple of years.

The lightning journey to Cornwall passed without incident, apart from a line of lorries loaded with hay bales swerving so violently when she undertook them on the hard shoulder that they nearly caused a multiple pile-up. Three hours later she was back home, tapping her fingers until, some considerable time later, Davinia's dear little Mini gently pulled up outside.

'Right, not a second to lose.' The poor young woman hardly even had time to get out. 'We're off to Penislow Palace, pronto.' The sleepyheads at MI5, less impressed than they should have been by Miss Mism's obvious seniority in the spy hierarchy, had told her the security detail wouldn't make it to the location until tomorrow at the earliest. Which was why the gap needed plugging right away.

Sure enough, there was a bunch of louts gathered outside the old stone walls encircling the property, shouting half-brained slogans like 'Inger-land for de Inglish', and 'fuck off foreign scum'. A troubled-looking local bobby was busy licking the end of his pencil and writing things in his notebook, which didn't seem to scare them off.

'Well?' Miss Mism was breathing fire. 'This the best you can do?'

'Er ... you see, Miss,' the not very tall, not very figure-conscious, and not very brave-looking young man muttered. 'They're not trespassing, and, er, you know, free speech and that. So they're not actually breaking any laws.'

'Get in that vehicle of yours and leave this to me. Or, rather, us,' she snapped, pointing at Davinia. Weedy though the bloke was, he showed he was at least human by dribbling at the sight of her. But, at the bellowed command 'Go!' he leapt into his patrol car as if he'd just been bitten in the bum by an XL Bully.

When Miss Mism marched up to the gang and demanded to know who was in charge, they scoffed in her face. 'Wot's it to you, Granny?'

'I'll tell you what it is to me. So will these.' Because the bloke had already turned his back on her, he didn't spot the gleaming knuckledusters she'd whipped out, but did feel one of them. The geezer next to him felt the other one, and the others swivelled round in shock and amazement at the sight of their fallen comrades. They also gawped in a grubby blokey way at Davinia, but when four of them stepped towards her with heaven knows what evil intent, they quickly wished they hadn't.

Two seconds later she wished that, before going through her "leaping into the air and doing the high kicking" routine, she'd taken off her hat. But almost immediately Miss Mism was more dazzled than she'd dream of letting on by the way the elegant young woman stooped slightly while remaining upright, swivelled her arm in a circular motion like a human wind turbine, scooped the thing up and popped it back on her head. Then, patting it neatly into place, she smiled as she lit a Sobranie and watched their defeated enemies running for their lives into the woods.

Miss Mism sauntered in a theatrically leisurely way back to the Tesla before getting the AK-47 out of the boot, aiming it at the three minivans that the yobbos had obviously driven down in, and taking out all their right-hand tyres and windows. Next, she stepped just as casually round what was left of them, and did the same on the other side.

'Silly to settle for half-measures,' she announced, as she blew the smoke, cowboys-and-Indians style, from the barrel of the gun.

Davinia smiled delightedly, and followed suit as best she could. Not having a shooter of her own, she settled for blowing smoke rings from her ciggie. Seemed to do just as well.

CHAPTER TWENTY–ONE
REVELATIONS

'Well, d'you want the good news or the bad?'

Miss Mism raps out the question as she marches through the front door of Jiminy and Maeve's monumental pile. Normal people knock before barging into other people's homes, but such a silly nicety really isn't for her. Any more than in any way acknowledging the gigantic splendour of the Mountie-Molehill mega-mansion.

'Er, the good?' Percy inquires tentatively.

'We saw them off.'

'And the bad?'

'They will be back.'

Once again, any normal person would explain in more detail, indeed in any kind of detail, what the hell they're on about, but the Penislow family is well used to having to join the dots for themselves. The same can't be said of their hosts, who stare at her as though she's just wafted in on the back of a unicorn. Davinia also attracts some attention, as do the smoke rings she's blowing in her usual – or, rather, unusual – way. Jiminy is particularly struck.

He knows perfectly well that he looks like a pantomime toff in his standard get-up of starched white wing-collared shirts and bow ties. The finishing touch, or final straw, according to taste, is the monocle. But at least the lens is prescription, and, he fondly imagines, it's less ageing than glasses. Besides, because it always hangs on its silken thread round his neck, he never has to hunt for it. Handy right now, as he's determined to get a proper look at this gorgeous creature.

Though he's faithful to a tee to Maeve, and is perpetually chuffed at having bagged such a beauty, he does have a short-sighted eye for the ladies. More than that, he's fascinated to see another human being in the twenty-first century who wouldn't look out of place in the Roaring Twenties. He's already registered that Viv, with her neatly bobbed hair and cloche hat, could have passed muster in the same period. But the newcomer, with her languid manner and tight-fitting between-the-wars dress, does more than that. And the ebony cigarette holder seals the deal.

'By Jove, d'you know you're Juno's double?' He's sounding like a little boy looking in a shop window at the best toy ever. 'Regarding the, ahem, little local difficulty,' he shoots a surprisingly shrewd glance at Percy and Viv, 'an Englishman's home is his castle, what? Ours is yours as long as you need it, egad!'

Trudi wants to ask whether Fangle and Lady Casement are included in the package, but decides it'd be better to discreetly sound out Tristan instead. To soften him up, she says she's ever so sorry about the surprise attack, and really didn't mean to bash him quite so hard. Happily, he's got over it with a bit of help from Daddy, who told him he'd been a jolly good sport, so he gallantly tells her she's up there with Boudica and Joan of Arc. But there's also method in his madness, as he knows she's going to be flustered by what he's about to say.

'I say, old thing, Mummy says it's time to dress for dinner. Everyone's invited, including divine Davinia and ... er, mad Miss Mism.' He's right. This sudden blast of formality certainly is another prod at Trudi's already fragile sense of who or where she is. It's one thing to hole up for a day or so in a secure environment, quite another to time-travel back into a different century. She quite liked the way the characters in Downton Abbey gradually got their heads round the way times were changing in front of their eyes, but it strikes her this lot must have missed the later episodes. And somehow got stuck, like when the needle in an olden-days record player does that annoying clicky thing, and keeps playing the same bit over and over again.

Fortunately, she does have in her suitcase the particularly pretty pink party frock that she'd packed on a just-in-case basis, but she really can't wear the same thing every evening. Meantime, she'll have to tap Mum up for a string of pearls or something.

Given that Percy tends to wear long, Edwardian-style jackets at all times, he's pretty confident he'll get by tonight, if he borrows some of Viv's gel and puts a comb through his normally unruly hair. Hopefully no one will notice that the lower half of his clothing is not actually suit trousers but black jeans. A nice buttonhole, and maybe even a tie, will help. As for Miss Mism, she'll be fine in her dramatic dress, though it's perhaps a statement of the obvious that she really wouldn't give two hoots if everyone thought she looked like Cinderella before the Fairy Godmother makeover.

Just over an hour later, everyone's assembled in what the guests are given to understand is the Little Drawing Room, and maids in neat black uniforms complete with neat white headpieces circulate with silver trays laden with cocktails. Trudi wisely decides a spot of Dutch courage would be no bad thing, but, also wisely, waits till Mum and Dad are looking the other way before she grabs a glass. Though the young serving woman nearest to her pretends she hasn't noticed, she does give her a saucy wink, which feels like a good omen.

Percy, too, is feeling reasonably chilled, as Jiminy has already shown he can flit happily between centuries and belief systems. Besides, he's sufficiently dinosaur-retro to positively encourage smoking, which ticks a big box. It does with Tristan too, now that, at the age of sixteen, he can officially come out as a part-time puffer. But everyone's a little anxious, as Maeve has yet to put in an appearance. Though her husband is a perfect century-old time warp, what with his pencil moustache, slicked-back centre-parted hair, ramrod posture, aquiline nose and sharply defined jawline, Maeve is harder to pin down. And a lot more besides as she appears at the top of the wide, sweeping staircase leading down to where they're all standing.

She might have got away with it if she'd just stuck with the Scarlett O'Hara *Gone with the Wind* look, but peppering it with so many pink frilly add-ons, that wouldn't look out of place on a

Christmas tree, does take things a bit far. Especially as everything clashes so vividly with her billowing mane of wavy red hair. Under it all, Percy's already noticed, she's a strikingly good-looking woman who could just about pass, maybe at a stretch, as Tristan's older sister.

'I say, what a corker of a cracker you are, my dear,' Jiminy calls out, tactfully. His mind wanders to the toe-curling scene in Daphne Du Maurier's novel *Rebecca*, when the second Mrs de Winter appears at a ball looking just like the first Mrs de Winter. He's not furious like the fictional husband, but does look forward to Maeve looking like her real self again, when they're snuggled up in bed. In the meantime, he makes a point of not putting his monocle to his eye. The blurriness is a comfort.

It's a teenage thing to find parents embarrassing, and Tristan's used to Mummy sometimes taking things a bit far. But this is beyond cringeworthy. He spots that Trudi's eyebrows are looking as though they're about to float upwards towards the nearest chandelier, and deftly leans forward to catch, just in time, the glass that's fallen from her seemingly paralysed hand.

Pretending they haven't noticed a thing, Percy and Viv step dutifully forward when Jiminy waves them towards what he assures them is the smallest, and definitely most informal, dining room in the house. Ideal, he adds unconvincingly, for an informal little do like this.

'All things are relative, I suppose,' Percy whispers, as they pass through into yet another absurdly high-ceilinged room, which is perfectly proportioned to accommodate the glimmering Louis XV dining room table, that's perfectly proportioned to easily fit at least twenty-five people round it.

Although, thanks to Tristan's quick thinking, Trudi did manage to down her cocktail, her heart sinks as she spots the immaculately spaced and horribly elaborate place settings. The rows of engraved silver knives, forks and spoons round the lavishly decorated plates leave her wondering what the hell you're supposed to do with them. The various different-sized glasses dotted all over the place are also something of a puzzle. At least, she thinks, the maids who now seem to be darting around everywhere might put something in them. Whatever it is, it'll help.

But Miss Mism has something else on her mind. She's struck by what might be an alcove, enormous, of course, lurking behind a sweeping swathe of embroidered velvet drapes. Blessed as she is with telescopically sharp eyesight, handy in her line of work, she can just about make out that the tiny figures dotted about the rich fabric are all wearing beaver-fur hats and waving six-shooters. As she marches towards it, the stolid-looking butler, whose face is so impassive that he could have been dead for hundreds of years, tries to block her path. But the zombie-zapping look in her eyes forces him to stand aside, leaving her free to sweep apart, in two overarching arm movements, the entire curtaining camouflage.

Behind it, in astonishing contrast to everything else in the house, is a life-sized statue, painted in vividly realistic colours, of a desperately gaunt-looking couple, scantily clad in rags. Their haunted look fills the space and billows out into the opulent dining room. Behind them, the wall is dotted, not with portraits of lavishly clothed and well-fed forebears, but cheaply-framed sepia photos of bare-footed, frightened kids in torn and tattered cast-offs.

'It's her – dash it all – her shrine to less happy times,' Jiminy murmurs, the moment his wife's gathered up her skirts and swept out of the room with a haughty look that doesn't fool anyone. 'You see, things were a bit sticky for her jolly old ancestors back in the old days, back in the old country.' He then gives the rundown on the potato famine nearly wiping them all out, before they managed to swap the new world for the next, and on how the Texan oil well had eventually dragged them out of the gutter.

'The money changed everything, of course, but she still sometimes feels she's got something to prove, poor love.' He looks sadly at her empty seat, but then stares defiantly round the room. 'I fly the flag too, though, I'll have you know, because before Maeve and I hooked up, my rellies were like the jolly old Russkie nobility after the Red Revolution. All mothballs, baloney, and bugger-all else, dash it.'

'Aha, your own dress code.' Viv smiles understandingly. 'Keeping up appearances?' Percy spots his wife's clever refence to a TV sitcom, but, typically, takes it to a whole other level, with a line spat at one of Shakespeare's characters when he'd got a bit muddled about his station in life.

'Some are born great, some achieve greatness, and others have greatness thrust upon them?'

'Question is, who's who round here? Know the feeling, mind – my lot had seen better times too, before my dad succumbed to the inevitable. In his case skipping the mothballs, and the country, when it all fell apart.'

Jiminy looks at him curiously, and is on the point of asking a whole load of questions when he's interrupted by Maeve's sheepish but normal-looking reappearance. In point of fact, the russet-coloured jacket she's wearing over pale brown skinny jeans show off her figure to great advantage, and tone wonderfully with her flowing Irish locks.

'Ah, my dear, so glad you're with us after all, for our dear little informal gathering, what?' Jiminy's kindly expression, as he looks at his wife while indicating to the maids that the soup can be served, is meant to set her at her ease. But sometimes sympathy's the last thing anyone can cope with, and certainly in this case it makes matters a whole lot worse.

Not like Trudi's never been there, which probably explains why she reads the look so clearly in Maeve's watery eyes. And why she takes the surprising step of hopping down from her chair, skipping round to her hostess, looking her full in the face and telling her she looks really, really sexy. Teetering on the brink of floods of tears, the woman stares back at her for a full half minute, then gives her a great sloppy kiss on the forehead and bursts out laughing.

Trudi's triumph? The first of many, dear reader. You'll see.

CHAPTER TWENTY-TWO
TANKS FOR THE MEMORY

Trudi's next clever move is to catch the eye of the maid who winked at her earlier. As she doesn't look a day over sixteen, and still less comes across as some zero-personality person who hates posh people, it seems worth risking an appeal for help with the cutlery.

Nothing's said of course, but by allowing her hands to hover uncertainly over the many knives, forks and spoons while looking in a worried way at the young woman, she asks her question nicely. And by looking meaningfully and very specifically at the one to go for, the maid answers it. Also, her flicker of a smile strongly suggests there'll be more vital intel where that came from. The understanding glance Maeve shoots in Trudi's direction suggests equally strongly that mealtimes were an ordeal for her too in the early days.

Although Davinia's upbringing was nothing like as top-drawer as she makes out, she's read enough nineteen century novels and watched enough period movies to get the idea. It's easier for Percy and Viv, as they've both been around a bit over the years, while Miss Mism makes two things abundantly clear. One, she fully understands the etiquette of all social classes, up to and including royalty. And two, it's her own divine right to follow or flout the rules as she thinks fit.

'It's a birthright thing,' she announces haughtily. 'It happens that I too am descended from one of England's oldest families. Like you, Cricket, or Jiminy, or whatever you call yourself, we also came over with The Normandy Bastard. Like you too, it became more convenient over the centuries to anglicise the name somewhat, but we were originally Les Mis-Mérables de Glurm.

'We were all very noble, very valiant, to a man. And woman,' she adds stiffly. 'And luckily the line never quite petered out, in spite of its speckled and unfortunate history of frequent suicides. I say frequent... Of course each of the unhappier members of the family only managed it once, but the numbers did mount up, or, rather, pare down.' The stunned silence that greeted these announcements is eventually broken by Percy, whose face has broken into an impish grin.

'Glurm, you say, my dear? Surely you'd have been better off with plain old Glum.'

Trudi doesn't think it's all that cool to admit that Dad's gags can be really funny, but can't help laughing out loud. Others vaguely titter, even though the joke is in rather bad taste. But both Jiminy and Tristan go quiet, as they're obviously thinking the same thing, and are both keen to check something out, pronto. Anyway, that subject's put on hold by Percy's following up Miss Mism's announcement about her unlikely background with a question about the equally unlikely pairing of his host and hostess.

'Splendid writer of yesteryear, Nancy Mitford,' he begins, thoughtfully. 'You remember, dear chap, how she'd refer to people being "U" or "Non U"? Very much upper class, or very much not. Terribly snobby of course, and perhaps wrong of me to ask. But you see ...' He tails off as he feels two pairs of eyes fixed on him, and wishes he'd kept his mouth shut. But Jiminy lets him off.

'Upper class, yes, old boy, but, like I say, utterly, utterly on our beastly uppers. The dear old Mater and Pater even had to pawn the mothballs to get me to university. Got me studying ghastly old Business Management, hoping I'd at least be able to make a fist of dismantling the jolly old estates. When all the old feller really wanted was to see me following his footsteps into Sandhurst, to wave the jolly old flag, what?

'Just a stroke of luck, really, that dear young Maeve was on the same course. And what a course!' His eyes go misty at the memory, his reserve floating away like a little paper boat in a stream. 'Course of true love, never did run smooth, eh? By Jove it did for us! That first day we met! We cut morning lectures and were in the jolly old sack by lunchtime! Never looked back, egad!'

'Sure was a humdinger,' Maeve chips in. 'Starry, starry nights ever since. Sure, Mom and Pop wouldn't hear of it at first. But I told them I'd got a better beat on my heartbeat than them. So they could, like, like it, or piss up a rope. Then when I sweetened it with the English milord's Irish connections, boy were they eating outta my hands. So ya see, the good girl got the guy. And the good guy got the girl. You better believe it – it was, like, some party. Goodness gracious, great balls of fire, that's what it sure as hell was.'

Viv glances at Trudi, not entirely sure that the tone of this conversation is suitable for a twelve-year-old. Yes, she and Percy are still at it like rabbits most nights, but she's never going to share that sort of thing with her daughter. Or at least not for a long, long time. However, judging by the giggly look in the kid's eyes, she's reasonably confident no permanent damage has been done. In fact, it's the girl herself who asks the next question. Mercifully, not about great balls of fire.

'So did you carry on with your boring course, even though the Yankee rellies had sorted your money problems? Don't think I would have done. Actually, I'd love to tie my geography teacher to a tree and set fire to him. And give up smelly maths.'

'Jolly good question. You're a bright little filly,' Jiminy drawls. 'I did stay at the university, as Maeve was going to, and wild horses and all that. But I did switch to history. Much more to my liking. And then when we both graduated, we moved down to Berkshire, to be together while I did a spot of swotting at Sandhurst. Jolly good fun it was too. We had such parties. Even learned one or two things.

'Bit of bonus, that, in the circs,' he adds, giving Percy a meaningful wink, which for the moment doesn't seem to mean anything.

But all conversation halts when Miss Mism's phone goes off. Needless to say, the ringtone is the distinctive James Bond *bum bu-*

bu-bum/bum bum bum theme music. It also hardly needs mentioning that taking calls at table is thoroughly bad form, not that she gives a tuppenny tiddle.

'I see. Right … Right … Right. Right, we'll see about that.' She's sounding like an alligator, snapping away at anything in range. 'Come, young woman, we have places to go, people to see. And kill, if necessary.' Fortunately, the main course has by now come and gone, so Davinia's already enjoying her third intercourse cigarette and isn't worried about going hungry.

There's another stunned silence as Miss Mism marches, and Davinia, in her sensationally high heels, clip clips across the marbled floor towards the door. Jiminy pops the monocle in for one last squint, then, by raising his right eyebrow, pops it out again, before clearing his throat and saying something surprising.

'Guessing things have got a bit sticky, what? Happens we Mountie-Molehills have always had a soft spot for military memorabilia. Got a fair few juicy bits of whizz-bang-wallop kit stored away in one of the jolly old barns, don't y'know? Some of it in perfect working order. The big beasts may come in jolly handy for what you're up against, what?' He then adds, as though he's just mentioned nothing more remarkable than closed-cup mushrooms being on offer in Waitrose this week, 'Spot of dessert, anyone? Cook does a lush jam roly-poly, and her custard's sans pareil, egad. We've had swells swooning over it, over and over, over the years.'

Trudi's not sure what's got to her more. The idea of getting whizz-bang-wallopy revenge on horrid men like those who shouted horrid things at her in London, or the thought of getting the best pudding ever. Even nicer now that the silly rows of knives and forks have been cleared away, so she'll know exactly what she'll be able to eat it with.

Less easy to stomach is the load of reminders she's been getting all evening of how much there is for her to learn about practically everything. Ok, the Mountie-Molehills are pretty extreme by anyone's standards, but still it's been a shock to discover that not far from where she's always lived there are parallel universes which she couldn't even have guessed at. On the plus side, she's pleased that what she did about Maeve's problem turned out as well as it did. Half makes her wonder if she is actually getting the hang of some bits. Trick must be to watch, listen and learn, instead of rushing to judgement. Evaluate the info carefully, and then, and only then, take a chance on her instincts.

Without even noticing she's doing it, Trudi's stroking the two sides of her neatly pointed little chin, as though she's tidying up a neatly pointed little beard on the end of it. Once again, it's something she's done since she was quite little, though unlike the nose-tweaking it suggests she thinks she's getting somewhere with something.

Percy smiles at her knowingly, though he has to admit to himself that he too has been on a learning curve. Not only is there more to Maeve than first met his eye, but Jiminy's also full of surprises. As well as the man's leap of understanding about what the hell's going on outside Penislow Palace, there's the offer of maybe game-changing help. But one important detail does need clearing up.

'Point of interest, old chap, do you have the faintest idea how to work any of this seek-and-destroy stuff you say you've got stashed away in your barn? May seem like a detail, but it'd be handy to know.'

'Oh, rather, by golly.' Jiminy's a little boy staring at best ever toys again, except that Mummy's now gone into the shop and bought them all for him. 'During my stint in the jolly old Guards they put me in charge of the jolly old museum. Had lots of fun making sure it was all tickety-boo. Of course the kit they use now is ever so much better, but too jolly boringly efficient for my taste. Besides, the best of my bunch get a jolly shifty on. You can get forty out of these beauties, don't y'know? The memsahib hates it, because the makers called the model "Cromwell", by the way.'

Maeve tenses, but Viv distracts her with an interesting thought.

'My journeys to London and back do take a while, but I get at least forty out of my little beauty too. Nearly fifty with the wind behind her.'

'By Jove,' Jiminy splutters, 'you mean you've got a tank too? Doesn't it rather churn up the jolly old motorways?' Viv looks puzzled for an instant, then feels her face warming alarmingly. She really, really isn't given to blushing, but there are times ...

Percy's mind bounces back and forth between wanting to give his wife a little squeeze and his host a huge hug. Tristan gets the first thought, but goes with the second. It's a lark trundling the Cromwells round the grounds to flatten buildings that aren't needed, or trees that're looking seedy. But blasting the hell out of a bunch of smelly ruffians will be ever so ever so much more fun.

Trudi, too, is scenting good times ahead, but she's also taking note of what Mum's just been through. It confirms that her new technique of weighing up all available facts before pronouncing on them really is the way forward. Not to say she'll always stick by it, but it's a start. And the job of keeping schtum is certainly made easier right now by the arrival of the jam roly-poly and custard. It would have been tempting to blurt out something to the effect that posh people aren't supposed to enjoy anything as non-posh as this, but she grew out of talking with her mouth full before she turned four.

It would have been impossible anyway, with it crammed quite as full as it is right now.

CHAPTER TWENTY-THREE
OPENING SALVOS

Though Trudi's brain can go into freefall under extreme influences such as jam roly-poly and custard, Miss Mism's is more like New York. It never sleeps. Which is why the anxious call from the bulbous bobby sent her synapses into action-this-second mode. And as the Tesla hurtles into the lane leading to Penislow Palace, she can see that the bloke had a point.

In place of a few dozen disgusting-looking thugs, there are now hundreds of them. Buzzing and milling like massed mosquitoes, coalescing, she mutters out of the side of her mouth, as 'An existential ectoplasm of evil.' Davinia knits her brows, then quickly un-knits them as this is not a good look. Instead, she drops the jaunty angle bit with her ciggie holder and points it directly in front of her face, like the big gun on the turret of a tank. Next, as this definitely isn't a moment for wafty rings of smoke, she blows a shaft of it straight ahead, as an opening shot, straight into the enemy camp.

But Miss Mism is more into dropping bombs than hints. First job, then: lose the bobby, as her plan of action won't strike him as standard police procedure. Turning away and discreetly slipping out her phone, she goes into settings and makes the ringtone go off. Then, turning back, she pretends to listen carefully and anxiously before speaking.

'I see, but that's terrible, Chief Inspector.' She sounds genuinely shocked. 'A deranged dairymaid, you say? In the next village? On the rampage? Armed with a three-legged stool, three machetes, three shotguns and a crossbow? Yes of course. I'll tell him to get along there. Right away, sir.' She touches the screen as though ending the call and stares him right in the face.

'Well, you heard what the man said. Hop it.' Of course he didn't hear a word, but is scared of authority in any shape or form. He has unhappy thoughts about frying pans and deep blue seas as he pockets his silly notebook, gives the tip of his pencil one last despairing lick, and heads for the motor. And, as its wailing siren fades out of earshot, Miss Mism gets the AK-47 out of the boot and eases the Tesla forward, forcing the yobbos to clear a path for her. Naturally curious that such a fancy motor should be driven by a dribbling old biddy, and naturally eager to get to know the really hot bit of stuff in the passenger seat, they gather round as close as they can without actually getting run over. Their reaction's just as natural as Miss Mism opens the door, swings her surprisingly shapely legs out, unfurls herself to her full height and points the gun right in their faces. Then, when she tilts the barrel only a tiny bit upwards and comes within a hair's breadth of blowing their brains out, they yet again do the natural thing.

She takes aim not far above the leading fleeing thug's head and, crack shot as she is, takes out a (fortunately unoccupied) crow's nest. As it tumbles down on him, Davinia murmurs 'their ship's lost its way now'. Quite a clever joke, but Miss Mism really isn't in the mood.

'So far, so good, but they will be back, in greater and nastier numbers.' She's sounding like Eeyore on a particularly bad day. 'You can rest assured about that – or, rather, not rest. Vigilance is essential, and more firepower would come in handy.' The old saying about being careful what you wish for obviously doesn't apply in this case, as she'll discover when Jiminy tells her about his tanks. When he does, though doing cartwheels would be even less age-inappropriate for her than for Davinia, she'll be well up for it.

Meantime, the little fat bobby's soon back, feeling stupid and looking flummoxed. The way he's trying to restore his beat cred by giving his silly pencil an especially dignified lick doesn't work. Any more than his trying to sound ever so formal and authoritative. Which, as usual, sounds just plain daft.

'May I inquire as to the whereabouts of the undesirable individuals whose undesirable activities appear individually and collectively out of action?'

'I'd say the fucking fuckers have fucking fucked off.' Miss Mism doesn't normally need naughty words to top up her own natural rudeness, but knows the shock effect will shut the man up. Manning up, she's pretty confident, isn't what he does.

'Now I shall leave these essential matters in your capable hands.' Her words, delivered over her shoulder and clearly meaning exactly the opposite of what they're supposed to, make him feel even smaller, but no slimmer.

Miss Mism lowers herself back into the Tesla, like a giraffe folding its legs carefully in readiness for sleep. Except that in her case, it's a matter of being careful not to trigger another burst from the AK-47 that she's discreetly placed on the driver's-side floor. Next, skidding the car round, she hurtles back up the drive and onto the main drag, hitting at least sixty within seconds. As the speed limit is twenty in this stretch of road, the bobby gets his notebook and pencil out yet again, but, looking sadly at the fast-disappearing car, he chucks the bloody things in the ditch. Not that he's a "WTF" kinda guy, but maybe he really is in the wrong job.

In what feels to Davinia, confusingly, both like half a second and several lifetimes, they're back at the mansion. The journey in dear little Minerva Mini would take at least six times as long, but at least she wouldn't get there feeling like her hair's turned grey, her back's developed a stoop, and she's grown wrinkles all over her body. Still, she makes a point of sparking up a Black Russian and trying not to let the smoke rings she's energetically blowing look too afraid. It's a relief that she could light the bloody thing at all, given how much her graceful and elegantly poised hands were shaking. But now, shoulders back, head up, she clip-clips in after Miss Mism, who ignores the butler's pleas to please be permitted to announce their return, and sweeps back into the dining room. There, everyone's having a lovely time working out how best and how soon to bring out the big guns.

When Jiminy first introduced Maeve to the place, he emphasised that it was customary after the dessert for the ladies to retire, to leave the gentleman to discuss affairs of state and other important manly matters over brandy and cigars. But when she pointed out that this was 'a goddam stoopid pile of horseshit', he did admit that the idea was perhaps a trifle dated. Also, he could hardly deny, if it were just the two of them dining, it would be a trifle lonely.

So there they all are, with Trudi feeling particularly light-hearted as she's topped up the cocktail with a fair few discreet glugs out of Dad's glass. Each time she did it the maid who'd helped her with the cutlery had to leave the room for a minute, as the way she burst out laughing would have completely given the game away. She was still a bit red in the face, and her little hat was a bit skewy, when she finally risked a sneaky wink at the naughty girl, who immediately winked back. This would have marked the beginning of a beautiful friendship if Trudi's brain hadn't gone a bit skewy too.

'Good Mishtriss Mishm, whatsh the new newsh at the new court?'

Percy's impressed at her riff on a line from Shakespeare's *As You Like It*, but puzzled at the way she said it. Viv, ever quicker on the uptake, guesses straight away what's going on here, shoots her a deeply disapproving glance, and curses herself for not having had the foresight to make sure the two of them weren't sitting anywhere near one another. Not that Miss Mism gives a monkey's about manners. Trudi's any more than her own.

'The monsters are massing for attack.' She's sounding like Winston Churchill doing his "blood, toil, tears and sweat" routine. 'My weaponry has proved equal to the task, so far. But in the very near future, we're going to need much more, and much more potent, retaliatory measures if we're to hold the fort and repel invaders.' To Percy, Jiminy and Tristan, this cuts both ways. On the one hand, Penislow Palace is a very nice place, and the idea of it getting trashed is a bit sad. One the other, the thought of deploying the tanks and the howitzers on these ghastly people is sheer bliss. Trudi is very much with the optimists. Also, she's showing signs of getting into the swing of Mountie-Molehill males' way of life.

'I shay,' she chortles, 'letsh give theesh binders what for. Blowing them to shmithereens will be wizard!'

Though it's a boy thing to take time to cotton on to things, Tristan can hardly miss the way Trudi's spectacularly wide-open eyes are looking like planets that're going out of orbit. He lays a gentle hand on her arm and suggests she might like a caffeine top-up. Though she's in full body-armour precision-weaponry mode, Miss Mism, too, registers there's something not quite right going on, as it's part of her spy's training to be ever on the lookout for odd things, like variations in patterns of behaviour. And barely a nanosecond later her protective instinct towards the girl kicks in. She leans across the table, grabs Percy's, Viv's, Jiminy's and Maeve's elegant porcelain cups, lines them up in front of Trudi and orders the maid to fill them, to the brim, immediately, with black coffee.

'But I shay,' our young heroine protests, 'I'm not really frightfully shirsty.' Miss Mism shoots her the kind of look guaranteed to fell several platoons of heavily armed advancing infantrymen, and tells her hers not to reason why. Hers but to do and ... well, just get on with it. At long last, Trudi, too, is getting the picture, not least because she's starting to lose track of whether she's in a dining room or a dungeon. Luckily, the coffee isn't too hot, and many slurps and several hiccups later she's looking a bit more normal. This is a great relief to Jiminy, partly because the sight of damsels in distress always troubles him, but mainly because he's been gagging ever since Miss Mism appeared to make his, in this case more or less literally, bombshell announcement.

'Help, dear lady, is at hand, don't y'know? High-speed trundling armour, and jolly old how's-yer-fathers lobbing out six-inch-calibre shells. Explode on impact, egad. Teach the blighters a lesson they'll never forget, by Jove! Be a jolly fine show, what?'

'You betchya sweet ass,' Maeve chips in, enthusiastically. 'We'll blow those goddam shit-for-brains limey bastards to hell and back, creepy motherfuck sons of bitches.'

Unladylike? Even Percy blanches a bit. But Miss Mism laps it up, demanding detail, chapter and verse. Listening intently as Jiminy spills the beans, she also notes that Trudi's not spilling her coffees. Plus, wonder of wonders, the girl's somehow managed to sit up straight and get her elbows off the table.

CHAPTER TWENTY-FOUR
LET BATTLE COMMENCE?

Trudi's the first to call it a night. She doesn't so much retire as fizzle out. And, flopping onto her giant ruby-red tapestry-draped four-poster bed like a deflated balloon, she has the feeling that she might have slightly overplayed her hand. More than slightly, she realises, when she eventually wakes up feeling as scrunched up as the dress that she's somehow managed to not take off.

She feels as ugly and smeary as the make-up splodged all over the pillows. Tempting to blame Dad for not protecting her from herself ... but, OK, it's not altogether absolutely his fault.

Much as she loves her dear, darling daughter, Viv reckons that what she must be suffering now serves her right, and might teach her a useful lesson. Percy's too busy wishing he'd also learned it to be any use for the moment, and although Miss Mism is feeling the kid's pain, she's focussed on her battle plans. Maeve is just as focussed on a good soak in the bath, and, because Tristan and Jiminy are far too gentlemanly to enter a young lady's bedroom, that only leaves Davinia.

But she's full of surprises.

During her crazy break-free-from-father first year at uni she gave the booze plenty of welly, and went through all the standard student morning-after remedies. In the end she decided that, fun though they were, a stiff Bloody Mary and/or a whopping great spliff didn't cut it, any more than a fat line of Charlie, however well cut. So, no beating it, the answer's a bowl of steamily bubbling thick noodle soup, washed down with a litre of Lucozade Sport. As she wafts into the room, remedies tray in one hand, Black

Russian in holder in the other, Trudi glares at her as though she were a hump-backed rhino that might charge at any moment.

'Darling.' Davinia's unfazed. 'You'll find this much more amusing and charming than you think. A little of what you fancy does you good. Even if you don't fancy, actually.'

Trudi hates her all the more because her sleekly fitted full-length deep blue dress looks so fabulous. But when the rebranded Florence Nightingale ditches the airs and graces, stubs out the fag in a saucer on the bedside table, fills up a spoon with soup and rams it down her throat, she'd have waved a white flag if there'd been one lying around. Given where they're at in terms of age difference, this no-nonsense nanny could just about be her auntie, or even her big sister. She'd often wished she'd had one, and regularly complained to Mum and Dad about their not sorting it before she was born. Only later did she realise that it was a bit late now, and they could hardly stump up any aunties or uncles either. Still, having Davinia in the family would have been nice.

That thought does as much to make her feel better as the stuff sploshing away inside her, and the hangover starts melting away like sleet when the sun comes out. Trudi doesn't care that she's acting like a baby bird that opens its beak at the sight of its mother, because each spoonful seems to have magical properties. But even there the surprises don't end.

'Under all my bullshit I'm a bit of a softie, really.' This is a new and totally different Davinia. 'But I'm relying on you, dear, not to tell the others. You will keep my little secret, won't you?' Trudi looks at her, eyes fizzing and sparkling like a box of fireworks that's been set off by accident, and tries to nod. Quite difficult when there's a spoon jammed in her mouth.

A few minutes and many glugs later there's a discreet tap at the door, and Maeve asks if she can come in. Davinia looks at Trudi meaningfully and puts her fingers to her lips, then snatches up the ciggie and gets it going again, along with the bullshit. 'Do join us, darling, we're having a simply marvellous party.'

'Sure as goddam hell looks like it.' Actually it strikes her as goddam weird. 'Well, you sure better join the party downstairs, where we're figuring out how to, like, get the wagons in a circle. Just as soon as you hitch up your breeches.' Her crooked grin matches Trudi's dress. Intentionally. The two women sweep out of the room, Davinia giving Trudi a final mum's-the-word wink over her shoulder, and the girl heads for the bathroom. At the sight in the mirror of what a state her hair's in, she nearly has a relapse, but the thought of her new bosom buddy helps get her big-girl pants on.

Some forty-five minutes later, repackaged via an even more thorough soak than Maeve's, a good brush, masses of make-up and a pale pink full-length dress cut just like Davinia's, she pats herself on the back for having had the good sense to trust Tristan. At home, she plays safe by washing before lying back in the bath in case the water gets cold. But here she can top it up with as much hot as she likes, for ever if needs be.

She also gives herself a round of applause for having got the lady-what-does to slip into Penislow Palace before hell broke loose to fish out lots of nice things for her to wear. Viv and Percy were grateful that the woman grabbed stuff for them as well, though Trudi was cross with her for claiming the credit when she wanted them to think all of it was her idea. Nor is she all that chuffed when she strides into the enormous, ornately-ceilinged and oak-panelled drawing room, and no one says how fab she looks. But, huddled in one corner on a little circle of Louis XV studded blue velvet chaises longues, they're far too busy plotting their next moves.

Miss Mism's grateful that she's no longer reliant for intel on the silly bobby who really should face up to not being up to the job. Little does she know that he's already torn between going for something nice and safe like a pet shop, or hanging onto a uniform by working as a traffic warden. But what she does know is that the thug count outside Penislow Palace has swollen to many hundreds, a tent city has sprung up in the woods, and the brutes are keeping a round-the-clock vigil. Little wonder there's now a massive police cordon round the place, and a fair number of MI5 agents, who're monitoring the situation with drones. Inevitably, there's a massive media interest in the story, with TV crews staking out the demo and Percy's main mobile flooded with requests for interviews. Lucky he's got a spare, which means he can at least make outgoing calls without that annoying "call waiting" sign endlessly flashing across his screen.

And all that's nothing to what'll happen when the news sinks in about what Spectacle really means in the news conference he's holding in Number Ten. First off, he explains that, in part thanks to compelling polling evidence revealing more and more buyers' remorse about Brexit, and in part thanks to strikingly popular campaigns on social media, it's clear that relations with the European Union need more than just a reset. There are no plans, certainly at this stage, to actually try and get back in, because the people voted to leave. But of course that was, he adds pointedly, by a wafer-thin margin. Hence the irrefutable case for breaking down all manner of barriers.

'Well, slap my face with a wet kipper.' Percy says the oddest things sometimes. 'The sleepy sod's actually pulled his finger out. He can't see further than the end of his own nose, which, admittedly, is some distance from his eyeballs.' He smirks at Trudi. 'But what he's doing is ditching the referendum result bit by bit. And by stealth, the cunning old goat.'

'And in the process driving the swivel-eyes to extremes.' Miss Mism's back in Eeyore mode. 'What we're seeing outside your highly vulnerable spread is nothing to what's to come.' Viv thinks about not fully thought through consequences, given how much of the polling evidence Spectacle's on about was supplied by her own company. She'd better fess up.

'Afraid I've played my part in making us homeless. The info I passed on to Downing Street revealed overwhelming support for binning Brexit from small business organisations, and widespread backing from larger companies. Concerns about short-to-medium-term uncertainty were substantially outweighed by the gains they'd make in the end. And, needless to say, pretty well everyone under the age of twenty-five thought leaving the Union was a stupid idea in the first place.

'Also, astonishingly large numbers of Tory voters from the leafy suburbs and affluent shires were very keen on the idea of cutting back on the hassle with their expensive overseas holidays, and maintaining their expensive overseas second homes. Plus they hate having to shell out for proper maids instead of getting European au pairs on the cheap. Could be that the real possibility of political gain is what finally got Spectacle's rear into gear.'

Percy's all for that, but not for what might come with it.

'Must admit my old chum Mick McKnackered has told me he's a bit worried. Stuck with a crisis like this he wishes they'd never made him Chief Constable, as he reckons he'd need a bloody army to get these buggers off his back.' Jiminy feels the poor fellow's pain, as his own old chum, the Lord Lieutenant of Cornwall, told him if there had to be a civil war he'd rather it didn't get waged on his patch. Bear in mind, the man added darkly, if not really relevantly, Trelawny did die in the end.

'But, stiff upper lip and all that.' He tweaks the tips of his pencil moustache, reassuringly. 'We can beat the bounders hollow with our own private army, what?' At this, Trudi has a brainwave, halfway between a lightbulb and a flash-of-lightning moment. This could be because, safely surrounded by her nearest and dearest, she's feeling daring – or because, for all Davinia's delicious efforts, she's still a bit off her face. Either way, she was thoroughly miffed that Spectacle didn't give her a name-check when he spoke of strikingly popular social media campaigns – meaning, excuse me, *mine*. She gets up and plants her feet a decisive distance apart, which is quite hard, as her dress is rather tightly cut. Still, it looks convincingly commanding.

'I think we should make him hold another press conference. Only this time make it a joint job. Him in his stuffy office in London, and me, down the line, from the battlements of this fabulously fortified place.' Everyone gawps for what feels like forever, and Trudi wonders how much longer she can keep up this girly version of the Napoleonic posture. But just in time, and in the teeth of almost everyone else's horror, Jiminy saves the day.

'By Jove, she's got it!' The booming bellow would get any regimental sergeant major sobbing with jealousy. 'The girl's a genius! We'll draw the bounders into our line of fire, egad! And jolly well give them what for! Teach them a lesson they'll never forget! By the left, quick … wait for it … blast!' As a grownup, he really couldn't give a monkey's about Brexit, but the little boy in him can't wait to play with his toys. What's more, because he recruited many of the estate's manservants from the other ranks of the forces, he really does have a private army under his command. They'll be gagging for a scrap, especially as many of them missed out during their years in the service. Meantime, they'll love getting all the mothballed tanks battle ready.

'Yee-haw!' Maeve's well up for it, no matter what the others think. 'It'll make Custer's last stand look like, like, goddam chickenfeed. Only this time we sure as hell beat shit outta them goddam redskins. Whaddaya say, pardner?' Jiminy's look also says "yee-haw". But, for the benefit of the limeys, he slips back into English. Or at least his version of it.

'I say, chaps, tally ho! By golly, it'll be such a lark.'

CHAPTER TWENTY-FIVE
TRUDI WINS THE DAY

'Now listen up.' Trudi does her best to bellow, in the nearest she can get to a sergeant-major voice. She thinks the "up" bit is stupidly American, but is keen to keep Maeve onside.

'Jiminy here is absolutely right. If we can lure these horrid, smelly people into a trap of our making we really can frighten the life out of them.' She's carefully skirting round the possibility that the man's tanks might also shell the life out of them. Hateful though they are, she can see that mass murder might have repercussions. Viv can too.

'Yes, darling, the idea of drawing them away from our nice home does have its appeal. But I do fear His Majesty's Constabulary might have something to say about piles of dead bodies scattered everywhere.'

'Oh, don't you worry your pretty little head about that, dear lady.' Jiminy has a way with words, including annoying ones. 'My chaps are crack shots. Cannon to right of them, cannon to left of them, cannon in front of them, what? They'll volley and thunder like it says in the jolly old poem, but we'll make sure their chaps *do*, but don't *die*.'

Patting a few stray hairs back in place, Viv recognises that her head is quite small, and, catching a glimpse of it in one of the huge mirrors dotted around the room, she likes to hope it's tolerably pretty. But she's satisfied that there's plenty of room in it for working things out. Hence the hint of Vivienne in what she says next.

'In a confined space? Shells exploding everywhere? And you're telling me no one gets hurt? Really?'

'No, no, no, my dear.' Jiminy's doing his best not to sound like a crusty colonel ordering the chaps out on a suicide mission. 'We let them pour in through the outer gatehouse to the wide-open space in front of the keep. All the time keeping our powder dry and well out of sight. Then, when we've got them where we want them, by Jove, we raise the jolly old portcullis, lower the drawbridge and roll out the tanks. That'll put the fear of God up the blighters, egad. Cracking good sport, what?' He turns to Maeve for support.

Though her "yee-haw" is sparklingly unoriginal, she does liven it up by blowing smoke out of the barrel of an imaginary six-shooter that she pretends to be holding in front of her face. In a show of solidarity, Davinia blows an extra-large smoke ring at everyone. Percy would love to do the same, but knows he's no more got the hang of that than learning when to ease up on the brandy. At least he can manage to be interesting.

'Choosing exactly the right spot to fight a battle is very often the key to winning it. Think Henry V and the Battle of Agincourt. Luring the French cavalry into a narrow, muddy space between woods was an act of military genius.

'It enabled him to follow up with volley after volley of armour-piercing arrows, and secure victory against stupendous odds.

'The story goes, our archers were convinced the enemy planned to cut off the first two fingers of one of their hands, to make sure they could never draw a bow to fell Frenchmen again. So they held them up in defiance, and, in so doing, invented the rude gesture that we use to this day.

'Not a lotta people know dat.' He's switched from top prof to Michael Caine, and offered up a V-sign, in case anyone didn't get it.

'Thank you, Percy. Very helpful.' Viv's full Vivienne. When they first met, all those years ago at uni, her degree course was strictly vocational, while his doctorate was about something ever-so elevated. At the time she was dazzled that he seemed to know everything, and to this day he often surprises her. But right now, he's a bloody Jack-in-a-box who needs to be shut back in. Not that

Miss Mism sees it that way.

'The survivors will tell their friends.' Oops, slip of the tongue there. 'The toe-rags will tell their friends.' Vivienne's eyebrows don't look convinced, but she presses on. 'The psychological impact of them running for their lives will be profound, especially if we film the fear. We'll shoot it tight, in high definition, and pass the vids on to the television networks.'

'Perfect.' Though Percy couldn't miss the gunmetal glare, he's back in his stride. 'It'll be a neat little riff on Admiral Byng's execution for not winning his battle, and what Voltaire had to say on the subject. *"Pour l'encouragement des autres."* That's roughly it. These fellers' terror will be a great encouragement to the others to bugger off and not come back.'

Miss Mism thinks better of mentioning the support they'd get from top bods in MI6, who'd pressurise Spectacle into turning a blind eye to any subsequent cover-up in the event of accidental injury. Or wholesale slaughter, if things didn't go quite according to plan.

Fortunately, that hasn't occurred to Viv, which is why she finally throws in the towel. Not altogether unwillingly, mind, as she has a real and heartfelt respect for her daughter's creative imagination.

'Ok, Trudi, you're a clever little minx, and I really do admire your loopy lateral thinking. And your courage.' This last bit comes out rather wistfully, as, for all her good looks, deadly efficiency and occasional scariness, the very thought of appearing in front of cameras gives Viv the willies.

'Oh, it's nothing, Mum.' Though Trudi obviously can't manage a mass of tail feathers, she is in all other respects preening like a peacock. 'Remember, I am a seasoned small screen artiste.' Viv can't work out which was the more galling, the girl's assured performance on FUCK News, or the fact that it was her very first go at it.

'Well, you're clearly your father's daughter.' She's hopelessly conflicted. While it's appalling the way the pair of them love lapping up attention, and manage it so effortlessly, she does sometimes wish she had it in her to be just a bit more of a luvvie. Trudi gives her a grin which may or may not be taken as sympathetic, then gives a bow which is definitely ironic, and everyone moves on from talking about things to doing them.

Maeve's off to rummage through an ancient and battered brown trunk filled with sacred family heirlooms that she hasn't been near since she showed them to Jiminy the night he announced he was off to Sandhurst. In it there's a pair of Colt Single Action Army revolvers, complete with a double holster that's still stuffed with real bullets. He was so impressed that he bought her a whole load more, which might at last come in handy. Dragging a decrepit, framed oil painting of Big Chief Sitting Bull down to one of the many dank, damp but nicely soundproofed basements, she places it against one of the many stone pillars, and opens fire.

Given that the goddam thing is nearly ten feet square, it's a disappointment that the first thirty rounds completely miss it. But then, when at last she at least manages to graze the edge of the frame, she blows the real smoke out of the end of the real barrel really smugly,

On an arguably more practical mission, Miss Mism heads off, with Davinia, to get a visual on the Penislow Palace protest and report back to base, while Jiminy and his son make for the barns where the armaments are stored. En route they drop in on the servants' quarters, to let the butler in on his promotion to aide-de-camp to the head of the Monty-Molehill Mounted Munitions Brigade, while Tristan's to be his second-in-command. The older man's delighted, as it brings back fond memories of his days in the service. The younger man's well chuffed too, as he's never been a 2IC before. He puffs out his chest, straightens his spine, pulls his shoulders back, and holds his head erectly up. Then bumps it on a low beam that normally just brushes his hair.

'Don't worry, me lad, we'll get you a tin hat.' Jiminy's show of sympathy-not-sympathy is really annoying.

Viv, meanwhile, goes back to her and Percy's suite of rooms, which, incidentally, are about twice as big as her entire flat in Camden, to check on snap poll results designed to gauge public reaction to Spectacle's Brexit announcement. To be sure he's out of his wife's earshot, Percy goes into Trudi's huge room to make more than one phone call. Beginning with Sir Percival Spectacle.

'Well, me ole mucker,' he announces, in a back-slapping sort of voice. 'You certainly got the ball rolling nicely with your first getting-back-in outing.'

'Er, first, you say? What the hell d'you mean by that?' Percy can almost hear the man holding his head in his hands, pushing back his already fast-receding hairline and staring wildly about in the vain hope of spotting hundreds of ciggies all over his desk. It's no great surprise that the second he got home after their last brief, but gloriously satisfying, encounter, his wicked witch of a wife had smelt the fags on him, snatched his stash, flung the lot into the fireplace, and threatened another divorce.

When Percy threw him the lifeline, he felt like someone who'd spent his entire life chained up in a cave suddenly basking in the sunlight. When the woman did her worst, he felt more like he'd been shoved back in, and had his eyes gouged out as well. However, as Percy explains Trudi's idea of a joint TV appearance, with her in full view on the battlements of some castle or other in Cornwall, he can see the attraction. Of that at least, if not much else. The protests outside Penislow Palace are nothing to the billowing numbers regularly bringing traffic to a standstill in Whitehall, and there had been talk at the COBRA meeting earlier of deploying water cannons to disperse them. But just getting the wretched people to wander off of their own volition would be less likely to provoke full-scale rioting, which could lead to insurrection, and – much, much worse – to calls for his resignation.

'Thing is, dear chap,' he falters, 'we both know the silent majority is with us, but the clue's in the name. And the silence is inconveniently short of golden.'

Of course, Percy knows that, and, having seen the footage of the ongoing demo at the end of Downing Street, is equally well aware of Spectacle's difficulty. What's more, knowing the man as he does, he can also see how he might be tempted, purely selfishly of course, to go along with the Trudi plan. The plan, that is, as far as has been explained to him. If he'd had any notion of the tank angle, he'd probably have had a heart attack, or ponced a pack of ciggies off the copper on the door. Or both. But not in that order, obviously.

'Well, promise me you'll at least think about it.' Even down the phone, Percy's voice smells of nicotine. 'Screw your courage to the sticking place, old boy. You know you want to.'

'Er, well … give me a day or so to mull it over.' It's a guarded response, but enough.

Timing is as important in politics as it is in joke-telling, Percy muses. Which is why he will let the silly old sod stew on it for forty-eight hours. At that point the dam of his anxiety will be ripe for breaching. And the four full cartons of fags that the Labour Leader in the Lords will drop in to Number Ten will rip it apart in seconds.

With a deeply wicked glint in his eye, Percy picks up the phone again.

CHAPTER TWENTY-SIX
TRUDI'S SIXTH SENSE

At the thought of two whole days doing diddly-squat, Trudi feels like a lioness forced back into a cage after having had the run of an entire wildlife park. But the pacing back and forth stops when Tristan mentions something that he and Jiminy have been thinking about for some time now.

'Thing is, old thing, can't say Daddy and I are great readers, but we have been trawling through some old stuff in the library. Particularly stuff about the history of the great families, like ours, and maybe yours, who used to run Cornwall in the olden days. *We few, we happy few, we band of brothers.*'

'And sisters!'

Not having ever come across the cross-between-anxious-gnome-and-shrivelled-peach look, Tristan laughs. Then wishes he hadn't. But luckily for him, Trudi unfolds her face pretty quickly, because she's impressed that he must at least have opened the occasional book to get the Henry V bit right. Besides, it picks up nicely on what Dad said about the Battle of Agincourt.

'Er, yes, and sisters.' Tristan thinks of racecourses and first hurdles, but stumbles on anyway. 'Thing is, Daddy and I have been starting to wonder whether we aren't related, loosely, to loopy Miss Mism. You see, there's loads and loads about Les Mis-Mérables de Glurm, and about their not-terribly-top-hole tendency to top themselves.

'Seems they got so worried about the line disappearing altogether, that one of their lot got hitched with one of our lot. Judging by the hordes of little horrors my ancestors were always spawning, we looked a pretty safe bet.'

Trudi's flexible features switch to the eyebrows-off-to-outer-space thing. Worried that she might be about to faint, or have some ghastly fit or other, Tristan gently takes her arm and gives her the "steady-on-old-girl" routine. This does at least bring her back to the here and now, as even a hundred years ago the term "old girl" would have grated. She gives him a bit of a telling-off glance, but a big hug all at the same time, because the news is so stunning that she is prepared to let him off, even though he's pushing his luck.

'I say, old girl,' he goes all pink, 'a trifle de trop, perchance?' He's as confused as Fangle sometimes gets when Trudi tells him he's terribly naughty, which he so often is, but kisses him anyway, because he's so sweet.

'But you see, old, er, friend,' Tristan's not taking any more chances, 'it doesn't stop there. The Mis-Mérables de Glurm records go right on to quite recent times. There's even a suggestion that our lovely loopy friend might have had a twin sister. Who might even have had a baby before the family proclivity prevailed. At this point, alas, the jolly old trail jolly well peters out.' Trudi stares at him fixedly, her eyebrows behaving more alarmingly than ever. Tristan wonders, rather idiotically, if in the event of their actually popping over to the back of her head, they'd finally land the right or the wrong way up. But Trudi quickly brings him back to earth.

'Is it possible? It can't be? Surely not? But what if... ?' Her mind flits back to that curious hint of a feature shared between Miss Mism and Davinia. That subtle, but distinctive, kink in the left earlobe. Of course the theory's preposterous. Simply too far-fetched. But then again, the very possibility is dizzying. So much so – literally in this case – that she, too, starts to worry about fainting, or having some ghastly fit or other. She slumps down, relatively carefully, on one of the striking-looking Epstein armchairs dotted around, though they really shouldn't be, in her view, among the Louis XV chaises longues. Quite beautiful in their own right, with their purple velvet cushioning and gloriously symmetrical upturned tulip heads on their remarkably high backs, but ever so easy to fall off. She grips the sides, wisely, at what Tristan says next.

'Oh, and by the way, forgot to say,' he breezes, 'there's an awful lot to be found about the De Pens-Le-Bas family. Could easily have been modernised into Penislow, don't you think? Whatevs, these chaps ... er, and chapesses, hooked up with the royal family of Munster, around the time Good Queen Bess was on the throne, then, a fair bit down the line, settled in Cornwall and started mating with our lot, would you believe? As it happens, the De Montagne-Petitescollines had also sided with the Irish back in the day, and later had their disagreements with that rotter Oliver Cromwell. So it was only natural the two families would have plenty to talk about.'

'Well, bugger me with a rusty bargepole.' Trudi was appalled when she first overheard Dad use that expression, but now, having very sensibly moved on to one of the chaises longues, she feels it fits the bill nicely. After all, if Tristan's right, then this being-related thing doesn't stop at Miss Mism and the Mountie-Molehills.

'You're telling me we might actually be cousins, cousin? Distant, but, well, in our way, sort of, close. How does that make you feel?' He scratches his head and ponders. And ponders. And ponders. For so long that he must be suffering from an aneurysm of the brain or something. She leaps unsteadily to her feet.

'Hello? Tristan? Hello? Hello? Can you hear me?' As well as saying this in a tone usually reserved for ever-so old people in the last stages of Alzheimer's disease, she grasps his wrist, stares at her watch and tries to check his pulse. This doesn't work very well, as, apparently coming to, he snatches it away and wraps his arms round her.

'Wouldn't normally do this, old, er, er ... friend,' he splutters into the nape of her neck, 'but it's not quite so against propriety, now that you might be family, don't y'know?'

'Yes, the idea had occurred to me.' She's beaming like a cat that's spotted an open-sided crate marked "small flightless birds". 'And it's a jolly nice feeling, don't y'know?' No, of course she hasn't morphed into a snobby little snit, or even just given herself a social upgrade, but she is suddenly more willing to go along with his silly olden-days ways. Just a shame she never thought to ask Dad about his parents, and their parents, and so on, as, if she could have managed to keep him to the point, he could have given vital clues about whether she and Tristan really are related. Typical silly kid thing, she thinks, pointedly ignoring that silly grownup habit of seeing twelve-year-olds as kids.

Still, her latest brainwave will make up for everything.

Last term, at school, the normally pretty daft English teacher had the bright idea of taking the class on a visit to a really, really olden-days local newspaper, that goes back ever such a long way. The bloke with the odd-looking green eye shade, that Trudi privately thought at the time was not a good look, proudly proclaimed himself to be Editor-in-Chief, News Editor, Chief Reporter, Chief Sub, Chief Stone-Sub and Chief Librarian.

Unfortunately, as Chief Engineer, he'd had to rule that the paper only comes out on a now-and-then basis these days, because the relatively mature shiny brass-and-metal printing press needs a bit of a rest between editions. But he was happy to report that the paper's library was as fresh as a frisky little lamb, making sure it stored every story covered for well over a century. Although Trudi still has no idea how old Miss Mism is, she thinks on balance it's more likely that she's less than a hundred. Meaning there's a chance of picking up the trail on the twin sister's suicide, and the baby, where Tristan's left off. Her sensible self tells her she's flinging herself down a deep hole after a rabbit that's fretting about being late, but at least it's something to do.

'We're off on a jolly jaunt now,' she announces. 'That's if you have a spare moment, dearest maybe-cousin. And a spare bike.'

'Well, actually, I jolly well have,' he answers, with a flush of pride. 'I'd sort of grown out of it, so it should be just your size, old ... er, young thing.' Faced with the irrefutable fact that he is the taller of the two, by several inches, she's prepared to overlook this possible slight, and four chocolate biscuits and a nice glass of milk each later, they're on their way.

Some four miles and an awful lot of pedalling later, they're outside the old and weary looking stone building, complete with gaping cracks in the walls and missing slates from the roof, that houses the Kernow Bellow, est. 1899. They're both rather obviously hot, but, Trudi's quick to point out, not in the same way.

'Dear maybe-cousin, I see you're perspiring. Of course I, as a lady, am merely glowing.'

'Golly gosh, I'd say I'm a bit more than perspiring, old, er … young thing. Positively sweating, what?'

'Oh no, my dear,' she does her best to drawl, 'only horses sweat, didn't you know that?' He didn't know that, any more than where the original line comes from. Impossibly silly though Dad often is, he is good with the old Oscar Wilde quotes. And Trudi well knows that, if used in the right way and at the right time, they can make her sound even cleverer than she is. Though she'll never be as posh as Tristan, it's good to keep her end up.

After a fair few muscular yanks, he manages to open the stiff and unkempt front door that leads through to the dusty and unkempt front office. A lick of paint here and there would help, though several gallons over every visible surface would be better. At least the ancient bloke in the green eye shade looks vaguely alert, as he peers at them over his nicotine-stained half-glasses, puts his silver-banded briar pipe in his mouth, and takes quite a decisive pull at it. Taking it out again, he briefly studies the bowl, which is shaped like the face of King Edward VII, then fires a question at his visitors.

'Do you come bearing news? A scoop, perchance? If so, you're in luck, as we're just in time to get it into the late edition. Comes out in less than a month, y'know,' he adds, briskly.

But the poor chap's features slump, making him look like a disappointed bloodhound, when Trudi tells him it's not a new but an old story they're after. But the please-feel-sorry-for-me look in his eyes subsides a quite a lot when she explains that it's a job for the cuttings library, as the old story in question dates back at least thirty years. If not a fair bit longer.

'Ah, there I can help you,' he beams, with perhaps the tiniest hint of relief playing round his grizzled features. The thought of actually having to write something tends to make him jumpy these days, especially when he's up against a tight deadline, all things being relative.

'Do step this way.' He leads them down a musty corridor, slips off his news editor's green eye shade, and slips on his librarian's trilby. He hasn't got a tail, obviously, but Trudi has the sense that if he had it'd be wagging, in a weary and ancient sort of way. 'Let me see now, thirty or forty years ago, you say? Seems only yesterday,' he sighs, as he flips surprisingly swiftly and adroitly through mountains of yellowing half-open envelopes containing sheaves of rapidly decaying cuttings.

Trudi well knows this is a long shot, as there's every chance the Miss Mism whose suicide they're interested in might have got married, and acquired a new name into the bargain. But where there's life – or in this case, she reflects, death – there's surely hope. This steadily fades, however, as trilby man thumbs through more and more mouldering envelopes. She reminds herself that he is going through years and years of material, but doesn't find the thought particularly comforting until … until … some two hours later … yes! He looks up triumphantly.

'There, dear lady. What did I tell you? Everything at my fingertips. Knew it wouldn't take a minute.' In her delight and, let's be honest, astonishment, Trudi doesn't point out that it's actually taken around a hundred and twenty minutes. She takes the cuttings with great care as it'd be a shame, having got so far, to see them crumbling to bits in front of her face.

"Shameful Hussy's Shame Shock", the headline reads. And the story's strapline continues, in gross and lascivious detail. "Well-born young woman betrays background, bearing baby out of wedlock. Takes own life. Shall not be missed."

This is becoming a habit, Trudi thinks, as she becomes aware, as she reads on, of her eyes doing their best to pop out of their sockets. Eventually she manages to focus, and discover that, after this Miss Mism killed herself, the illegitimate child – the paper regrets, it sanctimoniously points out, having to use the word "bastard" – was deposited in a local churchyard, in the hope that it might be adopted by the clergyman and his wife. One can but hope, the Bellow bellows, that these good God-fearing folk will teach the unfortunate foundling the error of its ways. To save them any future embarrassment, the editor declines to name them. A setback, from Trudi's point of view, but nothing next to the confirmation that the woman really did have a kid.

'Oh dear. I fear my predecessor had rather a nostalgic way of putting things,' her guide remarks, as soon as he's replaced his trilby with the green eye shade. 'Of course, he was perhaps a little past his youthful prime by the time he retired. Let me see now … ninety-eight, I think he was. Or it might have been ninety-nine. But I hope the Bellow's been of assistance.'

'More than you can possibly dream,' Trudi murmurs, dreamily. Once again, her hunch is a long shot. But if she's right it'll be the best bullseye ever.

CHAPTER TWENTY-SEVEN
THE BOOK OF REVELATIONS

'Time you got a motorbike, Trissie-baby,' Trudi pants as the two of them finally pedal through the giant, and painstakingly restored, medieval outer gatehouse that imposingly marks where the Mountie-Molehill land ends and the rest of the world begins. 'Preferably a two-seater,' she adds as she wipes a bead of glow-not-sweat from her dripping forehead.

'It's on the list, lady,' he replies gallantly. 'I am, after all, old enough. Just a matter of getting Daddy to see reason and jolly well fork out.'

'Yesterday would be a good moment,' Trudi sighs. 'The trouble with peddling around b-word Cornwall is that it's either an uphill struggle or downhill all the way.' He looks at her uncertainly, wondering whether she's really grumbling, or saying something terribly clever. Now that the two of them might be related he's much more relaxed with her, but less so at the thought that girls in general – and this one in particular – might be a jolly sight smarter than he is. Nonetheless, he doesn't question the command she gives him as Davinia appears in the distance, cocktail glass in one hand and ciggie in holder in the other.

'I'm going to have a nice chat with my nice friend.' Trudi's muttering out of the side of her mouth, aware but not fussed that she might have seen one too many American crime B-movies in her time. 'And while I'm doing that you are going to sneak into her room and have a good rummage. You've got your phone with you? Yes? Good. While you're snooping around, I want you to take pics of all the family photographs you can find. The more you can get of her with her parents the happier I'll be. Is that clearly understood?'

'Why, absolutely,' he nods, emphatically. 'Makes perfect sense.' Needless to say, it makes absolutely no sense, as he no more understands this peculiar request than the finer points of quantum physics or the mating habits of crocodiles. He consoles himself with the thought that he does have the edge over her on tech wizardry, if not a lot else, and, in his new role as super-sleuth, he can see the need to make himself invisible. After pressing a tiny knob that makes a bit of oak panelling slide to one side to reveal the entrance to a secret passage, he's satisfied, as he disappears into it, that he has at least managed that bit.

'Ah, lovely Davinia, my secret-softie bestie, how d'you fancy a turn or two round the moat?' The question mark sits oddly at the end of this sentence as Trudi firmly grasps the young woman's arm and steers her off on what she's obviously determined will be quite a long walk. She loosens her grip as they get moving side by side, which is a relief to Davinia, as it means she can now get her lips round the end of her ciggie holder without having to stoop for it.

'You were so kind to me when I was so wretched, and now I want to know all your secrets.' Though Trudi's doing her best to sound more like a lovely agony aunt than a Gestapo interrogator, it's a close-run thing. 'What was home life like for you, before you went to uni?'

Davinia's instinct is to copy those touch-me-not plants whose leaves fold inwards when anything brushes against them. Little wonder, as she finds it hard enough to even put this question to herself, let alone answer it. She wishes it wasn't quite so embarrassingly easy for a trembling hand to spill drinks from a slightly overfilled triangle-shaped glass. But while Trudi's face isn't doing its shrivelled peach bit, her eyes have switched to don't-you-dare-try-and-evade-the-question mode. She gives up even trying to try.

Layer upon layer of nonsense, from the priggish little swot of her early years to the aloof poseuse of her adult life, blown to smithereens. Just by one simple question – and from a kid at that. Maybe that's it, she thinks. The girl's just about young and fragile enough to feel the pain I've lived with for so long.

'Tell you the truth, it wasn't very nice.' Her voice is a mixture of relief that the dam's giving way and terror at where the flood waters might end up. 'My dad was so overpowering and, well, unforgiving, that I just pretended to be who he wanted me to be. And he was so remote. Which is odd, as well as terribly sad, considering he's a vicar. They're supposed to be kind to people, aren't they?' As these words drag themselves out, Trudi spots what look like the beginnings of tears in Davinia's eyes. She almost wishes she hadn't begun, but can see she's nowhere near the ending.

'I wasn't allowed to call him Daddy, or Dad, or even Pater. He insisted on 'Father', the word used by all his parishioners. Respectful, yes, but so impersonal. Made me feel like an add-on, not like his own daughter at all. And, you must know, every girl craves her daddy's love.' Trudi struggles to hide a smile, as she knows full well that not only does Percy put her on a pedestal, he almost seems to enjoy the way she wraps him round her little finger. Sort of a weird masochism strategy, she's always thought, but rather sweet.

'You wonder why I hide behind so many airs and graces? So much silly posing bullshit? Fact is, I've never quite got over all that. Being so, well, invisible, for so long. So you see, I've sort of made myself up, to get my own back.' At this she pulls her arm free, slumps down on the grass, chucks away her ciggie, and starts to cry. Deep sobs, that could be rumbling out of an ancient and long-lost mineshaft.

Better out than in. Trudi can almost hear Viv saying it. But this is way, way out of anything she's ever had to deal with. She tries hugs and pats, then ups her game with loads of oh-you-poor-loves and oh-please-don't-crys, and oh-I-think-you're-wonderfuls. A bit obvious, but maybe it is all in the delivery. Certainly her ever-so-real sincerity seems to be helping, as the poor woman eventually cheers up just about enough for her to dare risk one last question.

'But your mother? Wasn't she able to help?'

'As if!' The misery morphs into anger, as Davinia turns into a cat that's been chased into a corner by a dog, and suddenly realises it's time to get the claws out. 'She just trotted along in his wake, like a well-trained spaniel. As invisible as I was. If I ever dared tell her so, all I got was "don't be silly, father knows best". Father, that bloody word again! But there it was, trying to get anything out of my mother was like punching a bowl of blancmange. Don't know if you've ever tried it, but, trust me, it doesn't get you anywhere. Did you know, by the way, I've never shared any of this, at least not quite so openly, with a single soul?'

Of course Trudi didn't know. And she's shocked that it's down to her to act the grownup. Time was, she'd lovingly get her Barbies out of bed in the mornings, give them their breakfast, tell them to sit up straight at table, tell them off if they were naughty, give them treats if they were good, and read them bedtime stories. But that was playtime, and this is real. Still, at least the look Davinia's giving her, as she clasps her hands and somehow manages a watery smile, suggests she could be doing worse. Also, what's she's hearing is starting to make her hunch look like a no-brainer.

Then again, there must be loads of horrid vicars all over the place who're so busy loving God that they haven't got any left over for their kids. And it's obviously never occurred to this poor woman that her so-called father may not actually be Daddy at all. Besides, there's the worrying possibility that he might, if challenged, just lie outright, or even produce a birth certificate. Forged or otherwise. Being wrong is not something that Trudi does, but to be on the safe side she whispers a prayer to a much nicer god than the one that this old brute seems to like, that the photos she's after will pretty much prove her case.

The two of them sit holding hands and letting all this shared information settle, like the dust after an earthquake. But the luxurious silence is smashed to bits by the sound of gravel flying everywhere, as the Tesla shudders to a halt some little distance off. By the time Miss Mism's strode up to them, Davinia's leapt to her feet, adjusted her face, lit another ciggie, put her fingers to her lips and given Trudi the most pleadingly trusting look she's ever given anyone.

'What news, Comrade Commandant?' she airily wonders in the older woman's direction, as she marches into earshot.

'Can't decide if there's method in their madness, or madness in their method.' Miss Mism's in full snort mode. 'Generals always fight the last war, but this lot's taken it way over the top. You remember Worcester Woman and White Van Man?' Trudi doesn't. 'Well, Batty Tory Ladies have now joined the fray. Of course they want their au pair girls back, but what's really got their goat is the number of different ways the horny-handed sons of toil have managed to spell their own call to arms.

'I mean, just cop this lot.' Miss Mism whips out her phone like a fairground conjuror flourishing rabbits out of a hat, and scrolls through pic after pic of white vans, all daubed with really quite creative variants on the message they're trying to get out. "Keap ingerlernd wite" and "ceep iinglond whyt" are the two that strike Trudi as the most deserving of a gold star for originality. At the same time she worries that if their brains really are that small, their heads might be as well, which would mean dunce's caps would probably just fall off. But what she's thinking is interrupted by what she's hearing.

'These buxom tweedy women are challenging these bloated weedy men to battle, in a place and time of their choosing, where they seem certain their rolling pins and knitting needles will stitch the buggers right up. Probably right up the jacksie.' Miss Mism's not given to switching from King's English to cockney slang, which adds impact to what she's saying.

For what feels like at least the millionth time today, Trudi can feel her eyebrows fluttering around like the washing on the line on particularly windy days. At the same time, she can also almost feel the saliva slopping round her mouth at the thought of how this might play out. Dad once told her about enterprising locals at Tyburn charging for the seating they'd set up, so everyone could have a good gawp at public executions. Her view, from the Mountie-Molehill mansion's battlements, of these blue-rinsed belles beating seven bells out of the pot-bellied bastards, will be even better.

'Goodie, goodie, goodie! Yummy, yummy!' She's squealing and clapping her hands together just like she used to, as a little girl, at the thought of a really lovely treat. Miss Mism and Davinia look at her curiously.

CHAPTER TWENTY-EIGHT
MOMENTS OF TRUTH

By now it's nearly time to dress for dinner. Though Trudi still thinks all this ceremony's silly, it's not so bad now that she has the cutlery thing sorted, and no longer feels the urge to snatch up her food, dive under the table, and scoff it any old how. More importantly, though, she's gagging to get the latest from Tristan. And, if he's got what she's after, to get Davinia on her own again.

After she's climbed out of the enormous Victorian bath, with its enormous brass taps that spit out enormously hot water so enormously dependably, she slips on her nicest pink frock with its pretty *Alice In Wonderland* images dotted about the bodice, and distracts herself by fixing her face. Not that it needs any help, what with her totally clear complexion and already quite defined features, but it's a matter of principle. Suddenly, just as her mind's wandering onto some jokey line that Dad once came out with, about style mattering more than sincerity, she hears a soft but definitely eager knock. Satisfied that she could just about get by at a débutante ball, she hurls herself towards the door, nearly but not quite loses her footing, and nearly but not quite says something frightfully unladylike.

She doesn't need to say anything, as Tristan's beamingly smug smile tells her all she needs to know.

'Mind if I come in, old girl?' In his excitement he's forgotten he's not supposed to call her that, but in her excitement Trudi doesn't even notice. Instead, she grabs his arm, drags him into the room, kicking the great oak door shut behind her, and lunges at his iPhone.

'I say, steady on, dear maybe-cousin.' He's minding his language but savouring his moment. 'How about I show you what I've found?' Trudi takes a deep breath, not sure whether to hate him for keeping her in suspense or love him for what he's found, and croaks in a really weird voice, 'Do, before I kill you'. She sounds like his great grannie used to after she'd turned a hundred, but Tristan doesn't feel it polite to say so.

Instead, he just opens the picture function, and enlarges and reduces an image. Staring at them out of a rather shabbily framed photograph are three people. A repressed-looking kid who can just about be recognised as the young Davinia, an anxious little mouse of a woman and, towering over them, a man wearing a dog collar and an expression that's as reassuring as a two-handed sword. There's all the warmth in those eyes of the iceberg that took out the Titanic. The fact that they look as comfortable in one another's company as three complete strangers who've been trussed to the same tree to be executed is a detail. It's the lack of so much as a glimmer of resemblance that gets Trudi clapping her hands together again, in that puzzlingly girly way that she really should have grown out of by now. But switching almost immediately to something closer to wifey mode, or at least big sisterly, she absent-mindedly reaches out and straightens the bow tie that Tristan often wears with his wing-collared shirts in the evenings, and every bit as often leaves looking a bit squiffy.

'WhatsApp it to me. What with that, and the pix I took of the article in the olden-days newspaper, she'll have to face up to it. And a face-off with her beastly not-really-father-at-all.'

Trudi's sounding more sure of herself than she's feeling, probably thanks to a definite dose of the collywobbles about how Davinia's likely to react when the moment of truth (or otherwise) comes. It's less complicated for Tristan, who simply stares at his maybe-maybe-not cousin in awe. The terrifying twenty minutes he spent rummaging round Davinia's room struck him at the time as being just a silly indulgence of a silly girl's whim. But now that the penny's finally dropped, he's struggling to put his feelings into words. A boy thing – especially an upper-class boy. Still, he does his best.

'I say old, er ... brainybox, aren't you just the jolly old bee's knees, what? Top marks, you fearsome filly.' Trudi smiles back at him in a kindly way, because he obviously is doing his best to say the loveliest possible things to her. But then the dinner gong goes.

'Ah, for whom the bell tolls, it tolls for us,' Trudi misquotes, slightly and deliberately. This brings back poor Tristan's insecurities about girls in general, and this one in particular. Though the line is vaguely, somehow, familiar, he's damned if he can place it. But it just trips off the tongue of this scary little filly who should, by rights, have a clear four years' worth less information stored in her brain than him. But he has at least got one thing over her. She can't drive a tank, and he can, which could come in jolly handy jolly soon.

Still more so, he thinks, as Miss Mism leads off the dinner table conversation with news that the women of Worcester have set up counter demonstrations, both in Whitehall and outside Penislow Palace. The standoff here in Cornwall is particularly difficult to police, as it covers an area that's much wider, and the mood is much wilder. And, when the ladies are not actually shouting rude things at the slobby blokes, they're regrouping in their shiny Volvos and hooting their specially modified horns that bellow out slobbering farting noises at them.

'Not long to wait now.' Percy's having his very own full gloat, as at this very moment his man in the Lords is delivering to Number Ten his package of untipped, high-tar, nicotine-charged thumbscrews. 'I know for a fact that Old Speccie's going to drop the word tonight about his press conference in the morning, with someone we know and love beaming in from right here.' Appropriately, he beams at his daughter. She tries to beam back, even though she's ever so nervous about what to wear. And about what blend of make-up is right for an open-air shoot. She's even more scared about the tête-à-tête with Davinia that she's got to squeeze in before bedtime, but is distracted by what Jiminy suddenly blurts out.

'I say, Percy old sport, young Tristan and I have been poring over the musty old books in the jolly old library, don't you know?

And d'you know what we've come up with?' He doesn't, obviously. 'Well, we found bits'n'bobs bobbing up everywhere about an ancient family called De Pens-Le-Bas. Ring any bells?'

'Clamorously.' Percy's grinning. 'My dad was last but one in the line. Was all a bit embarrassing when he dodged the final tax rap by fleeing the country forever. Granted, he didn't murder anyone, but it was a bit of a Lord Lucan moment. That's why I went for the dynastic disestablishment, exemplified by the anonymized nomenclature.' Tristan wonders what any of those beastly words mean, but guesses Trudi probably does. He was puzzled a while back when she started going on about cultural capital, but is getting the idea now.

'Anyway, he left me the title, precious little money, and the family ruin, which is now a branch of Lidl, incidentally. Could at least have been Waitrose, but barons can't be choosers, eh?' He sniggers at his little joke, and so does Trudi, which puts them in a minority of two. 'Still, I am actually a "U" lord, as well as "non-U". Besides, the Doctor handle I'd already got always helped get upgrades on aeroplanes, and a PhD isn't exactly a bar to high office.'

'Ah yes, by Jove, you got to be PM. Jolly good effort, what?' Jiminy runs his forefinger across his pencil moustache, one side at a time, which Tristan knows often means there's a joke coming.

'Explains everything, old bean. Your chaps were chummy with the royal family of Munster, right? They owned Blarney Castle, right? And their ducking and weaving made Good Queen Bess so cross that she reinvented the word "blarney", to mean anything that wasn't the truth, the whole truth, and nothing but the truth, egad.

'And there were you, in Downing Street. Keeping up the jolly old family tradition, what?' Viv looks at him sharply, her eyebrows tilting upwards like mediaeval lances poised and ready to charge. But then she spots the good-natured grin playing round the corners of his lips, and pokes him in the ribs. Quite hard, mind, so he doesn't even think about getting uppity.

In fact, nothing could be further from his mind, as he shares the info that Tristan's already passed on to Trudi, about the tie-up between Percy's and his ancestors, and their shared hatred of Oliver Cromwell. When he mentions that this enmity was born of their every-bit-as-shared solidarity with the Irish, Maeve leaps up from her chair, bounds round the table, puts her arm round Percy and Viv and gives each of them a great big slobbering kiss.

'Yee-fucking-haw,' Percy mutters before he can stop himself.

'Well, I'll be blessed,' Viv adds, a little bit more demurely.

Miss Mism watches, looks on and says nothing. All this talk's broken something open in her mind, like when a sixteen-ton truck smashes into the side of a house. Worse, it's exposed a walled-up room that hid a terrible secret that no one dared even think about. But she comes to with a start when Jiminy thrusts an overfilled balloon of brandy into her hand, and tells her she'll jolly well need it when she hears what he and Tristan have dug up about her family history. He decides to leave the bit about her ancestors hitching up with his lot for another day, but doesn't hold back about how tricky things got for the Mis-Mérables de Glurms during the period that King George III went bonkers and his son took over as regent.

'The records showed that the milord of the moment was so fond of gambling, drinking and womanising that he squandered most of the family fortune, then shot himself, by accident. Dashed shame, I say.'

'By accident, you say? That makes a change from the usual pattern.' Miss Mism manages a snort.

'Ah, yes – I was coming to that, dear lady,' Jiminy replies, then abruptly changes both his mind and the subject, on the grounds that any mention of her late twin sister might provoke a display of emotion, which would have been jolly bad form at the dinner table. In the event, Miss Mism's training at spy school made good and sure that she never gives anything away, at least not outwardly. Excessively good form, that, as inwardly she's feeding as stable as a ton of plutonium.

It was Percy's talk of his ancestral pile that brought it all back. Dim, almost dreamlike memories of where her ancestors hailed from. She has a sense that during her nervous breakdown all those years ago, there was a reason why she hysterically insisted MI6 help her relocate to where she's living now. It certainly suited them to get her well out of the way, though for the life of them, they couldn't figure out what made her plump for that desolate spot. Nor could she at the time. But now, suddenly trickling back to her like a heavily polluted stream, are stories she was told as a kid about a family seat that got pulled down. Could it have been ... the question's gnawing at her like a nasty bout of toothache ... could it have been on the site of what's now a factory manufacturing top quality pianos, a bare half-mile from her cottage?

At this point, the shutter shudders down. She knows there's something dark on the other side, but can't bring herself to even try and see what it is. Trudi, who's spent more time alone with her than anyone else in the room, discreetly sidles up to her side. Gently taking the poor woman's hand, which she can feel quivering on her lap, she hopes she's got enough mothering in her to get her through the night. The time spent with the Barbie dolls was a useful rehearsal.

CHAPTER TWENTY-NINE
DAVINIA'S DILEMMA

Miss Mism hardly says another word throughout the rest of the meal. The others assume this is only because she's thinking about how things might play out in the morning, but Trudi knows better. She's also been pretty quiet – most unusual for her – but she has got tonight to get through.

As everyone rises, she gives Davinia a definitely I-need-to-see-you-alone look, and sidles after her as she heads in the direction of her bedroom. This typically huge space is exquisitely done out, but unlike everywhere else, is decorated and furnished in 1920s Déco style. It was Jiminy's idea to make this her billet, and she's touched, and quite surprised that he seems to have got such a clear handle on where she's coming from. Or, rather, where she wants everyone to think she's coming from.

No sooner has she opened the door than her young friend, apparently appearing from nowhere, slips in in front of her and hisses an instruction to come in, sit down, and pay careful attention. Amazed, she looks up and down the otherwise empty corridor, shuts the world out, and does as she's told.

'There's something you need to know,' Trudi whispers, unnecessarily, given that the oak-panelled walls are so thick and soundproofed that no one would hear if a hand grenade went off. 'Something that may shock you deeply, but you need to face up to anyway.' Whipping out the pink iPad that she's kept more or less out of sight all evening, she opens the photo that she took of the article in the Kernow Bellow. Davinia's baffled, and anxious.

'Now gather and surmise.' Trudi's so nervous that she's hiding behind Miss Mism's Hamlet-quoting trick. 'Just read this carefully, before I show you something else that's every bit as relevant.' Having enlarged the image, she zig-zags slowly down the page to make it reasonably easy to take in the words. Davinia's dark and deliciously full eyebrows normally rest at something like the normal height. But now they're right up there with Trudi's.

'Well, my dear lovely friend, can you guess why I'm showing you this?' The look on Davinia's face as she gets to the bit about the adoption by the vicar strongly suggests that she has, which makes the thought of how she might react to the family-not-family photo all the more scary. Trudi really, really wishes she were somewhere else. Even somewhere quite stinky would do, so long as it's a long way away. But now, firmly hooking on to the *in for a penny, in for a pound* thing, she opens the picture of the three uncomfortable-looking people who don't look the slightest bit like one another.

Davinia's eyes dart desperately round the room, like a hunted fox when the baying hounds are closing in, and options for escape are narrowing to nil. Her expression's a mixture of fear, despair and hatred. But maybe also — just maybe — the tiniest glimmer of hope.

'What. Are. You. Implying?' A cross between a hiss and a croak, the sound's almost as weird as Trudi's great-granny voice.

'I. Think. You. Already. Know.' Without realising it, Trudi's scrunching up the sides of her dress, her clenched knuckles turning lividly white and the delicate fabric not looking too happy either.

'Time to phone home, perchance?' Her shoulders droop, her words tail off, her eyelids dip and she looks down at her toes, which are pointing, slightly embarrassingly, inwards. Randomly, she thinks of the title of an old movie Dad once told her about. *All Passion Spent.*

In Davinia's case, the spree's only just beginning, and she's terrified of where it might lead. It's been years since she rung home, and keeping well away has always been a blessed relief. Nor is it like she's being asked to just put in a casual "hello, hope all's well" kind of call. Rebuilding a city smashed to bits by an earthquake feels like nothing next to sorting the chaos inside her. And she's got to do it alone. Pulling herself bolt upright, she stares at Trudi, points at the door and raps out one single word. 'Goodnight.' Not meant to be harsh, but certainly sounds it.

'Er, sleep on it?' Trudi simpers in an ever-so-little voice as she turns tail and flees. She's halfway down the passage before Davinia finally collapses onto the bed and lets the tears and mascara splurge all over the duvet. She's beyond caring what a fright she must be looking, which shows what a state she's in. But the good cry does work its magic, and some half an hour later she's imagining the confrontation with the man she's always known deep down she's never even liked.

So what it's late, she'd be telling herself, and the old brute's probably fast asleep? It'll help catch him off his guard. She can see herself keying in the number, which she wishes she could but somehow can't forget, then tapping the fingers of her left hand furiously on the spiky-shaped glass-topped dressing table as the beep-beeps carry on beep-beeping for what feels like at least twenty years. Eventually, just as she's on the point of giving up, and maybe flinging her iPhone on the floor and stamping on it, she pictures a grumpy and extremely sleepy old man muttering, 'Yes? Who the hell is it?' At this point her brain flaps aloft like an eagle and makes up the following conversation.

'It's me, er ... Father. Davinia. Remember me?'

'Who? Oh yes, you. Again. Why couldn't it wait till the morning, you wretched girl?' This gruff and unforgiving tone would be less than friendly from anyone who hasn't heard from a supposedly loved one in such a very long time. From someone who claims to be a parent, it's inexcusably horrid. Inexcusably, but not altogether inexplicably, as it turns out.

'You're not my father, at all, are you? Why did you never tell me I was someone else's child? Didn't I have a bloody right to know, damn you?' Davinia spits the words out, really getting off on the rude ones, with such pent-up hatred that the man's thrown utterly off balance. To the point that he's beyond even trying to lie his way out of the situation.

'We were trying to protect you, stupid creature.' He's so up on his high horse now, he's right up there on the right hand of God. *'Did you*

really want to bear the hideous shame of your sinful begetting? To know you were tarred with the unspeakable, the unforgivable, brush of illegitimacy?

Spiteful, yes, but exactly what Davinia was dying to hear. Gives her the opening to answer back with yet more rude words that she'd been dying to use on the old hypocrite for half her life.

'So I'm a bastard then? So bloody fucking what, you self-righteous, sanctimonious sod? And all that untruth for the love of me? Love? You wouldn't understand the meaning of the word, or even see it if leapt up and bit out both your eyeballs.'

'May God have mercy on your erring soul.' Her father-not-father's doing his bunched-up eyebrows fire and brimstone from the pulpit bit. Not that it does him any good.

'May God piss on your head from a great height. And poo down your throat, while he's at it. You should have just left me in that stinking churchyard for someone with a shred of human compassion to do the honours instead. I couldn't have done worse than you, you monster, you ... miasma.'

With that parting shot she imagines herself cutting him off, astonished, exhilarated, and shocked at herself, all at the same time. She never was one for swearing, at least not in anger, and indeed has never been that deliberately rude to anyone, to their face, in her whole life. But, telling herself it's all true, she fantasises about managing at some point in the future a teeny bit of forgiveness. Maybe trying to make amends, if not to this hair-shirted brute, then at least to his poor little wife, who in lots of ways is a much of a victim of his cruelty as she was. Male machismo, misogyny, and rigidly sticking by the savage God of the Old Testament make for a poisonous cocktail, she thinks. Certainly robbed her of most of her youth as well as her own identity, until this wonderful moment.

If only.

She's already confessed to Trudi what a softie she is behind her brittle exterior. But now she's questioning whether her kindness isn't just a form of cowardice, because it's much easier to be nice to people than dish out home truths.

Then there's the horrible thought that the old brute might have actually been telling the truth all along. Yes, Trudi seemed convinced he's not her dad, but Cornwall is stuffed full of churches.

So the story in the paper could have been about any clergyman adopting any baby all those years ago. No reason, really, why it should be her. Face it, lots of people don't look like their parents, and lots of dads are stinky and horrid.

She's back on the bed again for another jolly good cry. But this time it's different. These tears are of disappointment, not just at herself in not having dared sort things once and for all, but even more so at the very thought that Trudi might be wrong. It's this final flip-flop, the realisation that she really, really wants the vile old man not to be her father, so she can strangle him with his own dog-collar, that gets her tottering across the room to find her slinky little girly hip flask. In the event the gulp of brandy isn't so much a pick-me-up as a tuck-me-up, as all this trauma finally catches up with her.

Realising that if she doesn't lie down straight away, she'll fall asleep where she's landed, slumped in a chair. Hardly a brilliant beginning to her newly liberated life. Minutes later, safely snuggled up half-on and half-under the duvet, her knees quite close to her chin in a comfortingly unborn-baby position, she dreams of fumbling for the phone, keying in Trudi's number and tremblingly tapping out a four-word message. *'Mism mission accomplished! Yay!'*

Of course, it having not been sent, Trudi spends much of the night tossing, turning, and fretting. At one point she even thinks about ringing the nice pet-sitting lady and asking her to put Lady Casement on the line, in the hope that the silly bird might for once say something helpful, or even just funny. And even when exhaustion does finally win out, her dreams immediately start arguing with one another. In one, a furious Davinia tells her she'll never speak to her again, because her saintly father proved he really is Daddy by producing her birth certificate. In another, she announces that the fiend fessed up to being a smelly fibber fox, and smothers her in hugs and kisses.

But eventually Trudi's mind floats off towards the calmer waters of Brexit, and her plans to fix it. She's on an olden-days sailing ship with loads of pennants fluttering gaily in the breeze. They have lovely, exciting things written on them, like "lights", "cameras", "action", "adoring fans" and "a grateful nation".

CHAPTER THIRTY
A STAR IS BORN

Trudi's eyes snap open like giant blue saucers, about three hours earlier than they normally would. She's not so much a bit wired, as fizzing like a spaceship's booster rockets. And, though terrified about Davinia, she has managed in her sleep to work through the knotty problems of hair, make-up and costume for her world-stage debut.

After springing out of bed, she saves time by skipping the wonderful wallow in the enormous bath, settling for a quick, but obviously thorough, shower. Then, in what seems a matter of seconds, she's fixed her face, slipped on her best-ever fuchsia frock, and patted her hair into shape. She's also patted herself on the back for having persuaded the mother of a friend of hers, who's both a passionate remainer and a ceramic jewellery maker, to upgrade the European Union flag. The screaming pink stars on the brooch stand out beautifully against the pastel pink background, and the matching chunky pendant and dangly earrings tie in perfectly.

All a bit of a shock to Percy, as he taps tentatively on her door, then creeps in with a nice glass of slightly sugared warm milk, which usually helps ease the pain of trying to wake Trudi.

'Bloody hell, babe, you sure you haven't had an identity transplant?' The question strikes him as perfectly reasonable, and her as utterly ridiculous.

'What the hell do you mean?' It's not just the shrivelled peach look that frightens him. Even her toes look put out.

'Well, er … er … Oh, never mind, darling. Just that you're making Boudicca look like a scaredy-cat little mouse. In fact, I'd say you're, ahem, too cool for school.' Trudi raises one eyebrow, a little further up than usual.

With the ice, if not actually broken, at least looking reasonably skiddy, Percy risks giving her the crib sheet that he and Viv put together before bedtime last night. To Trudi, most of the bullet points are statements of the obvious, though she does give credit where it's due. Particularly at the suggestion, printed in bold type, that it's not just young people like her, but also anybody who tries to trade, buy their groceries from the supermarket, get an au pair, settle, or even just take a holiday on the continent, who'll benefit from ditching Brexit. Always best to read the room, or, as in this case, the stonking great field. She nods approval, and, given that Number Ten was on the blower within minutes of the ciggie delivery, and the joint press conference is due to start in less than an hour, this is a great relief.

With her usual efficiency, Viv has supervised the laying of cables and setting up of microphones, lights and cameras, supplied by a nervous-looking local TV crew. Time was they'd also have needed satellite trucks manned by scruffy looking techies as well, but even out here in the sticks they can do better than that these days. Standing on the neat little podium that she's had placed on the battlements, she carefully calculates the angles to make sure the distinctive and site-specific gatehouse will be plainly in vision behind Trudi, beyond the sweep of the area round the keep.

She's also taken the precaution of placing, on a neat little table close at hand, a glass of water, starched napkin, hand-held mirror, and a plateful of doughnuts. Playing extra safe, she's chosen the type that can't splurge out blobs of red jam. When Percy wondered, accidentally out loud, whether a couple of lines of Charlie might also be useful, the Vivienne brows knitted dangerously until she realised he was only joking. Well, up to a point. Like his wife, he doesn't like leaving things to chance.

But when Trudi glides up the not-exactly-olden-days lift, everyone stops fretting. The camera operator and sound man are just as gobsmacked as Percy was, at the sight of his fully awake and dolled up daughter. The make-up lady can't think why she even bothered to get out of bed.

No surprise that there's no sign of anyone else. Davinia's caught up in about thirty years' worth of identity crisis, while Miss Mism's glued to her phone in the ad hoc operations centre, in the barn that houses the tanks and howitzers. Jiminy and Tristan are there too, issuing last-minute instructions to the chaps, and making sure final checks on the equipment are carried out with due diligence. Jiminy has also, for the umpteenth time, raised, lowered and raised again the radio-controlled, cast-iron, and definitely-not-olden-days portcullis guarding the outer entrance, that one of the many movie production companies with more money than sense insisted on having installed a fair few years back.

At the time, a very much younger Tristan wondered why fortified gatehouses to all mediaeval castles weren't operated digitally, and was told by his father he was a 'dashed silly little nincompoop of a whipper-snapper'. Like Trudi when she's in the mood, he's learning how to laugh at his former self, though it's taking him longer to get the knack. Maeve, meanwhile, is in her favourite basement, still trying to get the knack of getting bullets from her six-shooter to land anywhere near their target.

It's for the best that Miss Mism still has no idea about what might be happening on the Davinia family front, because she needs her full focus on the running commentary from the rookie agent heading the MI5 detail outside Penislow Palace. He's spotted a slight lull in the massed farting from the Volvos, less fist-shaking and name-calling from the blobby males, and a scaling-down of the needle-and-rolling-pin brandishing from the stout females, and is wondering if that could be anything to do with the news flashing up everywhere about a very unusual broadcast in the offing.

'Well, well, you could have fooled me.' Miss Mism can't believe the man's that slow on the uptake. 'Perhaps you'll manage to register any developments when the thing gets going. Particularly when the surprise element surfaces.'

'Roger that.' The poor chap clocks that he's been a bit dim, but is trying to stand on his dignity anyway. He hates this haughty woman – the more so as she's always right about everything.

Suddenly, all the political commentators in all the news channels in all of Europe are cut off mid-sentence, as the famous black door of Number Ten swings open, and Sir Percival Spectacle steps out. He's just stubbed out his thirty-fifth ciggie of the morning, and texted Lady Spectacle to tell her if she insists on a divorce she can blasted well have one, as he's definitely given up giving up. Fired up both by this ultimatum, and the smokes that he's so loving, but mainly by them, he makes it to the miked-up lectern without stumbling once. A good start, his only regret being that he'll have to wait until he's safely back inside before he can light up again. This at least focuses his mind on keeping both his spiel and his answers tight. He crosses his fingers that the kid will do the same.

'I crave the indulgence of ladies and gentlemen here present, and viewers and listeners who might have just tuned in.' He's sounding like a Prime Minister on Pathé News in the old black-and-white days. 'I have detected the wind of change about this royal throne of kings, this sceptre'd isle. A day like today is not a day for soundbites, but I feel the hand of history upon our shoulder. A week, after all, is a long time in politics.'

Having binned the speech drafted by the Foreign Office, on the grounds that it was far too long, he's speaking off the cuff. Succinct and to the point, though he's wondering vaguely why some of it's sounding vaguely familiar. Meanwhile, the collective special advisers' eyeball-rolling muttering, two hundred and fifty miles away, is joined from right next to where Trudi's standing.

'Bugger me shitless,' Percy explodes, 'what's he going to offer next? Blood, toil, tears and fucking sweat?' Viv looks at him sharply, but it's The Talent who rises to the occasion. First by cupping her hand over the mike whose cable she had to thread through the inside of her dress so they could clip it to the neckline, and then hissing at him.

'B-word being b-worded, Dad. Just b-word off. They could cross to me any second.' He backs off, struggling to get his head round how much more of an old pro his daughter is than him, when she's so much less old than him. Not only that, she was right, as barely two minutes later a clichéd out Speccie explains, with as much of a flourish as he can manage, that this sensational little influencer is the anti-Brexit voice of Britain's youth. Trudi smiles, in a humble way that fools everybody except her parents, looks straight down the barrel of the camera, and says all the right things. The last bit's the best bit.

'Of course I did my ever so best to get everyone thinking about how hard life under Brexit has been for poor little young people like me. But I do ever so hope ever-so-sensible grown-up grownups like you will be so kind as to give a moment of your valuable time to the thought that it might be more than just a matter of, well, you know …'. Deliberate stage pause, followed by insincere but hopefully convincingly wistful gaze. 'Well, you know, suffering little children.

'I know we kids can be ever so silly, but we'd also so like to be a help to everyone else. Particularly anybody who tries to trade, go shopping, get an au pair, move to, or even just take a holiday on the continent. You see, you lovely adults would be ever-so-much richer if we go back into Europe.

'That'd be nice for us too, as it'd mean you'd be able to give us more pocket money.' Delivering this final, light-hearted line, she copies the clever thing she's seen Lady Di do on old TV footage. That butter-wouldn't-melt but beguiling way the lady had of lowering her eyelids always got people on her side. Worked for that princess, should work for this one too.

Her performance is followed by several seconds of silence, while the camera stays on her but steadily pans out, showing yet more clearly exactly where she is. Then, as instructions come through to the crew from Master Control in London that it's a clear, the lights switch off and Trudi gets through her earpiece a breathless little speech from the producer back at base. 'Love your work, darling! Pure television gold! Big time awaits! Have a wonderful rest of your life!' Then, before she's even had time to unclip her mike, Percy's rushed up, hugged her and shouted, "Love your work, darling! Pure television gold! Big time awaits! You'll have a wonderful rest of your life!'

Once or twice in the past, Trudi's felt her vision go weird when she's been a bit naughty with Dad's brandy, and for a moment she half wonders if something similar's happening now. Then she remembers that he, too, cut his teeth in the business, and was on the box for so long that the lingo's lingered. Such a relief, as it's a scary thought, hearing as well as seeing double.

CHAPTER THIRTY-ONE
MORE DEADLY THAN THE MALE

The action outside Penislow Palace began the second the camera started panning out from Trudi, and got rid of any last doubts about exactly where she was. Like discovering, as dawn breaks, that you've been driving in the right direction all along.

First the fatties lumbered towards their ugly vans and started noisily revving them, as overgrown schoolboys do. Then, as they headed off towards the road, the stocky ladies levered themselves into the Volvos. No knowing for now whether they're planning to defend the girl or attack the men. Logically, probably, both. Certainly they're only a couple of minutes behind as they career towards the outer gatehouse, whose portcullis has slithered up to allow the blokes to head straight through the gate to the main building. There, the leader's slewed to an untidy halt, partly on and partly off the drawbridge, it never having occurred to him that it might actually work.

As the others form a vague semicircle a little distance back, and the Volvos (and the ladies in them) do more or less the same, like the top layer of a cut-in-half sponge cake, the man marches across the drawbridge and tries to bully this second portcullis into being as obliging as the first. Endless kicking doesn't frighten it, which is hardly surprising, as it's managed in the past to hold back hordes of heavily armoured troops. He also tries headbutting it, which, even less surprisingly, really hurts.

Insults shouted through the square holes only go to prove that words aren't always mightier than the sword. Not even when his mates gather round and threaten it with ordinary, right-thinking people rising to defend England from filthy foreigners and snobby upper-class bastards, does it take the slightest bit of notice. Half an hour later the noise level goes down because they've all got sore throats, then peters out completely when one of them spots the hawsers attached to the outer edge of the drawbridge going rigid.

'Fuckin' 'ell, strewf, strike a fukin' ligh', looks like da fukin' fing fukin' works.' He has a way with words.

''Kin' 'ell, Jon, yer fukin' righ', bettah fukin' scarpa', like, stryt awhy.' So does his mate.

It's obviously too late to try and rescue the motor, which starts moving forward when the front wheels get firmly hooked onto the edge of the rapidly rising drawbridge. Then, when it finally snaps shut against the castle wall, the vehicle simply plops back into the moat. Round one to the ladies then. The blokes are hopping mad.

Then there's a standoff. Trudi gleefully watches the action – or rather, inaction – between the outer and inner walls through a small military periscope, handily positioned behind one of the keep's arrow slits. But she soon gets bored and reaches for the nearest anything-but-authentic-medieval intercom.

'Any chance of something happening? Sometime soon?' As usual, this isn't so much a question as an instruction. And it's well timed.

'On it, old ... er, young thing.' Tristan's sounding wildly excited, as any chap would when he's firing up a heavy-duty killing machine for his first outing onto the battlefield.

'Give 'em hell, babe.' Testosterone Trudi even surprises herself. 'And don't take prisoners.'

'Roger that,' Tristan breathes. Like Percy with telly talk, he's getting into the lingo.

The first hint the opposing armies outside the walls get of any change in their situation comes from a distant rumbling, somewhere behind the double-barred entrance. It gets louder and louder, but no less mysterious, until Miss Mism, who's dashed from the control centre to the keep's entrance, pulls two ancient but well-oiled levers. As the portcullis slithers up, and the drawbridge rumbles down, the men and the women gather in two separate crowds and gawp. And gawp. And gawp.

After all, how often does anyone see a line of tanks trundling out of an olden-days castle?

But the shocks don't stop there. As the great fume-belching monsters rumble towards them, their guns start firing. And, weirdly, as the blokes and the ladies try and pull further apart, the shells start landing in a pattern that's driving them back towards one another. Like when a collie darts around to make sheep do as they're told.

It's soon obvious they're going to have to fight it out. A problem for unarmed men faced with women brandishing rolling pins, knitting needles and – this war's equivalent of the atom bomb – rolled-up copies of the Daily Telegraph.

If that's not bad enough, the tanks are busy zig-zagging their way through the parked vans, smashing nearly all of them to bits. Soon, apart from the truck already gathering rust at the bottom of the surprisingly deep moat, there's only one left. But there's a roar and puff of smoke from the howitzer perched on one of the towers, and then there are none.

Nothing for it then. The blobbies run for their lives. Problem being, the remote-controlled portcullis in the outer gatehouse has suddenly shot down, cutting off their only means of escape. The ladies lash out to their hearts' content, and carry on slashing, stabbing and bashing until the blokes are crying out for mercy. Or their mums. Or both.

Eventually Miss Mism decides that'll do. No sympathy there, just that that she's bored at the sight of them. Reaching for the microphone that has a direct radio link to the loudspeaker, cunningly concealed between the gatehouse's two battlements, she clears her throat loudly and gives them a piece of Hamlet's mate's mind. Adapted for the occasion and dripping with irony.

"Now crack, ignoble hearts. Goodnight, not very sweet princes; and flights of demons sing ye to your rest.'

The men who're still conscious look up pitifully, pudgy fingers locked in a collective prayer for release. Which, lo and behold, opens before them, as Miss Mism presses the little button that makes the portcullis slide up. Given that the railway station's a good sixteen miles away, and they're not ones for a brisk pace, even on a good day, they're not so much looking at a long march as a weary hobble.

A very different picture back at the mansion, as the winning women definitely do march back to the keep. On the way they pick little posies of flowers to give to the heroine of the day, along with gift vouchers for their local classy little charity shops, and invitations to become honorary president of their branches of the Women's Institute and Conservative and Unionist Clubs.

Spotting that a victory lap is called for, Trudi takes the lift to the ground floor, skips up to the tanks and lightly vaults onto Tristan's.

'Come on, comrade-in-arms.' She gives him such a blokeish poke in the ribs that he almost falls off the gun turret. Grabbing her arm to get his balance back he nearly pulls her over too. For a while they sway about like the masts of a galleon during a storm. But somehow they both manage to right themselves.

'Best not snatch defeat from the jaws of victory, eh?' Trudi feels more victorious the ever. Tristan doesn't.

'I wish I knew a millionth of the clever things that you've got stabled up, ready to trot out whenever you fancy.' He looks like a deflated balloon.

'Actually, that was quite clever, Trissie baby. Stabled up? Trot out? You've got the bit between your teeth.' He's partially re-inflated, even though she's still out-clevered him with the bit bit.

'Right. Let's give 'em their money's worth.' Trudi gives him a hug, which makes up for everything.

'Roger and out.' Tristan giggles. 'Or should that read Rosalind?' Quite smart, that. For the second time today, Trudi gives credit where it's due. But as he lowers himself into the body of the tank she gives his hair a tweak, just so he doesn't get above himself.

As the machine lurches forward, some of the ladies wet themselves, as they've used up their entire supply of bravery on the men. But they quicky stand up, and hope nothing's showing, when they spot their star player, legs positioned deliberately apart, balanced precariously on the slow-moving but wobbling gun turret. As she gets closer, Trudi risks a sweeping bow, and, because she still hasn't fallen off, a fair few more, with flourishes, as the caterpillar tracks nose up close.

Unwilling to give all the credit for what was, after all, a collective effort, Jiminy fires up his own tank, orders his men to follow, then trundles out after Trudi and Tristan. Stepping rigidly to attention, he gives an impeccable military salute, and the chaps in charge of the rest of the cavalcade do the same. But the chapess standing on the one bringing up the rear looks and acts very differently.

Kitted out in her best chewing-gum-pink Stetson and cowboy boots, Maeve has rounded off the effect with shiny Buntline six-shooters holstered to each hip. Now that she's given up trying to fire accurately, she hopes the revolvers' long barrels will at least make it less likely she'll miss the sky and end up killing people on the ground.

Whipping the pistols out like Wyatt Earp, she bellows her usual 'yee-haw' at the top of her voice and opens fire. Unfortunately, what with all the racket going on, she hasn't heard the small helicopter whirring away not far above, and, for the first time ever, manages to hit a target. Just a shame it's an unintended one.

Sir Percival Spectacle, terrified at all times of air travel, reaches in panic for a strictly forbidden fag as a couple of bullets tear through the chopper's windscreen. But luckily the thing's so close to the ground by now that it manages to land safely. Meaning he can stagger out and enjoy not being dead. Ducking the whirling rotor blades, he sticks the ciggie in his mouth and curses that the draught they're creating would make it impossible to light the bloody thing, even if he could find his bloody matches. Which he bloody can't.

Percy, Viv and Miss Mism had been tipped off that the Prime Minister was planning to drop by, though not, as it so nearly turned out, literally.

Speccie had thought it'd be a nice idea to motor down and shake Trudi by the hand, but his head of communications insisted he fly there, to be with the ladies as well as the girl for the photo-op to die for. Those words were haunting him, again almost literally, as the windscreen started turning into a jagged jigsaw puzzle. He's a gentle soul at heart, but while his life was flashing before him he wished he could have had a rerun, with the pistols in his hands and the entire press office in his sights.

But, crisis over, he still can't fire up the fag. Biting the end of it, he's slapping his pockets and rummaging in them as though his life really did depend on it.

'Need a guardian angel, old chap? Grinning from ear to ear, Percy steps forward, skips the usual handshake and holds out something far more useful. His lighter.

CHAPTER THIRTY-TWO
ACTION THIS DAY

Speccie puffs and puffs and puffs, as though he's drinking the elixir of eternal youth. The fact that the stuff's supposed to protect the body from harmful substances, not pour more into it, passes him by. All he cares about is that he's got a fag in his mouth and he's alive to smoke it.

Although he still hates the Downing Street publicity machine, he's prepared to admit that pix splattered all over the papers of him with Trudi are nothing, next to a Labour Prime Minister being cheered on by a horde of true-blue Tories. No harm then in implying it was all his idea.

'I feel like Old Nick surrounded by hundreds of bowing and scraping Christians.' He's looking so pleased with himself that Percy doesn't have the heart to point out that Jesus being worshipped by Satanists might have been a better way of putting it.

Viv, meanwhile, has had the foresight to get a load of blue rosettes express-delivered to the mansion, and made sure Jiminy has masses of cases of champagne ready for just this moment. On the nod from her, he gets the chaps to slip out of their military gear and don their best butlery togs, ready to do the rounds of the ladies. Heads held high, starched white napkins gracefully draped over outstretched arms bearing booze and prawn vol-au-vent-laden silver trays, they float around like sprites at a teddy-bears' picnic.

The guests repay the favour by pinning on the rosettes and talking at the tops of their voices about how Speccie's almost up there with Maggie, and as the cameras roll and the boom-mikes mosey in, everyone gets exactly what they want. Trudi goes into charm overdrive for the benefit of the stills, and Sir Percival Spectacle risks giving her a clumsy hug and virtually no contact peck on the cheek. No one's to know that the adoring look she gives him is a thank you for not damaging her make-up.

Also, while she's happy to mingle for a bit with the starstruck Tory ladies, she's secretly hoping they'll sup up and sod off without too much hanging around. This, happily, they seem minded to do, probably because after all this excitement they wouldn't mind getting in nine holes at the golf club before lunch. Or maybe because they really fancy a bit of zizz in their own comfortable homes at last. Camping out in a good cause is all very well, but there's no beating Laura Ashley bedding. To send them on their way, Speccie delivers a little speech, about how grateful he is for their support and about how determined he is to obey their instruction to fix Brexit.

'Action this day', he says in conclusion, with a vague sense that he's not the first person to have used the phrase. Percy rolls his eyeballs, but is impressed that Trudi's spotted the wartime slogan too.

'With that little chin of his, surely he'll never be able to stick it out like Churchill used to? But, is it me, Dad? Or has he at least managed to poke his nose out a bit further?' Next to her cattiness, Fangle looks like a moggie on Mogadon, but what finishes Percy off is her wide-eyed innocent-little-girlie look. It's like Vlad the Impaler making out he's sorry about having people skewered.

Percy pulls himself together a bit when he spots what Speccie's doing to his bow tie. Ever since he's known the man, the poor thing, or, rather, succession of poor things, has had a beastly time of it when he's upset. It's as though this perfectly harmless piece of cloth is personally responsible for anything that goes wrong. That includes old mates laughing, as this one so obviously is, at him. And right now he's tugging so hard that its life expectancy looks set to be measured in minutes.

After strenuously adjusting his face, Percy holds out both an opened packet of fags and the spare ciggie holder he's been meaning to give the man for ages. This'll obviously eliminate the telltale nicotine-on-fingers evidence, and so maybe get the missus off his case. As goodwill gestures go, it's up there with Earl Grey and Abe Lincoln abolishing slavery, and although Speccie has pretty much given up on his marriage, forgiving and forgetting is one of his nicer qualities. This is partly because of his naturally good nature, but more thanks to his appallingly bad memory. Not that he's going to lose track of the horrors of helicopter travel in a hurry. Or of the fact that the new windscreen won't be delivered for hours.

'I say, is there any chance I could stay on for a bit? Maybe even kip down here? Of course, my security detail followed on by road, so I don't suppose you'd have room for these fellows too?' There's an edge to his questions, even though they're meant to sound casual.

'Oh, I daresay we can slip you all in somewhere.' Jiminy has most politicians down as complete idiots. What he's just heard proves he's right.

'Actually, there's enough room here to billet half a regiment. Just take a look around you.' Speccie does. And takes the point. And heaves a deep sigh of relief. A whole day and night away from Downing Street, and the dowager duchess, as he often calls his dear – if these days more off than on – wife, is a blissful thought. Besides which, he'll be able to travel back in a nice, safe Range Rover Sentinel instead of that beastly flying contraption, which, he slightly weirdly announces, makes his heart feel like a singing bird whose nest is in a watered shoot.

'Opening lines of "The Birthday", Christina Rossetti, Victorian poet,' Percy whispers, in answer to Trudi's eyebrows. 'Amazing. Never realised the bloke got beyond the Beano.' She sniggers, but slightly distractedly as she's suddenly realised that she's starving hungry, as well as desperately worried about Davinia. There's been not a peep from the woman since yesterday, and there's no telling what she's going through, or when, if ever, she's likely to come out the other side.

Lunch on the lawn is a distraction, as is the sight of the fleet of towaway trucks dragging the remains of the silly men's vans off, presumably, to a scrapyard somewhere. It's eventually decided the vehicle sunk in the moat can stay where it is, as a monument to human stupidity. Like the Titanic on the seabed, Percy suggests. And, as the menservants clear away the bits of accidentally broken glasses, discarded rosettes, half-chewed vol-au-vents and battle-scarred copies of the Daily Telegraph left by the ladies, order seems finally to be restored. Maeve claps her hands, manages to not draw the Buntlines, much to everyone's relief, and tells them what they're going to do tonight.

'Yee-haw, we gonna party! A swell party! Like you don't doggone see every day! Yes, siree! We sure as hell beat them goddam Johnny Rebs! Now we sure gonna paint the town red!'

Jiminy's pleased that she's remembered this time which side actually did win the American Civil War, and also rather likes the idea of a bit of a knees-up. Percy and Viv do as well, not least because the MI5 detail has informed Miss Mism that there's no sign of any of the protesters coming back to Penislow Palace. Starting to seriously sort Brexit is grounds for celebration, but so's the thought of being able to go home again. Trudi, too, likes the sound of that, though it brings about a strange add-on to her usual missing-things thing.

'I really, really want to see Fangle and Lady Casement again.' The poor love's almost whimpering, which is so unlike her that Viv gives her a comforting hug and promises to do what she can. Though she's on absolute tenterhooks waiting for the results of the instant poll she's commissioned to gauge public reactions to Spectacle's stuff this morning, she's quite sure she can get hold of the pet-sitter and make the necessary arrangements.

As a rather eerie afternoon-after-the-morning-before calm descends on the mansion, and tonight's partygoers disappear to their various quarters to doll themselves up, Trudi's nerves continue to jangle. And Tristan, who knows exactly why, eventually taps tentatively on her door.

'I say old, er … oh blow it, *young* maybe-cousin, are you decent? Mind if I come in?' Trudi, who's looking more than decent in her very prettiest pink frock laced with gold lame flounces, snatches the door open, drags him in by the sleeve, absent-mindedly tidies his bow tie, and gives him a pitiful look.

'Not a word. Not a b-word bean.' She's mumbling, miserably. 'I don't do scared, as you well know.' A half-hearted attempt to get back her big girl cred. 'But I do feel a certain … er, inhibition about disturbing her.'

'Don't blame you,' he murmurs understandingly. 'Mind if I give you a bit of hug? Got a feeling you need it.' She does, and is very grateful, even though it doesn't solve anything. There follows a long and embarrassed silence, as neither boy nor girl knows what to say next, until they hear the gong summoning the household to dinner. As Trudi slips on her very best and most sparkly pink shoes with diamante buckles, it's on the tip of Tristan's tongue to say what a nice change they make from the trainers that she so often wears, even with quite formal dresses, but he settles for saying how jolly charming they look. Which shows he's getting the hang of things at last.

Some considerable distance away, Davinia, who's been laid out nearly all day on one of the art Déco divans dotted round the room, rouses herself from her stupor. She has managed to sort her particularly striking costume and makeup for the evening, but not much else, apart from reliving in her mind practically every experience she can remember throughout her entire life. Pretty obviously that hasn't left much room for anything else, given that it was about twenty-nine years less than the ideal time frame for the job. One last glance in the gracefully curved metal-framed full-length mirror on the back of the door, one last check that the glittering star-shaped diamante brooch is centrally positioned on her tight-fitting jet-black dress's plunging neckline, one last pat of her carefully coiffed curls, one last lightning look to ensure her jet-black cigarette case is fully loaded and the jet-black holder is neatly stored in her small, glittering black clasp bag, and she's as ready as she'll ever be to face the world.

For Miss Mism, too, there's been an awful lot going on – in her case, fragments of yesteryear and up-to-the-minute stuff all jumbled up together. It feels like one of those awful dreams when you've really, really got to get somewhere but find your feet are stuck in clods of cloying earth. The debrief from the bosses back at MI6 got a little confusing towards the end, as they'd been at the bubbly. Perhaps only to be expected, after Spectacle had opened the doors to something approaching the intelligence access they'd enjoyed back in the good old pre-Brexit days. But still, given that she hasn't touched a drop in twenty years, it struck her as seriously irritating, like on the rare occasions that she goes to parties. Within half an hour or so all the sensible grownups she's been talking to turn back into children. Stupid ones at that.

At the same time, there've been endless fleeting, but hard to pin down, visions of something that happened in her life many, many years ago. Something bad. Very bad. So bad that she's blocked it out all this time, successfully, up until now, but which seems to be hacking its way back to the front of her mind. Forget unsettling, it's terrifying. Not that she *does* fear, at least not as anyone would know. Which is why, when the gong goes, all she does is straighten her spine, pull her shoulders back, give her hair a telling-off kind of pat into place, and stare sternly at her reflection in the mirror. It's such a fierce look that even she's a bit scared of it.

For Maeve, meanwhile, it's been a busy afternoon, what with all the party arrangements to sort out, and servants to order around. Jiminy, too, has had his work cut out, going through his wardrobe to find something suitable for Speccie to wear. Prime Minister though he is, he's still rather flustered by all these posh folk and their posh ways, and horribly aware that his very ordinary off-the-peg grey suit and tired-looking off-white shirt aren't quite the ticket for glittering occasions. Any more than the bow tie, which looks like it's begging for death after years on the rack. Not that Percy feels any shame about his part in all this.

Quite the opposite, in fact, as he and Viv spend a very happy couple of hours in their lush sleeping quarters, that come complete with the biggest, bounciest, and most richly velvet-draped four-poster bed that either of them has ever come across. Figuratively speaking.

The debrief that Percy's managed to get out of a jumpy and tetchy Speccie has put lead in his pencil, metaphorically speaking. Via a go-between mechanism, dreamt up by the French, called the European Political Community, the British government plans to pull all manner of Brexit-fixing tricks out of the hat. No need to frighten the horses with talk of formally reversing the referendum result, but with the swivel-eyed loons in open retreat, the back door's swinging wide open.

Just how wide, Viv reminds him, might depend on the result of her snap poll. Waiting for it's making her jumpy, though the excitement's also leaving her skittish, and oddly energised. She gives Percy a certain look, and what follows feels like a rerun of when they first got to know one another. Biblically speaking.

CHAPTER THIRTY-THREE
TRUDI'S TOTAL TRIUMPH

As the various diners march, skip, clippetty-clip, and swish towards the banqueting room, the pleasant but overawed pet-sitter lady hovers by the doorway. Imprisoned in the two smallish wire-meshed cages she's carrying are an irritable-looking Lady Casement, and a downright furious Fangle. But though they're her passport to the party, she doesn't dare join in. Yes, it does look to be, as Maeve put it, swell, but these swells will be a bit much for her and her Primark frock, even though it's the nicest one she's got.

'Oh, I'm so sorry you won't be joining us.' Trudi means this, but, thinking back to her own first brush with how the other half lives, can see the problem. 'There will be another party below stairs though, if you don't mind too much slumming it with a bunch of policemen and some of the staff.' Actually, the lady doesn't mind a bit, as the decree absolute freeing her from her horrid ex-husband has finally come though, and she's got the hots for the head footman, who she's seen around the village a few times recently.

As the cages are opened, Fangle springs out onto the huge, heavily laden, and exquisitely embossed rosewood table, and darts along its entire length, dabbing onto the floor every glass he can get his paws on. But because they're all empty, and this section of the room is lushly covered in thick-pile carpeting, this is hardly the Charge-of-the-Light-Brigade-style massacre that he had in mind. Shame, really, but he has made his feelings clear. Lady Casement does, too, by flying onto Trudi's shoulder, peering into her face and giving her a good-telling-off sort of stare, before haughtily fluttering off to the outer ring of one of the many sparklingly cut-glass chandeliers.

Though they're some way up she'll be able to hear everything, and already some of the weirdly cut-glass accents have got her thinking. Likewise, the unfamiliar and, to her mind, frankly bizarre turns of phrase. She once heard Percy describe himself as a "snapper up of unconsidered trifles", and, because she doesn't realise that he was quoting one of Shakespeare's shadier characters, she's sure that's her all over too.

Last to arrive is Davinia, whose extra-casual air is, to Trudi's eye at least, extra-obviously fake. There's even something forced about the deep drags she's taking of her ciggie, as though she'd whirl the holder around like a scimitar if anyone dared try to approach her. Not that it'd be much good in one-to-one combat, but there is a place for gesture politics. Sometimes.

As the food floods in and the drinks flow freely, even Speccie starts to loosen up, in spite of his being so unused to starched collars that the one he's wearing is bringing him out in a rash. And he struggles, when Percy can't resist teasing him, not to attack the immaculate black silk bow tie that isn't, after all, his. He keeps raising, then lowering, first his left then his right hand, like some demented mechanical toy soldier, but stops when Viv clocks what's going on, and stamps on her horrid husband's foot. Quite hard, actually. He gives her the look of pretend innocence that Trudi's so good at, and gets in return the full gunmetal glare.

'Ok, I surrender.' He is a bit scared. 'But the silly sod's so easy to wind up. So hard to resist.'

'All the more reason to give the bugger a break, and stop being such a bitch.' Overhearing things she's not supposed to is one of Trudi's many special skills, and she's struck by Mum's rude language, which only comes out when Dad's in real trouble. She's torn, as on the one hand it's always good to see girls on top, but on the other Percy needs protecting because he is only a man, so can't help being silly. For the millionth time in recent days, she's struggling with just how complicated life can be. It feels like playing snakes and ladders, only worse, as the ladders are really short and the snakes ridiculously long. But she's distracted when Miss Mism lets the side down by taking a call, not even during a ciggie break, but halfway through the second course.

The woman's already steely expression starts spitting sparks when she hears the familiar, at times disgustingly over-familiar tones, of Doctor Strangelove. He tells her he's fed up with living in the Philippines, and, judging by today's headline news from the UK, she bloody well owes him. Trudi's triumph is all very well, but he made it happen.

'Oh, all right then,' she raps. 'I might consider engineering your rehabilitation. Pave the way for your return, some day. More than you deserve, mind, you ill-bred toad.'

At the mention of breeding, Jiminy's eyes light up.

'Aha,' he begins, leaning across the table in a conspiratorial way that strikes everyone as odd, seeing as they can all perfectly well hear what he's saying. 'Been meaning to tell you about the jolly old genealogy, and how your chaps fit into our chaps' picture. Right down the jolly old line, don't y'know?' No, Miss Mism doesn't know, which is why her eyes fix on him like high-powered laser beams. But they just bounce off him. After winning this morning's battle, battle-axes like her can go to hell.

'Fact is, old bean, your lot and ours are kith and kin, don't y'know?' Because, once again, Miss Mism doesn't know, she fixes him with an even more scary stare.

'Well, get on with it then. Spit it out man.' Her nostrils are so flared that at any minute there could be smoke puffing out of them. From her vantage point on high, Lady Casement watches, fascinated, but doesn't say anything. Like the tank crews while the drawbridge was still up, she's keeping her powder dry.

'We've also established that the Mis-Mérables de Glurms' ancestral pile wasn't so very far from ours. Actually, just up the road from your bijou little billet. Everything went jolly haywire for the jolly old fam back in the Regency period, and the place fell to bits. It's a factory now, making posh pianos.' At this, Miss Mism's stony expression starts to fragment – frighteningly, to Trudi's mind. What she doesn't – well, can't – know, obviously, is that this intelligence is peeling away layers of protective covering, of deep-seated secrecy, within the woman's mind. Suddenly she's clocking why she was so insistent, when she went loopy, on shacking up in this precise location, in what seemed on the face of it such a remote and unlikely part of the country. Also, it fits with her turning herself into a nutty reincarnation of her once-rich ancestors, who were as brilliant with music as they were rubbish with money.

'What? What? What!' She sounds like she's being garrotted, each word sounding more strangulated than the last. 'Are you telling me we're all actually related then?'

'That's right ... Granny!' Trudi and Tristan's excitement's like a ticking timebomb that's got fed up with waiting and finally blown up. She stares at them, her face a fleet of tankers on a collision course. Utter delight at this news smashing headlong into panicky terror of something else. Something long crushed back into the shadows, that's finally threatening to drive her over the edge again. Lady Casement spots the warning signs, and decides this must be her cue. She flutters down and perches on Miss Mism's head, grateful that, like Percy, the woman has masses of thick and easily-hung-onto hair. Leaning forward, she peers into Miss Mism's upside-down face, marvelling, not for the first time, at how odd humans look, what with their visible ears and invisible beaks. Then, because parrots can't actually clear their throats before making a pronouncement, she just gets on with it.

'I say, steady on, old girl, bit of a rum do, don't y'know? Best buck your ideas up, what?' Everyone stares at her, especially Jiminy, who's never noticed how silly he can sound, what with his caricature posh ways of putting things. Not to mention his accent.

In spite of the intensity of this moment, or maybe because of it, Trudi gets a fit of the giggles. Viv, too, shows she can sometimes have no sense of occasion, by checking her phone that's just beeped, then rushing out of the room to make a call. A couple of minutes later she makes up for all Percy's horridness to poor old Speccie, by showing him the WhatsApp she got her London office manager to pass on as soon as he got it. It's the result of the poll and it makes lovely reading, as his efforts of the morning have been a soaraway success with the voting public. His face wreathed in smiles for once, he's the visible personification of absolute magnanimity.

'I only followed the lady's lead.' He's actually blushing, bless him. 'But all this is, surely, Trudi's triumph.'

She's got to hand it to him, he's not wrong there. Not that she even needs to say it. The ecstatic look in her eyes does the job just as well. And this in turn triggers a dam-busting burst in Davinia's mind. Probably true to say the loads of bubbly she's drunk has also played a part, but she suddenly leaps to her feet and announces that if Viv can be so rude as to make a call during a meal, then she can too.

Actually sprinting out of the room, not without risk, given how high her stiletto heels are, she prises her mercifully super-slim phone out of its hidey-hole under her left bra strap, and, the second she's out of everyone's earshot, taps in that dreaded number she's so long wished she could forget. The conversation that follows, with her father-not-father, is as truthful as it is terse, going on pretty much exactly the same lines as the fantasy she kept playing through her mind last night. Only, this being the real thing, she ends it with a scream of delight. Braveheart William Wallace might not really have shouted "freedom" before the executioner chopped his head off, but *she* does. The noise is so loud that it echoes down the corridor right into the banqueting room, and Maeve's so struck that she gives a "yee-haw" of her own. Though she obviously hasn't got a handle on the specifics, there's no mistaking the positive energy. Also, it has to be said, she enjoys yee-hawing.

All this time Miss Mism's mind has also been vaulting over hurdle after hurdle, risking all as she careers through a minefield of pain, and maybe, just maybe, hope. She's finally facing up to the memory of her twin sister, her untimely end, and the hideously unsolved case of the vanishing baby. And staking what feels like her life on what Davinia might have to say. Still, nothing could quite have prepared her for the young woman's hoarsely whispered words.

'Auntie! Auntie! Beloved auntie! Found you at last! And I don't even know your name. Silly, really.'

But there's nothing silly about the way she lunges forward, grips the woman in both arms and really does nearly strangle her with hugs. Trudi and Tristan join in the fun by holding both her trembling hands. Fangle leaps onto her lap, Lady Casement peers at her thoughtfully and everyone makes little lump-in-throat gulpy noises. And then are totally shocked by what happens next.

Shaking herself free, Miss Mism lurches to her feet, face ashen, features set, and heads for the door.

'But, but, but?' The question bombards her from all sides. Turning round briefly, and holding herself rigidly, she spells it out.

'I'm not having you lot watching me crying. Maybe even joining in.' Her words are at once defiant and an open invitation. Trudi and Davinia clasp one another, holding on as though their hearts are about to break, and sob uncontrollably. Their tears are like molten gold. Pure, delicious, blissfully unadulterated joy.

THE END

ABOUT THE AUTHOR:

After forty years covering Westminster politics, first for LBC then Sky News, Peter Spencer is now a freelance presenter on GB News, where he provides neutral (if at times frivolous) political analysis. He also writes a weekly column for Malestrom magazine. Peter has a waterfront home on Cornwall's rugged north coast, where he handfeeds seagulls and does exactly what granddaughters tell him to.